By Lawrence Schoonover

❄   ❄   ❄

THE CHANCELLOR

❋ ❋ ❋

❊

❊

THE CHANCELLOR

❊ ❊ ❊ ❊ ❊ ❊ ❊ ❊ ❊

LAWRENCE SCHOONOVER

LITTLE, BROWN AND COMPANY

Boston - Toronto

❊

❊

❊

❊

Published simultaneously in Canada
by Little, Brown & Company (Canada) Limited

PRINTED IN THE UNITED STATES OF AMERICA

To
RUTH M. KNIGHT
TRUE LADY . . . TRUE FRIEND

THE CHANCELLOR

✻ ✻ ✻

※ ※ ※ **1** ※ ※

E VERY MORNING of her life, punctual as the sunrise,
the dowager duchess of Montholon looked out of the
narrow window slit of the ancient Château Montholon to
assure herself that nothing had changed during the night.
Nothing, of course, ever had; but still there was always the
fear. Change was all around her.

Reassured, she would address a special prayer to Heaven,
through the likeliest intermediary, Saint Agathe, for whom
she was named: "I thank Thee, O Lord, that Montholon is
not like the others," and then she would prepare herself
for her duties of the day, hoping they would present no unusual aspects. Even a cow that aborted or a butt of wine
that went sour struck her as undeserved and unwholesome,
since normally the Montholon cows did not abort and normally the Montholon wines did not go sour. They were famous for their quality and constituted a goodly portion of
her generous revenues.

Quality; quality indeed was the test. How reprehensible,

3

how strange that the world nowadays, the reckless new world, seemed to forget quality.

In wine and in blood — what a solemn ring that had, like the bell in the chapel her ancestors had built during the reign of Louis the Saint! — quality was what counted. It was fundamental; it endured; enemies had never prevailed against it; time had tried it in a century of war against the English, now purged from the sacred soil of France. God prospered it. How else account for the curse on the king of England, who had no son? How else account for the excellence of the house of Montholon?

She had never experienced the slightest doubt that her way of life was unassailably correct: one's feudal responsibilities towards the good people who labored on one's estates; one's obligations towards those of one's aristocratic class.

But even in France, which she equated with the civilized world, the spirit of change was in the air like the sharp smell of lightning that hangs over the fields after a thunderstorm. The king himself, that disturbing young man, was unorthodox. Good heavens, not in the field of religion! Not like the heathen English and Bohemians and Germans, barbarians who followed the mad heresies of the renegade monk Martin Luther — one could see where the lack of quality led one. But in the silly Italianate way that the young king thought. Time, perhaps, would mellow him; she hoped so.

Why in the name of all the saints had King Francis chosen to be called *Francis?* That was what was so frightfully unorthodox. Why not a Charles, of which there had been eight? Why not a Louis, of which there had been twelve? But Francis! And to compound the eccentricity,

The First! It broke with the past. It flouted tradition. Surely in all his string of Christian names there must have been a Charles or a Louis. But he selfishly called himself Francis the First. Never before had a king of France had the gall to call himself Francis.

The estate of Montholon, viewed from the duchess's window, presented a comforting aspect. All was as it had always been; all was as it should be. Far off by the river the wheat was green around the mill, and the sails of the mill were turning full rigged in the gentle breeze, slowly, sturdily, steadily. There would be bread and to spare for her people. In the middle distance a peasant and his sons were plowing under a four-inch-high crop of a wicked Italian weed called maize, or Indian corn. The very name was an affront. Cattle sickened on it and humans foolish enough or hungry enough to eat it bloated and died. She had noticed the alien vegetation only yesterday and threatened the man with eviction if he did not destroy it forthwith. "That must go," she had said, holding a handkerchief to her nose to ward off infection. "That or you! See to it, tomorrow at the latest. Not a stalk must remain. It is understood?"

It was understood, he said, cap in hand and a frightened look on his honest face. By sundown tomorrow not a stalk would remain. He had been misled by a neighbor.

"One of mine?" she had demanded.

No, madame, not one of yours. Actually, a neighbor's neighbor, a nobody, a new man who had got the seed from a troop of gypsies who fed their horses on it, and very fat horses they were.

Likely enough, thought the duchess, and therefore even more suspect. Gypsies, witches! Plow it under!

Now, as she watched, the poor deceived man was indus-

5

triously plowing it under; all would be as it had been before. Indian corn, indeed! Why, it was as bad as tobacco and tomatoes and potatoes. Strange new weeds from barbaric new lands across the sea. It was a difficult century, a mischievous age. How stable, how secure the 1400s had been, how brazen these brash new 1500s, with French kings abandoning good old French names, and the 1500s had not yet run through their first quarter. Indeed, this was only the year 1523. God and His saints only knew what lay in store for the world in the next hundred years. Fortunately she would not live to see it.

The duchess Agathe, dowager of Montholon, aged thirty-seven, considered herself old, as indeed she was if judged by the life span of her contemporaries. Except for a few exceptional persons, chiefly clergymen like Uncle Duprat, who was fifty-two, one usually died before reaching the half-century mark. Battle or murder or plague, witchcraft or childbirth or fatal accidents like broken legs when the bone punctured the skin, life's natural hazards cut short the three score years and ten that the Scriptures held out as man's ultimate hope and sent him down to his grave before fifty. But Uncle Duprat, who had a mind for figures, said that in Caesar's time the life span of the ordinary man was only twenty-two: and Uncle Duprat was chancellor of the treasure of the realm. This constituted progress, he said. The duchess would reply, "I think, my uncle, that it is the quality and not the quantity of one's years that counts." He would answer, "Yours, at any rate, have been full."

Close by in the immediate environs of the château the familiar noises of squawking chickens and squealing pigs, necessary and close in her self-contained feudal economy, wafted up on the wings of a southerly breeze laden with odors that did not offend her unprejudiced nostrils and told her that all was well with the duchy of Montholon, if not with the world, as assuredly it was not.

It is not unnatural to be apprehensive in the morning. As day wears on and nothing out of the ordinary happens confidence grows; but on first getting out of bed one is prone to be a little frightened of another day with all its mysteries and challenges, particularly if one is a widow. But they are not the only ones. Armies are most successful with dawn attacks, as every good general knows. And Uncle Duprat said that he always waited till after a long holiday to announce new taxes because he caught the taxpayers by surprise, when they were least able to voice their anger. The dowager duchess had thought the remark in bad taste, but Uncle Duprat was certainly unpopular and she supposed he considered the taxpayers his enemies.

The walls of Montholon were three feet thick. The masonry was solid. The bars at her window chamber were a comfort. Modern walls were frail, barely a foot thick, just enough to support the weight of the upper stories; and of course nobody built bars into the windows of living apartments any more. In place of the iron was now fragile glass; a naughty boy's slingshot could shatter it with a pebble. But Château Montholon had been built two hundred years ago, a fortress against the marauding English. And as for the windows they built nowadays, they were huge, absolutely and absurdly huge. They let in too much light and they shut out the wind, to the ruination of ladies' complexions and the effeminizing of boys, who ought to grow up strong and who certainly never would in this hothouse atmosphere of Francis's Italianate château.

Hothouses, orangeries, Roman baths, brothels, that's

what this prodigal young king was building, not sturdy
French châteaux. But reluctantly she shared with all France
a warm admiration for the prodigal. Foolish he was and supremely opinionated, but he was remarkably handsome
and, by some magic, the more he spent the more France
prospered. Her own revenues bore witness. The prosperity
of the people, the big families and exploding population,
the general content and pleasure in life seemed to grow
every year. Insubstantial and suspect as the glittering new
era might appear to her she had to confess that life in 1523
was a great deal more interesting than in the secure and
gloomy days of her youth when nothing ever happened.

The trouble of course was not with France. The dowager
duchess was vehement on that score. She knew exactly
where the trouble lay. It was those dreadful Italians. They
were always singing and dancing and wenching and painting pictures and carving marble statues without a stitch of
clothing on them, not a stitch, copying nasty old Greek and
Roman things that they dug up out of their gardens. Every
Italian who had a garden, she supposed, must have dug up
a dozen, for some of them were already appearing in
France and becoming fashionable. The good Lord had
wisely, and most appropriately, buried them in the dirt out
of sight of Christian men lest their nakedness corrupt them,
and there they had lain for a thousand years. Now the
dreadful Italians were digging them up again and calling
them art. What nonsense.

The same thing was happening, or so she was told, in the
world of books. Pagan writings of the Greeks and Romans
were being translated, even into French, and this too was
in the name of art. Worse still, these foreign books were
being printed, multiplied by the thousand by an ingenious

device called the printing press. Another foreigner, a German it was said, certainly no decent Frenchman, had invented the thing. But France was flooded with printed books. King Francis was rumored to have three thousand of them at Fontainebleau. Well, that was all right for kings, since the rules never applied to them; they made their own, as was only right and proper. But as far as *she* was concerned, she was very glad that she had never wasted her time learning to read. She knew her missal by heart; in church she dutifully turned the well-thumbed pages, aided by memory and the exquisite little pictures. But the Latin and French in which it was written — hers was a beautiful manuscript copy, not one of those printed things — were equally mysterious and she did not know one from the other.

Her chaplain kept her accounts and would present them to her every quarter day for her signature. After listening to him read the complicated figures, which involved fees, rents and the current price of wine, she would trace a careful X after her name, *Agathe, duchesse de Montholon.* And woe betide the earnest young cleric if he should err by so much as a sou; for though she could not read she could carry in her head an entire column of figures and add them up in a flash. Not for nothing was she the niece of Antoine Duprat, chancellor of the king's *épargne,* a word that had superseded the old *trésor publique,* which meant only "the national treasury." The king's *épargne* meant "the king's economies." It struck the public ear more pleasantly for it seemed to promise that the king of France was an economical fellow with personal solicitude for Jacques Bonhomme, the common man. It was one of Duprat's great political achievements; it made Francis I the most popular king

France had ever had. What it made of Chancellor Duprat no one cared. The duchess would learn sympathy for her kinsman only much later. As of now she could only admire and hold him in awe.

As she dressed she glanced in her mirror; no, there was no change there either, not a single gray hair, and for that too she was thankful. She adjusted her widow's mourning cap, smoothed a wrinkle out of her skirt and turned towards the door, which opened softly before her approach.

"Good morning, Claudette," she said without looking at the girl. It was certain to be the waiting-woman, who was never allowed to help her dress or even comb her hair, the duchess insisting on doing everything for herself, but who risked a tongue lashing if she did not station herself at the door, listen for her mistress's light step and open precisely at the moment she was ready to emerge, which was always the same.

"Good morning, *madame la duchesse*," said Claudette.

Occasionally Claudette would hazard the hope that her mistress had slept well and would receive in reply the assurance that she had; but today Claudette was silent. Today was an important day, as the whole castle knew. They had had their orders for a week, from the cook whose fires were already roaring in the great kitchens below stairs to the major-domo, who was directing a small army of scullery lads and cleaning women industriously wielding brooms and mops. The major-domo himself, with the solemn air of a bishop asperging a cathedral, was whisking drops of peppermint water from a little besom about the halls and into corners where dogs had been. Uncle Duprat was coming today and Uncle Duprat had a delicate nose. The place must smell sweet and fresh or he would be offended, an unthinkable faux pas.

Breakfast was set in the great hall and there, waiting at the far end of the long table, respectfully standing, was the girl on whose account all the activity and excitement centered. The dowager duchess appraised her with a critical eye, sustained an unaccustomed maternal tug in the region of her heart and conceded that Marie de Montholon was satisfactorily presentable, indeed actually beautiful in a soft and innocent manner. There were so many aspects of beauty.

One expected in Marie, of course, the good manners of the convent. Her high color was natural on so important an occasion in her life. And, examine them as critically as you might, neither side of the family was unattractive. But the women somehow were inclined to present the appearance of competence rather than warmth and beauty. In Marie, by some magic of the mingling of the blood, beauty and competence were mingled.

"Good morning, child," the duchess said.

"Good morning, *madame ma mère,*" said Marie.

"Come sit beside me."

Marie did.

"You may kiss me, Marie," her mother said and turned her cool cheek. Marie flushed and kissed it.

The duchess gave her a little hug, which made Marie flush still deeper with pleasure. Her mother had never been so demonstrative before.

But then, never before had her mother faced a day when she must affix her X and her signature seal to her only child's marriage contract.

She had haggled with the old Comte de Tonnerre for a year, ever since Marie was sixteen. The old count was as ambitious for his son Henri as the dowager duchess was for Marie. Naturally, and quite properly, the young couple were not consulted while these delicate negotiations were in progress, nor had they ever set eyes on each other.

Patently old Tonnerre had had the worst of the bargain financially from the beginning, for Uncle Duprat had handled all the details. The formidable document was now complete, engrossed in triplicate, one for the duchess, one for Tonnerre, and one for Duprat. On its signing Marie de Montholon, already wealthy, would become one of the richest women of France.

"You will exert yourself to be sweet to your great-uncle, Marie," the duchess cautioned. "Without him I could never have managed the alliance so successfully."

"What is he like?" Marie asked, her eyes alive with curiosity.

"Who?" said her mother sharply.

Marie had met her great-uncle Duprat at least a dozen times, though admittedly not so often in recent years. He was climbing rapidly both in the state and in the Church. In addition to his chancellorship of the *épargne* Antoine Duprat was an archbishop, occupant of the episcopal see of Sens and already reaching for a cardinal's hat. No one would be surprised to hear of his elevation to the purple. His enemies whispered darkly that his grasping hand would reach out and snatch the papal tiara itself and clap it onto his own bald pate if he could only contrive to bribe the College of Cardinals. And even his friends, the few that he had, could not deny that Archbishop Duprat was as proud and covetous as Wolsey of England.

"I was referring to Henri, *madame ma mère.*"

"To Henri? Oh yes, dear, of course; Henri de Tonnerre, your affianced. He is quite suitable."

"Yes, *maman,*" said Marie, dropping her glance, her voice so small and submissive that the dowager duchess felt again the unwelcome twinge near her heart.

She relented.

There were, she remembered, other aspects of marriage, not so important as the financial arrangements and soon forgotten when one stopped being foolish and romantic about them. But before marriage they were likely to bulk large in a girl's thoughts — even in hers they had — before a girl became wife, mother and mistress of an estate and grew into maturity and common sense.

"He had to be suitable, dear," she said gently, "or your great-uncle would never have sanctioned the alliance. His war record is admirable; he fought bravely at Marignan and distinguished himself in sight of the king; the king knighted him on the battlefield that very day with his own sword, young as Henri was. Oh, he's quite suitable, my dear; and of course you know how prominent his family is, one of the oldest and noblest in France."

It was more than Marie had expected; her mother had disclosed that Henri was young and brave. Perhaps he was also gentle and kind. But knowing her mother Marie had feared these considerations might not weigh, and Tonnerre might be merely rich; and revoltingly old.

Marie brightened visibly and her mother, touched, added slyly, "And I *hear* he is nearly as handsome as the king."

"Is he coming today?" The stars in her eyes betrayed her; Marie was exultant, hoping she would see her betrothed.

"Good heavens, child, no! Why should he?"

"Oh," said Marie, her exultant mood somewhat deflated. But still it was wonderful, wonderful news, far better news than most of her convent friends ever heard. "Do you know where he is, *madame ma mère?*"

He was somewhere abroad, her mother said, shrugging.

"Is he safe?"

"Marie," she said sternly, "do you love him already?"

It was more of an accusation than a question.

"I think I do," Marie said softly.

"Don't. Not yet. And never too hard. Duty, of course; duty is expected. Often that is all that is expected. But never get hurt. One gets terribly hurt when one loves too hard and too soon. You have not seen the man. You do not know him. How can you say you love him? Later. Later, dear. When you know him, when you know him through and through, you can afford to love. And then it doesn't hurt."

Marie listened, shrinking back into her chair.

"I distinctly resent your trapping me into this emotional conversation," said the dowager duchess, recovering her composure. "I assure you that if Henri de Tonnerre were not safe Antoine Duprat would not be wasting his time to bring me a marriage contract to sign today. You can therefore assume that your husband-to-be is quite properly intact, physically, financially and as morally as any young man in this degenerate age."

"He can't be so bad if he's really all that," Marie said smiling.

He was heading a mission, the chancellor said when, late in the day, he finally arrived at Château Montholon, a mission on which King Francis set great store and which no one could discharge with the tact of Henri de Tonnerre.

"What is this precious mission?" the duchess asked, hop-

ing but far from convinced that it was something respectable: hanging some Italian brigands perhaps, or bringing
to heel some obstreperous baron. The dowager duchess of
Montholon, with all her distrust of the flashy new king, was
a staunch monarchist and despised the few remaining
feudal houses of France who still clung to their ancestral
privileges to the detriment of the realm.

No, her uncle said with a shrug of his elegant shoulders,
Henri's mission had to do with a painting. Yes, a painting;
pigments on canvas, a bauble to embellish the king's château
at Fontainebleau. He and his niece smiled an understanding smile. The vanities that were fashionable nowadays!

"I expected you earlier, *mon oncle*," she said.

He answered severely, "I should have thought you kept
better order on your estates, Agathe."

Everywhere throughout the towns and hamlets of the
duchy of Montholon he had been stared at, hooted at and
once actually threatened by an old woman in the crowds
which poured out to glare at the man they accused of op-
pressing them. They seemed to experience some slight sur-
cease of habitual hatred by viewing him close up as he
rode with his suite through their towns, like the sufferer
who must examine the forceps before it extracts the tooth.

"At least nobody stoned me," he said.

She said, shocked, "They wouldn't dare."

"Not yet, Agathe."

Some of the chancellor's immunity to physical harm was
owing to his clerical robes. Long ago he had had a wife and
envisioned a career in the law; but his wife had died, she
had given him no children, he took holy orders and now,
combining his legal and ecclesiastical talents, Antoine Duprat was the ablest administrator and diplomat in France.

15

It was he who had brought about a concordat between France and the Holy See at a time when it seemed likely that France would separate from Rome, set up a national church and fall into the heresies that were distracting the northern kingdoms of Europe. In a spasm of gratitude the Pope had permitted the French clergy to pay secular taxes to France for the first time in history. Rome was appeased; King Francis was enriched; and Antoine Duprat soared to the rank of France's leading statesman.

Whenever a difficult question arose King Francis would say, "Let Duprat decide this," particularly when it dealt with some unpopular new form of taxation; Duprat dutifully handled the matter; the king never was blamed and the realm of France benefited. But many there were who paid in gold, in forced labor, in confiscation of estates and even in blood for the chancellor's stern exactions. "The *épargne* is a winepress," wrote a chronicler of the age, "in which all the grapes of France are squeezed dry, and only the king holds the key to the cellars." Duprat twisted the screw of the press. Thus the chancellor received all the blame and King Francis reaped all the rewards, which provided funds to support the most brilliant, most exciting, most spendthrift court of Europe.

In the market place of the village of Montholon a crowd had gathered to witness a public execution, obstructing the cavalcade of the chancellor-archbishop.

A small merchant of no consequence was being broken on the wheel for committing a crime of unusual viciousness. He had been fairly tried and duly condemned. Popular sentiment ran high against him. The crowd approved, as the executioner applied first the lash, then the iron bar at each slow turn of the wheel to which the victim, spread-eagled, was chained. A tense animal "Uagh!" of pleasure went up from the massed spectators at each blow.

Two ways were open to the executioner, a compassionate man, to shorten the criminal's agony. He could call his assistants to speed up the rotation of the wheel, in which case the blows would fall faster; or he could apply the *coup de grâce,* a smashing blow with the bar that would shatter the ribs and crush the heart, bringing instant death.

But the crowd cried, "Slower! Slower!" when the wheel was speeded up, and "Not in the chest! Not yet!" when the iron bar poised above the ribcage.

"The unfortunate man was therefore fated to expire with maximum discomfort," Duprat said to the duchess, "to the great disgust of the hangman."

When the criminal suddenly died, however, without even the *coup de grâce,* the crowd felt cheated. They had but sipped their apéritif; their hunger was unassuaged. It was then that they turned, brutalized by sight of the unfinished torture, towards Duprat, who stood aside averting his ascetic face.

They remembered the sequence of personal disaster in the life of the shoddy little merchant who just had died. He had been robbed, he swore at his trial, of a warehouse full of merchandise. This could not be proved; it was suspected that he had robbed himself and disposed of the goods on the sly. He had then lapsed into tax delinquency; and this was abundantly attested by the local tax farmer with many sworn documents bearing the formidable seal of the king's chancellor of the *épargne,* though Duprat always delegated his seal and had no personal knowledge of the case. There were scores of them every day in France.

And then, confronted with the prospect of poverty, con-

fiscation of all his possessions and disgrace for himself and
his family, the merchant went berserk. He sawed off the
head of his only daughter, a pretty little girl aged three,
with a carpenter's saw, an item of the merchandise in his
shop. He murdered his wife also and similarly sawed off her
head. Then lovingly cradling the severed heads in the
crook of his arms, he sat on the doorstep of his house in the
evening, crooning, "Lullaby! Lullaby, my treasures. Lullaby,
my little cabbages, *dormez bien*. Ha! Cabbages! Come buy!
Come buy!"

He had been an esteemed and reputable member of the
community up to the moment that he collapsed, but thereafter he was an object of fury. When he died too soon on
the wheel the mob turned accusingly towards Duprat, and
one old woman shouted, "*You* murdered them," and had to
be restrained.

"I was greatly distressed, Agathe," said the chancellor. "My
men dispersed them of course."

"They went home, *mon oncle?*"

"Of course they did. Where else would they go?"

"I shall try to keep better order on my estates in the future."

"I do not burden the people beyond their powers of
endurance," said Duprat shrugging. "That would be woe-
some management. No more does a farmer overload his
beasts. The poor people saw in that miserable merchant — a
robber to the end, you will note; he robbed them of their
entertainment — the reflection of their own weakness and
fear. They pay their taxes; they do not go mad and murder;
but the merchant cheated, and the only way out was insanity. He destroyed himself and his loved ones. No question that he loved them. Every one of that bloodthirsty

mob imagined himself on the wheel. They hated the criminal but they hated also that part of themselves which they share with him. That was what they could not endure. When he died before they were appeased, having hate to spare, they vented it on me. It is one of the unpleasantnesses that go with being chancellor. I am used to it. But it matters not if they hate the chancellor so long as they love the king."

"I do not love him."

"Hush, my niece. The walls have ears. Concede that he is admirable."

"That I concede, but not lovable."

"Therein you differ from most women," he smiled, "and are somewhat old-fashioned."

"He climbs to glory on your shoulders."

"I have not suffered unduly in the process," the chancellor said, "and neither have you. Now, if you please, can we turn to a pleasanter subject?"

He spoke of Marie, who had not shared this confidential colloquy with her elders.

"Sign here, Agathe," the chancellor said, producing a beautifully engrossed and lengthy document on sheets of official parchment. "Here, on the last page," pointing with his jeweled finger.

With a flourish of her pen the dowager duchess traced her X where Duprat indicated.

"Now Marie does not have a single care in the world," the chancellor said.

※

※ ※ 2 ※ ※

MARIE DE MONTHOLON was Duprat's only concession to love. He could lavish on her the affection
denied him by his position. Everyone else wanted something from him, but not Marie. He was so placed in the
hierarchy of the state that he could grant immense favors,
make or break careers at will; he was keenly aware of his
power, and therefore he viewed with suspicion even a
simple "Good morning, Your Eminence," from a stranger at
his audiences. "Eminence" was a title usually reserved for
cardinals, but the Holy See had bestowed it upon the chancellor-archbishop for noteworthy services in the matter of
the Concordat. Marie, a mere infant in her great-uncle's
eyes, was far too unsophisticated to be self-seeking, beyond
suspicion even from Duprat, and hence, on her, he poured
out the pent-up love that he dared not bestow on anyone
else in France. He was sensible that she was his pet, like a
pet cat or a thoroughbred horse or a little canary. He saw
no impropriety in comparing Marie with a cat, since a cat
is exquisitely beautiful and incomparably graceful; with a

horse, since a horse has spirit born of the blood; with a bird, since a bird has wings and alone of all God's creatures except the angels possesses the power to soar above the clouds.

"I adore the child," he would say to himself chuckling. "She does not deserve it of course, but I've got to adore something." There was precious little else in the life of the chancellor of the *épargne* to adore.

This had not prevented him from reaping a thumping financial benefit to himself in the drawing of Marie's marriage contract.

A concession here, a concession there, and a bonus to himself from all concerned for making the concessions, such was the invariable pattern of Duprat's official administration.

Marie's *dot* to Henri was of princely proportions. The dowager duchess embarrassed herself to raise it. But Marie benefited, for in return the old Comte de Tonnerre deeded to her mills, towns and vast tracts of revenue-producing farms. The chancellor levied a small percentage on Marie's *dot*.

And the Comte de Tonnerre benefited likewise. Marie's *dot* was paid in gold and the chancellor remitted Tonnerre's taxes for three years, subject of course to a transfer tax and a tax on the remission of taxes, which made fiscal sense in the economy of France in the chancellorship of Antoine Duprat. Much of the complex outpouring of treasure filtered into the king's *épargne,* and the king, rolling in revenues such as no king of France had ever enjoyed, was delighted. Thus everyone benefited and no one was a whit the worse off save Jacques Bonhomme, who did not know it and, as Duprat truly observed, was never tried beyond his power of endurance except in the case of the mad. If one has always worked to capacity from sunup to sundown and beholds himself no worse off than he was while his country prospers as never before, one may grumble but one does not stone the genius who works the miracle. Thus reasoned Jacques Bonhomme, whose honest sweat was transmogrified into elegant royal châteaux and paintings like the Mona Lisa to the end that King Francis might wallow in beauty. The deep love Frenchmen bore their king was the envy of other monarchs who lacked his spectacular charm.

Duprat gave Marie a pat on the head, bestowed an avuncular kiss on her clear forehead, accepted as his due her deep curtsy and departed with his men-at-arms, his cross bearer and his coterie of clerks, who lent a stern monastic note to his otherwise glittering cavalcade.

"I have told Henri de Tonnerre about you," he called cheerily to Marie. "Unless I greatly mistake his nature he will be here soon."

By custom a prelate might ride only a mule, evidencing his ecclesiastical humility. Chancellor Duprat's was shod with silver shoes, and the animal's delicate hoofs were painted gold. Despite his humble mount an aura of power surrounded him.

He mused as he rode, "How can young Henri think about a picture when Marie is so much prettier!" To Antoine Duprat the Mona Lisa was merely the likeness of a somewhat supercilious girl; in area the painting seemed absurdly small to have taken four years to paint; and as for her so-called enigmatic smile, it moved him not at all, except to suspect she had, probably, repeatedly seduced old

Leonardo da Vinci, no easy task considering the master's multifarious other interests. Perhaps that was why it had taken four years. But King Francis thought it was wonderful, and paid four thousand gold florins for it.

Henri de Tonnerre was immensely proud of his mission to Italy. To be trusted to escort the Mona Lisa to France ranked in his mind with the military honors he had won on the field of Marignan when he knelt, all bloody and breathless, to be knighted by his victorious king, surrounded by heaps of the bodies of the slain and the captured battle standards of the enemy, waving in the soft Italian air that still reeked of gunpowder and death. It had been a glorious moment.

In all former ages, thought Henri, a man of my rank would scorn to act as escort for a mere painting. But that was because those ages were dark and devoid of appreciation of beauty. He, he knew, lived in a new era of culture, refinement and progress.

He was not ashamed that he knew how to read and write. He felt somewhat patronizing toward his rude ancestors. Granted that they were valiant; granted that they excelled in the rougher virtues; granted that they had made of France the premier state of Christendom — yet how primitive they seemed in retrospect, how cheerless their castles, how naive their pleasures, how monotonous their fare, how inelegant their wines. Even his father, by no means as old-fashioned as some elderly noblemen, still drank a heavy Burgundy with the chicken course and never had tasted the tart and tingling surprise of *vino di Napoli di Malvasia*. An experience! But one must be educated into appreciation of the new Italian imports.

It was not that the old virtues were wrong, or past, or entirely false. They were merely incomplete. It was still expected of a man, at least a French nobleman, that he prove himself strong in battle. It was not that something good had been lost. It was rather that something better had been added. Kings still wore steel in battle, still slew with the sword the foes of France. But when the battle was over they did not remove their armor and sit in their undergarments of leather and homespun around groaning boards heaped high with heavy meats and sop up the gravy with slabs of bread among purely masculine companions, often drunk and usually unwashed. Manners had improved and ladies were present; the king himself set the fashion; food was esteemed for its sauce rather than its quantity; and wines were prized for their bouquet rather than power of instant intoxication. There were forks. There were spoons. One wiped one's lips with a napkin. One did not — not at court — wipe one's fingers on one's doublet or hose.

Never before had men, valiant men, strong men, worn satin, brocade and jaunty feathers in their caps. Never before had Frenchmen worn ten jeweled rings at once or bathed so frequently or perfumed their hair and beards. The virile odors of sweat and blood and the smell of the stable were not despised, but they were relegated to their proper place: battle, the hunt, the joust. And then the men put on their finery and no woman thought them effeminate. Thus courtly life had the best of both worlds in the wonderful Renaissance dawn. King Francis wrote sonnets and, breaking with tradition that excluded women from court entertainments, gave his opinion, which set a fashion, that "life without ladies is like a year without a spring and a spring without a rose." Little wonder the ladies adored him. He set another fashion too, breaking drastically with the past. The reason Henri de Tonnerre wore his hair short-cropped was that King Francis, having received a head wound at Marignan, was forced of necessity to cut his own. The style took and persisted. In the provinces many an old seigneur, out of touch and stubborn, remained clean-shaven with hair that reached down to the nape of the neck, Crusader fashion, a hairdress that had lasted since Louis the Saint. But Francis the First, who changed everything, changed even the barbering trade. Change, change for the better was in the air everywhere in France and, what was remarkable, men like Henri de Tonnerre were aware of it. It was so sudden, so different, that even contemporaries, blind to the slower changes, were dazzled. *"O siècle,"* cried a contemporary chronicler, *"les lettres fleurissent, les esprits se réveillent; c'est une joie de vivre!"* "Oh my century," he rhapsodized, "letters flourish, minds awaken, to live is a joy!" And another contemporary, "The world smiles on the world, and the world is young."

Tedious scholars would trace this sudden self-awareness and appreciation of the beauty of the world to Constantinople, where the cultural treasures of ancient Greece had long lain dormant, locked away from the West throughout the centuries that followed the fall of Rome and Europe's descent into barbarism. In turn, Constantinople, gorgeous in decadence, shining with the phosphorescence of decay, fell to the Turks. A host of refugee scholars filtered into Italy, bringing with them the dusty manuscripts of the ancient Greek writers: poets, philosophers, historians, playwrights. In Italy the seed fell on fertile soil. The art that had hibernated for a thousand years burst forth, lush, floreate and sensual. Long passages of the pre-Christian poets, especially the dramatists, were delightfully salacious. Their plays were again produced after a millennium of silence; Medea again murdered her sons and Oedipus again married his mother, and the ghosts of the old Greek writers again heard the plaudits of an audience, but an audience new and unrecognizable, the Italians. The Italians forgave the wicked Greek plays because they were pre-Christian. But the stories were incomparably daring and no one denied that the lines were superlative art.

Italians were dimly aware that their art was Greek in origin, but Frenchmen were not. Good Frenchmen like Henri de Tonnerre knew only that Italy, Italy the enemy, Italy the beaten, possessed a brilliance as far superior to France as France was superior to the wildernesses of Canada.

Henri had changed his mind about the Italians now that he had made a second journey thither. On the first occasion he had seen the Italians only as enemy bodies, bodies to be shot down by artillery or run through with the sword. They had proved as vulnerable as any other bodies, and he had conceived a low estimate of their fighting qualities.

This, he now realized, hardly did them justice.

On his second journey to Italy, the mission of the Mona Lisa, he had caught a glimpse of their minds. He had stood amazed at their versatility. They were interested in everything. Nothing was too small to excite their curiosity, perhaps some exotic new herb in cookery; nothing was too big to dampen their enthusiasm for experiment, like the architectural problem of superimposing a dome on a drum, free from its abutments and crowned with a cupola.

"Let's try it," was their response. "Let's try everything."

They appeared to be under some lash of the old pagan gods to excel. Their minds were feverishly alive. Their morals were singularly low. In fact, they seemed by the old standards to have no morals at all. But this was perhaps not to be wondered at, since it is impossible to have morals without a sense of shame. The Italians were not even ashamed of defeat in battle, as witness their casual acceptance of the disaster at Marignan, which doomed the entire duchy of Milan to the overlordship of France.

Coupled with their extraordinary curiosity was an inexhaustible fund of energy, expressed in extremes that dazzled a Frenchman. Michelangelo worked for four years on a forty-foot scaffold lying on his back to paint a ceiling, but with equal enthusiasm he wrote love sonnets to the adolescent son of a neighboring nobleman. Benvenuto Cellini sweated like a peasant in a bronze foundry to cast a statue two stories high and weighing ten thousand pounds, stirring the molten metal with a heavy iron puddler as he shouted the formula to assistants who threw in the prescribed measurements of copper, silver and tin. But Cellini also won a prize by applying a coat of gold paint to the body of a slender youth and entering him in a beauty contest where he was adjudged the most lovely of all the girls before his sex was discovered. On which Cellini shook with laughter, exacted his due from the lad, got raving drunk, staggered out into the night, jostled a stranger who saved him from falling into a canal, took offense at the stranger's bad manners, stabbed him in the belly and left him to die, which he did, and went home without a wink of sleep and began to engrave a medallion. The die was steel; the artist's hand did not falter. The button that resulted was destined to rank as a masterpiece of delicacy and good taste and was admired on a papal cope.

Italy opened the eyes of Henri de Tonnerre and made him determined to emulate a people so superlatively confident that defeat seemed unimportant.

Rome awed him. Here was a city erected by a cultured and gifted race when Paris was a swamp. Here were marble columns reared by sophisticated engineers when in France his ancestors were building wooden palisades around their huts to keep out the wolves. Here was a people so gifted and vital that they shrugged off without shame even the loss of their independence, knowing that there were other ways to conquer, other ways to excel.

As with the men, so with the women. It had happened in ancient times with the rape of the Sabines, when the Sabine men were slaughtered and the Sabine girls enslaved, only to become the progenitors of the Caesars. It had happened more recently in Constantinople, when the city fell and Christian girls found themselves in the harems of the unspeakable Turk, only to become the mothers of conquering sultans of transcendent genius, now the menace of Christendom. It had happened in the New World discovered by Columbus where the men spoke a different language from the women. There, in those distant and mysterious islands, it was actually true that warriors spoke a superior dialect among themselves, while their wives spoke a dialect of slaves, and the reason was this: there was war in America shortly prior to the appearance of Columbus. The Caribs were slain by the Mexicans. The Carib men were exterminated, the Carib women reserved for other purposes, and after a few generations these women, now dead and revered, were remembered as respectable great-grand-mothers, and their descendants were the Indians who paddled out to meet Columbus's caravels: and the male Indians all spoke Mexican and the female Indians all spoke Carib. It was a Carib-speaking Indian girl who first introduced into Europe, in the loins of Columbus's crew, the most serious illness ever to trouble humanity since the Black Death. In England Henry VIII had already contracted it. Henri de Tonnerre had been warned against its prevalence in Italy. It had not existed in France in his father's time.

The world was a dangerous, exciting place, with surprises everywhere. There were greater rewards to be won; there were greater hazards to avoid. It was not enough to be loyal and brave; one had to think and scheme.

The Italian women were new and delightfully seductive. There is an ethos of the beaten. A memorial always arises to honor the forgotten slain. The daughters of slaughtered enemy soldiers are oddly more desirable than other girls in the eyes of the conqueror. When the men are exterminated the women, merely by existing, by their helpless availability, redress the imbalance of nature; and the bastards born of the first generation of the vanquished become venerated roots of some family tree in the land of the conquerors.

Giulietta Leone, whom Henri called Juliette, was orphaned when her father, a stonemason, was killed at the battle of Marignan. An aged aunt, widowed and desperately poor, took her in for a while, cackling and scolding and switching the child out to steal, which Giulietta learned to do expertly. When Giulietta was a little older the old harridan changed her tactics, sensing a greater use for the child than stolen fish and scraps of bread. *"Giulietta mia,"* she whined, with an ingratiating leer, "there are easier ways to get good things."

"Are there, my aunt? What ways?"

"I am very old," said her aunt, "and soon I shall die and go to Heaven, and maybe I can't get in because I taught you to steal."

"We were hungry, my aunt. Stealing's all right when you're hungry."

"My conscience hurts me," said her aunt.

"Mine does too sometimes, but what else is there to do? And I never got caught except once, and then I ran like the wind. I got away. I never got caught again. I can see out of the corners of my eyes and tell when I'm being watched and nobody knows I am looking."

"You have beautiful eyes," her aunt said, "big, black beautiful eyes. When you run you run like a gazelle. Oh, I've watched you, Giulietta. You have lovely long legs. That's why you can run so fast. How grand you'd look in shoes."

Giulietta blushed at the praise, and she had always wanted shoes.

"Such pretty little feet. Like a lady, a real lady."

"Some day I'll have shoes."

"How your eyes flash when you say that! No wonder men look at you as if they were hungry for supper."

"I'll have shoes if I have to steal them."

"It's all my fault," the old crone said, "I'll never get to Heaven. I taught you how to steal."

"Then I can't get there either," Giulietta said, without any particular fear of the flames, "because I did the stealing."

"You must not steal any more, Giulietta."

"I am old enough to work, my aunt," she suggested.

"Hm-m. I didn't mean quite that. There are quicker ways."

"Marriage!" said Giulietta. "Of course."

"Without a dowry, child? Oh no, oh no."

Giulietta hung her head.

"What do you know about men? How could you please a man? Marriage interests you? You think you're grown up. You are not grown up. Your body is grown up, but your brain is a baby's. You know nothing."

On this severe note, leaving Giulietta puzzled and ashamed, the aunt rested. But later she resumed the lesson. Giulietta had not stopped stealing, but she now concealed it from her aunt.

"They'll be bringing the poultry in from the country today," the old woman said. "How good a chicken and rice would taste. I am so weak."

It would taste good to Giulietta too.

"I'll get one from a cart," she cried. She did not say "steal." "There are so many. It'll never be missed. I know just how. I can wring its neck before it squawks. Oh auntie, let me!"

"It would taste so good. But it is wrong."

"And I'll get the rice too. We haven't any left. We ate the last last night."

"Thou shalt not steal," said her aunt, scowling.

"I know."

"Of course, if somebody were to *give* you the chicken and rice it would be different. Did a man ever try to kiss you, Giulietta?"

"Lots of them."

"Did they do it?"

"I wouldn't let them. I ran away."

"But if you liked a boy you'd let him kiss you, wouldn't you?"

"That's different."

"Is it?"

"It's different when you like a boy."

"You like chicken, don't you?"

"Of course." She paused. "Oh. Oh, I see."

"Well, then?"

"I wouldn't have to give my whole self to him, would I, auntie?"

Her aunt raised scandalized eyes to Heaven, invoking celestial aid. "For a lousy chicken? May the saints teach my little girl a sense of value! No, dear Giulietta. When it's time for you to surrender yourself it will be for princes! For a chicken you only smile and allow a little kiss and run."

"I'd think I'd run anyway for fear he'd take the chicken back."

"Not if you kept promising. Always keep promising. Men will give you anything if you keep on promising."

"Did you?" Giulietta asked, glancing at the poverty around her.

"I was stupid," her aunt said bitterly. "And I didn't look like you."

When her aunt died Giulietta was doubly orphaned, and mourned her like a mother. She had lived with her ten years and learned from her all she knew. Her beauty had matured and men had offered marriage knowing she had no dowry. But she stayed with her aunt, who was bedridden and helpless before she died. The little house was sold for debts; a smitten carter with whom she had flirted trundled the coffin off to the potter's field and asked no fee beyond "Giulietta, sometime?"

"Sometime," she said, conscious that her honest tears made her eyes shine with promise.

"You're mighty pretty," the carter said, moistening his lips nervously.

"Today I am sad. Sometime."

"I was a brute for asking today."

She thought he was a brute too, but she looked up at him with a wan appropriate smile.

The priest who said the prayer as the earth thumped onto the cheap wooden coffin glanced at the single mourner and said, "What will you do now, Giulietta?"

"I don't know."

He knew; and to avoid it he visited an orphanage that night and spoke to the Mother Superior.

"We do not take girls that old," she told him, stiff as the starch of her wimple, "and besides, Giulietta Leone has a bad reputation."

"All the more reason," he said.

Giulietta could cook, Giulietta could sew, Giulietta had cared for a disreputable aunt with the tenderness of a daughter. One should not believe all one heard, and in any case she could not be all bad. "She is exceptionally bright, and with a little teaching herself she can teach the younger children. In the meantime there are many duties she can perform in your household."

"She'd steal the candles off the altar!"

"She asked for one to burn for her aunt. I gave her a penny."

"*You* gave *her* a penny?"

"Yes."

"It should have been the other way round."

"Would Our Lord have said that?"

Reproached, the Mother Superior lowered her eyes. If Giulietta had started bewitching the clergy it was high time the girl was taken off the streets and taught to behave. Privately she thought the priest had been taken in.

But Giulietta charmed her too, with her willingness and eagerness to please; and presently she won over the teaching nuns also, whose lessons she soaked up like a dry and apparently insatiable sponge. When, in turn, she started teaching the children, they loved her. It was not discovered at once that Giulietta bribed them with forbidden dried fruits that she stole from the kitchen.

Shortly they trusted her with money. Save for that one candle she had never asked for anything, sleeping on a straw pallet in the kitchen till they gave her a tiny cell — after all, woodmen did come into the kitchens from time to time to deliver fuel. Nor had she ever stolen so much as a penny, though on several occasions the Mother Superior purposely let drop that the convent funds were hidden under a bread sack in the pantry. Once she left the pantry door unlocked and waited all night, spying, to see how Giulietta would withstand the test. A peculiar thing happened. Quiet as a thief in the night Giulietta slipped into the Mother Superior's room. The good woman dived into bed and pretended to be asleep. Giulietta found her keys hanging with her cross and rosary at the head of the bed. She detached the right key without a sound, slipped out and locked the pantry door. Then she returned and replaced the key.

"Did you hear a prowler last night, Giulietta?" the Mother Superior asked next day.

"No, Reverend Mother," Giulietta said. "Did you?"
She could not honestly say she had.

"I don't know how she manages to get such bargains," the Mother Superior wondered, but no whisper of scandal had ever reached her ears when Giulietta would return from the market place, gay and proud of her purchases. "It cannot be respectable, but I can find no wrong in it, much as I try."

When it came time to buy a length of new linen for the altar cloth — it had to be heavy and of finest quality to carry all the embroidery the nuns would lavish on it — Giulietta was solemnly given a gold florin to make the purchase.

"Mind you get something first-rate," the Mother Superior said.

"I promise to look at nothing but the best." She swept her a deep curtsy and the Mother Superior, smiling gently, felt she had reason to be proud of her handiwork. Giulietta Leone had come to them clever and quick but illiterate, ill-spoken and unwashed. Now Giulietta's manners were those of a lady, her speech was polished and she smelled so sweet from her constant baths that the nuns wondered whether they had not overemphasized this matter of cleanliness. But search as they might they could never find perfume in her cell. No one thought to look at the vanilla bottle in the kitchen or the bottle of rosewater in the chapel: the scent Giulietta concocted from a discreet mixture of the two smelled like neither and better than both.

When Giulietta did not return from the market place the Mother Superior was greatly distressed. But the search that was instituted yielded no results, and it was feared that she had met with an accident or foul play, both being common. In the convent chapel the prayers for Giulietta's safe return at length gave way to prayers for the repose of her soul.

She never returned.

The Mona Lisa was wrapped in a light covering of cloth and encased in a cedar box. Cedar was chosen because it did not exude gum, like pine, which might have spotted the surface, and cedar also kept out the cockroaches, which had been known to spoil many a painting by chewing upon certain favorite colors. The casing was ventilated to avoid mildew. Over all was a wrapping of oilcloth to keep out stray drops of rain that might splatter in under the gorgeous canopy that covered the litter on which it was being carried. Da Vinci's masterpiece was being escorted to France in the same conveyance accorded a visiting dignitary and with the same pomp. A squad of archers appareled in the lily-embroidered tabards of France's guard of honor marched in step beside it. Before and behind marched pikemen and musketeers, three men to each of the powerful new firearms: an expert to fire it, an engineer to load it and carry the muzzle, and a powder-and-bullet boy who carried the heavy butt end. Everything traditional, everything modern was represented. To the rear of the cavalcade was a rough-looking guard whose duty it was to ward off curiosity seekers and beggars who crowded about so rich and important a train. Last of all came the pack mules and supply wagons with a load of tents, provisions and cooking utensils, and servants walking or sneaking rides under the baggage: cooks, grooms, muleteers. As with an army, there were camp followers and other hangers-on, some female: gypsies, vagrant musicians and rapscallion entertainers, who would attach themselves temporarily to this tag end of the procession. They were not molested and were permitted to come and go as they pleased.

Leading the cavalcade was a group of cavaliers with Henri de Tonnerre at their head.

Once a day, with the archers at attention, their bows strung and arrows at the ready, he ordered the painting exposed and inspected it. Each day the Mona Lisa smiled at him; he experienced the sensation, stronger each day, that she was real, alive, and had granted him an assignation. "I am here," she seemed to whisper; "I shall always be here. I am safe, Henri de Tonnerre. Are you? What will you be like a hundred years hence? You are young and strong today; I observe you have acquired a becoming tan in this sun. I wonder what you will be like a century hence, a short, short century hence, Henri de Tonnerre. I shall be the same. Poor Henri. Poor tanned handsome Henri. Oh mortal! Beneath those lithe young muscles I smell the dead and rotten bones!"

"Ouf!" he said, passing his hand before his eyes and shaking his head as if to dislodge crawling things.

"Everything all right, chevalier?" his lieutenant asked.

"Eh? Oh yes, quite all right."

"The cloth's smudged a little, sir. The road was rough yesterday and the litter swung a lot."

On the road to Marignan the horses had frequently faltered and stumbled in the ruts still left from the military traffic and the packaged painting had rocked back and forth. The inner cloth was slightly wrinkled and discolored.

"I'll replace it at Marignan," Henri said. "There'll be linen there, I should think."

He would buy linen, pick it out himself. He smiled. In former ages a man of his rank would never have compromised his dignity by entering a market place like a woman. Henri was not disturbed by such old-fashioned scruples and, proud of his mission, walked among the hawkers and ironmongers and vegetable sellers to a booth with a cross where ecclesiastical fabrics were displayed: cloth of gold for chasubles, watered silk for monsignors' birettas, lace for frontals and skeins of gold and silver thread to be worked into embroidery for copes and stoles. Here, he thought, if I purchased a bolt of brocade for my own personal use everyone would take it quite for granted.

Rabelais, the good-natured rascal, had caught the spirit of the Italians and was writing enormously popular stories about them, which everybody was enjoying except, probably, his mother-in-law-to-be; and the burden of the stories was, "Do as you please." Why not? Was it so bad? At the moment he could think of nothing he wanted to do that would really hurt anybody, though *belle-mère* would probably disapprove. *Belle-mère* probably disapproved of everything. He had never seen her but he was already prejudiced. But then, what mother-in-law ever did approve of a son-in-law? They sold their daughters, invariably hideous, to the highest bidder and then had the gall to cackle and carp at their sons-in-law. Fortunately, sons-in-law were never expected to be faithful, even by a mother-in-law. He wondered what the Italian term was for "mother-in-law." With all their genius they could hardly have improved on the gay and cynical *belle-mère* of the French.

Henri de Tonnerre was therefore full of rebellious

thoughts as he jostled his way through the chattering bour-
geoisie of the market place to buy a piece of cloth. Looking
forward to making the purchase had been easy to ration-
alize. Looking back on it would probably be equally easy,
by reason of the dignity of his mission. But it suddenly
occurred to him that he had never actually purchased anything in his entire life: his purser took care of such things.
"It wouldn't bother an Italian," he muttered enviously.
"Why does it bother a good Frenchman?" False pride, old
feudal manners, an outmoded sense of shame, that was all,
that was the only explanation. Striding through the crowd,
which parted to let him pass, he approached the booth.

For the first time in his life he carried a purse. Its strings
were attached to his sword belt. He felt conspicuous. But
he saw many Italian *cavalieri* similarly accoutered.

It would be far more pleasant, he mused, if men chose
their own wives. Already he resented the burden of *belle-
mère,* growing angrier and angrier at her. *Belle-mère* and
the purse were much alike, both rich, both burdensome,
both dragging him down into a position of tutelage. Purse
strings and apron strings, both confined, both irked a man.

If they could choose their own wives, he was sure, all
men would choose orphans. Perhaps the time would come
when men were really free. No, probably not. Marriages
were arranged from top to bottom on the social scale.
Peasants consolidated grazing rights, enlarging their fields.
Kings negotiated alliances. Paupers and princes alike were
pawns in the games played by their ambitious elders. His
father's marriage with his mother had been arranged for
the good of the house of Tonnerre. For the good of the
realm of France, King Francis had married Queen Claude.
No, marriages had always been arranged and probably

39

always would be. Well, that left a man a certain freedom of action. "When it comes my time I too will arrange the marriages of my sons and daughters," he said to himself, solemnly as if he were taking a vow to perform some onerous duty. "But I shall also legitimize my bastards," he added, for his eye had fallen upon Giulietta, who was standing at the booth. His bastards were likely to have far more spirit than the lawful offspring he could expect from this Marie of Montholon. Chancellor Duprat had said she was a beauty, but no one who knew Chancellor Duprat wholly believed him. Marie de Montholon was probably as big and fat as her dowry. Ah well. He would do his duty.

Giulietta was haggling with the merchant over a length of linen that looked to Henri's unpracticed eye like the very sort of thing he needed. She wore the demure and respectable garb of a lay sister, but on the way to the market she had cinched up the belt around her slender waist and loosened her hair. Outside the convent walls Giulietta was a different person; she walked with the free abandon that came naturally to her lithe long legs, imparting a gypsy-like swing to her hips. The breeze ruffled and tangled her hair; she did not care, though she knew how it made her look; she liked the fresh feeling it gave her and regretted the moment that always came when she would have to put on again the confining headdress before she returned.

Henri had never seen such bright, alive eyes; he was not aware they had seen him too and swiftly appraised him. The girl seemed entirely absorbed in her purchase.

As he watched, the girl's bargaining became more animated. She tossed her head, and the sun struck sparks of dark iridescence from her hair, like the blue-black sparkle

of a raven's wing. Nay, a falcon's, for Giulietta was the bird
of prey and the merchant was the victim. She lifted her face
and brought it close to the merchant's and, taking a deep
breath, which strained against her bodice, let fly a flood
of Lombard dialect incomprehensible to Henri's inadequate Italian. She waggled a threatening finger under the
merchant's nose. Her hands were smooth and expressive.
It had been a long time since she had done any heavy work
to roughen them. It had been a long time since those strong
long sensitive fingers had filched a purse or wrung a stolen
chicken's neck before it could squawk. Her whole young
body seemed to enter the spirit of the argument, tense,
integral and full of the will to win.

Henri chuckled. She was unquestionably giving the merchant a hard time. Reluctantly the unhappy man was
measuring off more and more of the linen, foot after foot.
Then suddenly he extended his arms in an eloquent gesture
of abject defeat, pushed the whole rumpled length of fabric
towards her across the counter and said, "Take it all, you
vixen. You are ruining my day." Giulietta gave him the
florin.

Henri, who had stood aside watching the battle, laughed.
"Bravo! He capitulated!"

"Another such customer and I shall lose my license from
the bishop," the merchant said ruefully, pocketing the
florin. Then, turning to Henri, as one turns to a shelter
in a storm: "And you, chevalier? In what can this poor,
worsted and lowly servant of the Church be of service to
the young French lord's excellence?"

The transliteration of the polite Italian idiom, mean-
ingless to the merchant, sounded strangely flowery in French.

Giulietta answered, also in French with a halting and

oddly intriguing accent, "I did not steal from the Church. I bought it for the Church." Glancing shyly at Henri she said, "He does me an injustice." She lowered her eyes, ashamed of her boldness. She covered her hair with her prim little white headdress, which only added more luster to her complexion, already made richer by heightened color during the argument. "It is for the altar at the convent, as he very well knows, *mon seigneur*." Then she began to fold the linen, taking pains to smooth out every wrinkle. This took some time. Meanwhile she stood side by side with Henri, her sleeve occasionally touching his arm. He could smell her perfume. She knew he could.

"Watch your purse," said the merchant once when her hands strayed unnecessarily close to Henri.

"That was an ungracious remark," Henri said.

"Stupid, too," said Giulietta. "It's on the other side. Did you think I'd put my arm around and steal it? That's what I'd have to do."

Henri laughed. "I think I'd notice if you did. I should probably chastise you severely."

"How? What would you do?" said the girl. She had the reddest lips and whitest teeth he had ever seen smile. The Mona Lisa's smile was accusing and made you think. Not this girl's.

"I'd probably turn you over my knee and spank you," he said.

"Not here, if the *signore's* magnificence please," the merchant said uncomfortably. "Then I should lose my license for sure. Is there anything else in my booth that attracts your lordship's eye?"

Giulietta glared at him.

"I want some cloth exactly like the linen you just sold this young lady," Henri said. "Quite a lot of it."

Inwardly the merchant groaned. If he had not let Giulietta get the better of him he could have sold the same length of linen for five florins instead of one to this unsuspecting Frenchman. "I am losing my grip. I deserve to lose my license."

"She bought it all," he cried. "Every inch of it." There was genuine distress in his face. Giulietta smiled. "But I have other fabrics, your lordship, silks, brocades, cloth of gold, cloth of silver —"

"They'd smudge," Henri said.

"Alas, I cannot help your lordship."

"Maybe I can," Giulietta said.

"You?"

"What would they smudge, *cavaliere*? You?" She laughed softly.

"No, my little one," Henri said. "Frenchmen don't wear brocade next to their skin, in case you don't know."

"I only wondered."

The merchant concealed a cynical smile. No doubt she wondered; no doubt she'd find out.

"It's to wrap a picture in," Henri said. "A rare and beautiful picture."

"How I should like to see it!" Giulietta said.

"There's no reason why you shouldn't."

This young Frenchman would know much more than he did now, before he was through with Giulietta Leone, the merchant thought. He watched them move away through the crowd.

Henri placed her to his right in the French manner, but

she moved around to his left. "You are careless of your purse, *cavaliere*," she said. "Anybody could snatch it. I think you need protection."

"Now you can steal it," he said, "and I shan't feel an arm sneaking around my waist, I'll never notice, you'll fly away and I shall be deprived of the very great pleasure of spanking you."

"Here," she said, taking his hand. "Now I can't steal and you can't spank."

The wrapping of the Mona Lisa, Henri decided, could wait. There would be other bolts of fine linen to buy, but a Giulietta was not to be found every day. "I'd like you to see the picture," he said.

The sun was setting when they reached the inn. "I take excellent care of my little painted lady," Henri said, motioning with his head in the direction of a room with a guard at the door. "It would be unkind to disturb her slumbers, don't you think?"

Giulietta nodded, smiling. "And expose her to the evening chill, too! Most unkind. Keep her wrapped up, all nice and warm."

"Besides, the light would be all wrong. Candlelight wouldn't do her justice and she'd reproach me."

"Does she talk to you, chevalier?"

"Always reproaches me," Henri said, shrugging.

Giulietta laughed. "What a silly way to talk about a painting."

Henri said, "I'll just keep her wrapped up all nice and warm in the dark tonight; then first thing in the morning we can take a look at her if she's still here."

It was a question.

For answer Giulietta took off her prim headdress, shook

out her long hair and smiled. "Yes, she will still be here in the morning. But she cannot go back where she came from. You can never go back, Chevalier de Tonnerre." To Giulietta the Frenchman represented more than escape from the dead-end existence at the convent. She guessed he was older than she, most everybody was, but there was a simplicity about him, by Italian standards, that moved her deeply. Old auntie had said, "When it is time for you to surrender yourself it will be for princes." The Frenchman was no prince, but he was not far below princely status, his strong face was sensitive and his brow was high and thoughtful. No doubt in time, she thought with a mental shrug, he would grow gross and opinionated. But at the moment he roused her Italian blood, for the moment he could be trusted to be chivalrous. And at the moment he constituted a sure safe avenue of escape from the stultifying routine of the convent. He could be trusted and she needed help.

He had not treated her as a whore though he must have been aware how outrageously she had flirted with him. Indeed he had couched his proposal in delicate language, pretending to talk about the Mona Lisa. She compared him with the gross advances, the hip pinching on the street, the sweaty hands of street vendors that fumbled at her breasts and tried to untie her tight-fitting bodice, the wine-sour breaths, the foul words, the leers: oh, he was better, far better, Heaven-sent.

Giulietta said, "She will be here. Yes."

Late in the night gossip raced through the personnel of the French mission that Henri de Tonnerre had taken a mistress. He had closeted himself with the Italian girl at sundown. A supper of champagne and oysters had been served *à deux* at nine o'clock. At midnight she was still there. He had not turned her out like a common trollop to make her way home as best she could, alone or with some hanger-on of the tag end of the train who would exact his reward in turn. Clearly she was something more than a night's companion.

The archers laid bets on the outcome. "He'll send her packing by dawn with a florin or two. He's not safely married yet and the chancellor would throw a fit if he showed up with a mistress." Others wagered, "He's a fool if he lets go of a piece like that. He'll keep her under cover and the chancellor will never know. That's what I'd do if I was Tonnerre." "No, he'd be caught. How'd he keep her under cover? She sticks out like —" There were expressive similes. "Anyhow, who'd tell?" was the answer. They looked at one another; not one would tell; every one of them hoped that if Giulietta fell she would fall to him.

Late in the night Henri said to her as she lay beside him, "I was wrong about you, Juliette. I was sure you had known other men."

"No," she said.

"Many other men."

"No, Henri."

It was the first time he had heard No from her lips.

Early next morning the French cavalcade left Marignan lest someone at the convent institute a search for Giulietta which would have caused gossip that might get back to Duprat and prove embarrassing. It would not break the marriage contract but it would bitterly irk the old Comte de Tonnerre and make an enemy of the chancellor.

Henri wanted to keep her near him. He had expected an evening's entertainment. He had uncovered a treasure. She would present difficulties later on, no doubt, but the road to Paris was ten days long and could be stretched to two weeks — the Mona Lisa must not be shaken up and the pace could be slow.

He wrapped the painting in Giulietta's length of fine linen. The Mona Lisa's smile said to him, "Congratulations, chevalier. Do you know why you did it?"

"No," said Henri.

"No what, sir?" his lieutenant asked. "It seems a most excellent wrapping."

"You did it because Giulietta is beautiful, and Marie, the maid of Montholon, is ugly as sin. You have already decided."

"Quite so," Henri said.

"I thought so too," said the lieutenant.

To Giulietta the painted smile said, "Well, my girl, what now?"

Giulietta did not know, but whatever the future might hold it could hardly be worse than the past. And the present was delightful. "I will hang on to him," she vowed. "I will hang on to him though I know he will never recognize me as his mistress. I'll never be a princess but I'll never be poor again. I'll never meet his noble friends but he will visit me in some hidden obscure dwelling. He will not forsake me. He is not a man who will change."

"Sometimes I think that smile is the nastiest, most cynical smirk I ever saw," Henri said to her as the painting was locked in its cedar case and covered with the oilcloth.

"Didn't you like her today?" Giulietta asked.

"Not a bit."

47

"I didn't either. I don't like what's so hard to understand."

"She didn't talk to you, eh, Juliette?"

"Oh, Henri, paintings don't talk. She just looked mysterious as if everything in life were my fault and even the weather was going to be bad and I was too stupid to foresee it and it would serve me right when the storm came."

"The weather, my pet, is superb. I predict it will stay so for two precious weeks."

"What then?" In two weeks they would be in Paris.

"Nobody can predict the weather, Juliette." She saw clouds on his forehead.

Let him think, let him ponder what to do with her. She would make herself so essential to him that he would never cast her aside. She had had infinite practice in pleasing. She had pleased her aunt, the nuns, the Mother Superior, even the children. By all possible devices she had made herself necessary. Almost she wished she had taken lovers. She would have learned how a mistress makes herself essential to a man and fights off competition. She counted on her love to make up the deficiency. If his passion was brutal she would submit. If his weakness was a roving eye she would take what was left after the others and feed on him in her heart and be thankful. If he turned glutton she would feed him. If he got drunk she would clean up the mess and put a cold cloth on his head. If he fell ill she would nurse him back to health.

If she could have seen the Mona Lisa's smile at that moment she might have heard a wiser voice, "Many girls feel thus the morning after their first man. Are you sure you are quite awake, Giulietta, not still in a dream?"

He looked extraordinarily handsome, she thought, riding

48

straight and tall on his charger beside her. Vividly imagining how soon he would lie naked in bed with his bride, she twisted her hands in a wicked wrenching motion, ending with a jerk, and a chicken's neck was wrung before it could squawk. But she thrust down the emotion; it would be disastrous to bring up the subject of Marie; he would only hate her for it and, worse, lose respect for her. He was of the race of the conquerors, strong, full of a sense of old-fashioned honor. He would not desert her. She counted on him never to change from exactly what he was now. In his transports of pleasure during the night, pleasure she had given him, pleasure that hurt, pleasure that sanctified and absolved and made her proud of bestowing, he had vowed that he loved her. Frenchmen were not like Italians and love with them was deeper. Giulietta was certain of that, with all the certainty of her youth and the ghost of her virginity, sacrificed and pleading her cause like the incense of a burnt offering. And who could be more certain of anything than that?

What were his last words? Ah yes, the weather.

"I never beheld a more beautiful day," she answered.

He looked over at her and barely checked his hand as it reached out to caress her knee. But one does not pat the knee of one's page.

Giulietta's brilliant smile flashed; her dimple deepened and under her doublet he could still see the breasts that had bewitched him during all the long night after passion was appeased and her body had drained his loins.

"You wouldn't cause a bit of comment, chevalier. More than one noble Italian has a favorite page boy. You would only make the disguise more convincing."

He had dressed her in a page's doublet and hose. She

straddled her mount like a man. Her hair was tightly braided and hidden in a pert little hunter's cap. Many an aristocratic youth had features as beardless and fine.

"You don't look like a page boy to me," Henri said, laughing heartily.

"I do to everybody else."

"We'll have to be more careful in France, however."

"Henri, how far is it to France?"

"All my life, my darling."

She believed him.

※

※　※　**3**　※　※

THE ARCHIEPISCOPAL PALACE at Sens was hoary
with tradition. A grim and ancient structure, it stood
in startling contrast to the modern buildings that had risen
around it in the last two reigns. No Frenchman could look
up at its high towers and massive walls without feeling a
surge of pride in his ancestors of a rough but still venerated
age when these mighty fortress-palaces were erected as a
matter of common necessity, not to be beautiful but purely
to be functional.

Here Louis the Saint had danced with his bride. Thither
he had sent from the Holy Land the Crown of Thorns for
safe keeping till the exquisite little Sainte Chapelle could
be built to house it in Paris. Here were displayed in dusty
dignity the Mass vestments worn by Thomas à Becket when
he was slain on the steps of the altar in England. Here, in a
crystal reliquary, was a fragment of the wood of the True
Cross, a gift of the Emperor Charlemagne.

Here dwelt in studied simplicity the richest, busiest, most

grasping and best-informed statesman of France, Chancellor Antoine Duprat.

It was said that the chancellor never slept; assuredly he permitted little sleep to others. A continuous stream of agents and informers, each unknown to the other and often meeting but never realizing that they were playing similar roles, came and went inconspicuously, shadowy figures in his vast organization of spies.

Henri de Tonnerre was unaware that one of the tatterdemalion crowd in the tag end of his retinue had slipped away in the night and, armed with funds too large for an honest beggar, had hired a horse reserved for the king's post and ridden to Sens three days in advance of Henri's arrival at Paris.

At dusk at a postern gate, unlighted and unguarded because it was always barred, a ragged minstrel appeared, struck a chord on his cracked lute and was instantly admitted. He was travel-stained and weary. His chin was smudged with a three-day stubble of beard, and he reeked of the odor of the horse from which he had just dismounted.

He mounted the dark and dusty steps of a winding passageway like one who had been there before. He paused at what appeared to be a bricked-up window in the solid masonry of the wall and again plucked the chord on his lute. At the signal the wall opened and he was ushered into the brilliantly lighted study of Antoine Duprat.

The chancellor wrinkled his sensitive nose and motioned him to the far end of a long table.

"Pray, sit," he said, scanning him with an eye that was trained to see all, to reveal nothing. If an agent cringed there was usually no news of consequence. If an agent's manner was confident the news was usually bad, and it was then Duprat's habit to make a great show of discounting it, lest the agent conceive a puffed-up opinion of himself.

The minstrel lounged into the proffered chair, a smile on his face. The chancellor knew that the news was bad.

"Well?" said Duprat. "All goes well?"

"Alas, Your Eminence!"

"What do you mean by 'alas, Your Eminence'? You are not employed for your rhetoric. Kindly specify."

"All goes as ill as can possibly be imagined, Your Eminence."

"The painting is safe, not harmed, not stolen?"

"Oh, the painting is all right."

"And the Chevalier de Tonnerre? He is safe? No foreign agents have approached him, no Spaniards, no Englishmen, no one from the traitor of Bourbon?"

"No, Your Eminence."

Then the bad news was not international in character, Duprat concluded. He was particularly concerned about the traitorous Bourbon prince, but many foreign powers also had claims on Italy and might well have attempted to infiltrate the French mission.

"Then your news cannot be so ill after all," Duprat said with an engaging smile. "My dear fellow, from the looks of you you have ridden fast and hard. You could do with a bit of refreshment. I shall get you a glass of wine." He reached out his hand in the direction of a little silver bell on the table.

"Could Your Eminence make it a glass of brandy?"

"Of course."

Duprat's smile did not alter but mentally he scowled. The fellow wanted brandy, did he? Then the news was indeed something out of the ordinary. He rang the bell, and a servant materialized and dematerialized with a speed and silence astounding to Duprat's visitor, leaving on the table a generous glass of vintage brandy. The agent's ears were quick. The bell had scarcely tinkled in the chancellor's hand; it could not possibly have conveyed a signal for brandy. Therefore the servant was listening. The agent experienced an uncomfortable sensation that the empty room was full of watching eyes and listening ears — and who knew whether pistols also were not leveled at his heart? Some of his confidence evaporated. He drained the glass to steady his nerves under Duprat's hard and deceptively pleasant smile.

"Now," said Duprat, "this news you consider so momentous, what is it?"

"The Chevalier de Tonnerre has taken a mistress!" the agent declared.

Duprat betrayed no emotion. Slipping into his clerical role he remarked unctuously, "That is, alas, a failing the flesh is heir to, particularly in young men. You yourself are a young man; do not judge the Chevalier de Tonnerre more harshly than you would judge yourself in a similar lapse, unless you would have me believe that all during your travel in Italy you have observed absolute continence. Whatever the Chevalier de Tonnerre has done, I have no doubt he did it with circumspection." It would not be difficult, the chancellor thought, to dispose of one small mistress.

"Eminence, I do not pretend to be better than I am, but I did not flaunt my — my little lapses like Henri de Tonnerre. He has dressed up this Italian girl in a page boy's livery. She rides beside him every day. She shares his room every night. Everyone knows about it. The king's archers, the soldiers, the servants, everyone."

Duprat raged inwardly, "The young fool! He will break Marie's heart even before he marries her!" His first thought was for his grand-niece. It did him honor, but it was immediately smothered by a rush of other considerations, less emotional and more practical.

Everyone, even the king, would hear of Henri's affair. It would compromise the dignity of the cultural mission to Italy. Duprat would be blamed. "I am never given credit for the solvency of the realm of France," he thought, "but I am blamed whenever anything goes awry." He thought of the scapegoat of the Scriptures, how a ribbon of red, the color of sin, was tied round its throat and how the creature was whipped into the wilderness bearing the load of all the unworthy thoughts, words, and deeds of the whole tribe and the tribe was thereby purged of all its collective guilt. He thought of Wolsey of England, his counterpart, who was hated by all and who took upon his shoulders the odium that rightly belonged to King Henry VIII. Popular figures, like King Henry and King Francis, required their scapegoats too. In a changing world, where monarchs were becoming absolute, the fiction was arising that ministers were responsible when things went wrong, while the crowned idols got the credit when things went right. Little wonder the scapegoats grew hard and were forced to scheme for preservation of self. But such an existence need not be without its rewards. Wolsey was a cardinal; Duprat had high hopes of achieving the same exalted position.

Hence the self-preservatory thoughts that took place out of long habit in Duprat's busy brain:

55

Item: The dignity of the cultural mission dispatched to escort the Mona Lisa to France must not be compromised by amorous dalliances on the part of its leader, Henri de Tonnerre.

Item: The mistress Giulietta Leone was by now too prominent a personage to kidnap and shut up in a convent. Nor could she be sent back to Italy, where she would boast of her conquest of the conquerors and reduce the conquerors to ridicule.

Item: Duprat's fees were involved. The dowager duchess of Montholon might demand a revision downward in Marie's *dot,* complaining that Marie had got a bad bargain, a notorious profligate. And if she did that the old Comte de Tonnerre, Henri's father, might break off the marriage contract. Everyone would suffer in prestige, Marie would sustain an incurable heartbreak and, worst of all, the chancellor himself would lose money. This had never happened before; it was not in his nature to permit it to happen now.

His course of action was crystal clear. Henri and Giulietta must be separated. Antoine Duprat knew exactly how. When it is inadvisable to kick an opponent downstairs one kicks her upstairs.

Meanwhile it was important to minimize the whole shoddy affair, and again the clear sweet face of Marie de Montholon arose before her great-uncle's eye to remind him that at bottom his motive was good, and that it would be cruel and inhuman to hurt her.

To the agent he said, "This is a small matter; delicate, I concede, but small. The little Italian girl will be properly taken care of. The Chevalier de Tonnerre is about to be married; no doubt that is why he permitted himself one last fling. He will not hazard his entire future on a casual flirtation."

"He'd be foolish if he did," the agent said, "but that's how it looked to me."

"You are overly romantic," the chancellor said kindly. "From now on I shall find you missions that do not enkindle your artistic temperament." The agent already knew too much.

There was, the chancellor said, a place for an alert observer overseas in the New World, in Canada where there were few accomplished musicians and where one could do good work. The agent left with a heavy purse but with a heart almost as heavy, exiled to spy on a tribe of hostile savages in North America and report if there were danger, which there was, of their falling under the influence of the English.

Then Duprat prepared to smash the love affair between Henri and Giulietta before it assumed unmanageable proportions. "Their love can only be physical," he thought, "and that is the easiest kind to interrupt, since a substitute can so easily be found."

Giulietta was saying, "Henri, dear heart, we are approaching your homeland. What will happen to me now?"

Henri was answering, "I shall take care of you, Juliette." But he thought, I will take care of you on the sly, without recognition unless you present me with promising bastards, for you have begun to irk me with your everlasting subserviency. One grows surfeited with sweets, Juliette. "I'll take care of you, Juliette."

It wasn't enough.

She knew his every mood by now. Somehow, already, she had lost him. Perhaps she had given too much. She remembered back to the advice her aunt had given her; she remembered the stolen chickens, the wrung necks. I was a fool, she thought; and to herself she swore, "My next lover I will torture."

"You are sweet," she said aloud.

❊
❊ ❊ 4 ❊ ❊

THE MONA LISA had now entered the territorial
boundaries of France; it had not been stolen or de-
faced; King Francis could preen himself on the success of
the cultural mission to Italy. The handsomest, most chivalrous, best-dressed monarch of Europe had now added to his
other glittering qualities the distinction of being a patron
of the arts. He was making elaborate plans for a celebration in honor of the masterpiece that England coveted and
Spain, his old enemy, would have sacrificed an army to acquire except for the fact that the Spanish King-Emperor,
Charles V, had no feeling for art. Charles Quint of Spain,
son of a madwoman, was reactionary and he was a religious
fanatic. In all respects, thought Francis, I am the most fortunate prince in Christendom, for I am a fanatic in nothing;
I only demand the best of everything, for France, and if for
France, for me.

And I am well served, he remembered. Duprat serves me
better than a whole council of marshals. Duprat sticks at
nothing. What a jewel that man is.

A servant brought Duprat the silver-shod mule, but Duprat said, "Take that beast back to the stables and fetch me a horse." An escort of monks and prelates presented themselves to accompany him on his journey to Fontainebleau, but Duprat said, "Get me my archers and musketeers." It was not an ecclesiastical progress he had in mind today. Today Duprat was the representative not of the kingdom of Heaven but of the kingdom of France, and his agile brain was full not of prayers but of wily schemes.

His thoughts turned back to his younger days before he was an Eminence, when he was a layman, a lawyer, a lover, a husband, and he remembered the tug of the flesh, the power of a woman, how the heart is snared and the vision is distorted by emotions common to all men. He did not condemn them. He was glad that God or Fate or the State had given him large experience and understanding. How twisted one sees when one loses sight of the essential, when the man is young and the loins burn and thinking is fogged by the warm moist longing that stultifies logic and whispers, "Tomorrow, tomorrow I shall consider practicalities, but tonight a bed is warm and a woman awaits me. Tomorrow I shall think. Not tonight." How exquisite to contemplate is the hard sharp-faceted jewel of logic! What a pity it comes late, when youth is spent. Yet who would want logic in the young? If the young were logical there would be no place in the world for the old. Better, far better to remember, to understand their careless passions and guide — nay, outwit, dam and thwart when necessary — the passions' wild flow. And if one happened to be a mitered Eminence with a grand-niece whom one adored, one had the power to spare her sorrow and whip into line the young fool who was going to marry her. For Henri must marry her, Duprat would see to that, despite his infatuation for Giulietta, a lapse that must be covered up.

He spurred his horse towards Fontainebleau. It was good to feel the pistol in his belt. It was good to be surrounded by soldiers instead of clerics. He tired of them sometimes; they slowed him down. It was good to feel so hale. It was good to be chancellor of the *épargne*. What would become of Marie if Chancellor Duprat were only Archbishop Duprat? He would probably be telling her to look for her happiness in the next world. Duprat wanted the best of both worlds for Marie, both this and the next.

At Fontainebleau a wall had been stripped of its red damask and plastered over to provide an Italianate background against which to display the Mona Lisa. The rest of the reception hall remained as luxuriously decorated as before, but here all had been removed — every crystal mirror, every tapestry — anything that might draw the eye away from the delicate colors of Leonardo's precious and provocative masterpiece. The smallness of the painting would contrast with the large expanse of naked wall and dramatize its value. King Francis had already rehearsed a little speech, suggested by Duprat, for the benefit of anyone so crude as to say, "Sire, the thing is not very big. A man could carry it under his arm." If the critic were a military man the king would observe, "My friend, a spearpoint isn't very big either, but it devastates." If the critic were a prelate the king would suggest, "My reverend lord, it sticks in my mind that I have heard you preach from your pulpit that the kingdom of Heaven is like a mustard seed, which is the smallest of seeds but the greatest of herbs"; and if by chance the critic were a lady he would raise his hat and say, "Madame, your mirror has accustomed you to too much beauty, beyond the fortune of ordinary mortals." King Francis looked forward to the celebration, and to the dancing and fireworks that would follow.

Duprat did not present himself to the king immediately, but pleaded necessity for rest and meditation before the reception. He installed himself in his suite of rooms and sent for Henri de Tonnerre. By now he was dressed in his rich ecclesiastical robes.

Henri had expected a warmer welcome. He was met with a thunderous frown, the disconcerting odor of incense and a nearness of great power, greatly displeased. He was not invited to sit. Every chair had been removed from the room except the chancellor's own. He knelt and kissed the archiepiscopal ring.

"Your Eminence," Henri said, rising, standing like a man condemned instead of one about to be feted for a successful mission, "I can report that I have escorted the Mona Lisa to France without accident or blemish and I await your further orders, grateful for the opportunity Your Eminence had afforded me to be of service."

"It has come to my ears," Duprat said, the frown deepening, "that your mission was not entirely without accident or blemish."

Henri startled. Had some idiot workman damaged the picture uncrating it?

"I delivered the painting into the hands of the king's own experts, who will hang it," he protested.

Duprat's mask of displeasure was intended to intimidate; it did not express his true thoughts; his face seldom did. Actually he was far from displeased. He saw before him a well-knit young nobleman, scion of an ancient house, destined soon to become his grand-nephew by marriage; he saw a man high in the king's favor, who had been useful to him already and who would be more useful in the future. Moreover, the young man had just said a very gracious thing: he had said, "I delivered the painting into the hands of the *king's* experts," knowing full well that they were Duprat's, thus shifting the blame from Duprat if the painting had met with an accident or been blemished.

"The blemish to which I refer is not on the Mona Lisa, chevalier, but on your immortal soul."

Good Lord, Henri thought, the old fox has caught wind of Giulietta. How? Since entering France he had hidden her among the riffraff and hangers-on at the tag end of the cavalcade, visiting her on the sly and at night. He had thought his secret was safe.

"The blemish I refer to is Giulietta Leone," Duprat said. "Sin is not only morally reprehensible, Henri de Tonnerre; it almost always brings practical difficulties. It throws stumbling blocks in the way of legitimate ambition. It crops up unexpectedly to ruin a career. It sullies the purest intention. When, in your pride, you feel you have successfully isolated sin in some secret compartment of your life it gains its greatest hold over you. Then, like an acid, it dissolves the compartment and seeps into your soul and erodes your character; and the Devil laughs and says to the fires of Hell, 'O flames, how stupid are my children, who think themselves more clever than Lucifer, Star of the Morning, who fought and nearly won the War in Heaven against Almighty God! Prepare, prepare to consume yet another new member of the lost!' "

Duprat paused, pleased with himself. He would remember this apostrophe to the flames. It would make an excellent sermon one day. Henri, a congregation of one, was visibly shaken by it. The grand thing about the theme was that it would do for almost anyone and almost every occasion.

Forgiveness was now in order. Duprat permitted his face to soften.

"I adjure you, grand-nephew," he said, "put away this temptress, lest she cause great suffering to Marie, and lest she endanger your prospects, not only in this world but in the world to come."

Subtle, theatrical, spying old man! Henri thought. He wraps himself in his churchly robes and smothers me with the air of his cathedrals! Informed by his agents, and they are clever, whoever they are, he confronts me with my guilt and threatens me with the next world, as if *he* ever thought about that! But he is in deadly earnest. He means every word he says. How deeply he loves his grand-niece. Sincerity crackles from him like lightning out of a thundercloud. Antoine Duprat would be a dangerous enemy. Is Giulietta Leone worth it?

No, Henri thought, she wasn't. He had never really intended to marry her. But it irked him to be spied upon, and he was furious that Duprat, whose reputation for duplicity was notorious, should take him to task for a peccadillo. It was fashionable to keep a mistress, as it was fashionable to buy a new cloak every month, and they were discarded as casually.

Since the chancellor took the matter so seriously it would be dangerous, Henri knew, to seem to take it lightly. He would appear in the chancellor's eyes like a flighty young man whose affections ran shallow — did they? Henri had never wondered — and therefore unfit to be Marie's husband and grand-nephew to the chancellor of the *épargne*. Nor was the moment one for equivocation. He must confess the truth. Not all the truth, for he did not know how much Duprat knew about his liaison with Giulietta. But truth, like a circle, is perfection, instantly recognizable by a man like Duprat: a little truth is a little circle; the whole truth, if a man's mind could grasp it, is also a circle, identical in shape but infinite in dimension. Stick therefore to the truth when nothing else will suffice.

"It is the truth, Your Eminence, that I dallied with the girl," Henri said.

"Inexcusable stupidity," Duprat said, not unkindly.

"But it was not my intention that my indiscretion should cause pain to my betrothed, the maid of Montholon."

"You probably supposed you would not be found out," Duprat said.

"That is what I supposed, sir; I was wrong."

"Well, you are candid at any rate, Henri de Tonnerre."

"I will return her to Italy at once, Your Eminence."

"I'm afraid that's impossible, chevalier. No doubt you conceived yourself clever in hiding your little affair and dressing the girl as a page boy; but actually, everyone knew what you were doing, every groom, every scullion in the king's cavalcade, not to mention the elite guard of archers. The story is all over Paris by now. Only an innocent child like Marie will not have heard of it, and if she has, she doesn't believe it. Shame, shame, chevalier! Chevalier, indeed! How you degrade the fine old feudal style! Chevalier, knight, belted with the sword of chastity, fasting and praying before the altar, consecrating your sword in the cause of the weak before the ancient title is bestowed upon you, title of noblesse, title of the Crusaders. Shame, shame, Henri de Tonnerre!"

"I received my title at Marignan, on the field of battle," Henri reminded him.

"The greater shame to forget it between a wanton's legs," Duprat said.

"I would sacrifice everything, sir," Henri said vehemently, "if, by so doing, none of this might reach the ear of my betrothed."

"I assure you, young man, that my grand-niece will never hear a word of your paltry conquest unless you are fool enough to disclose it yourself. I have been at some pains to make sure that those who were privy to your indiscretion are scattered, so they cannot gossip. Only you can hurt Marie. If you do so, Henri de Tonnerre —" the chancellor's voice lowered and the terrible threat he uttered was soft, but it rumbled like thunder — "I will hurt you."

"I will send her back at once!"

"On the contrary, chevalier, you will dance at her wedding. Giulietta Leone is going to marry, an obscure but respectable member of the petty noblesse; it is all arranged; it will happen tonight. Above everything else your name must be cleared."

"Giulietta didn't object?" Henri asked, bewildered and a little hurt.

"She was delighted, and so, I have reason to believe, was the captain of the king's archers. Henceforth you will treat Giulietta with distant respect, as you would any member of your suite who contributed to the success of your mission, taking daily charge of the linen that shrouded the Mona Lisa during the journey."

He knew about the linen!

"You see," the chancellor said, "I have kept myself informed."

Henri sensed that his formidable great-uncle must know about everything. Rebelliously he feared and respected Duprat, like everyone else in France except King Francis. But there was no denying the chancellor-archbishop's intense devotion to Marie.

Marie began to interest Henri.

✱
✱ ✱ 5 ✱ ✱

"HE DID?" said King Francis. *"Incroyable!"*

S   "Assuredly, Your Majesty, she did," Duprat said.

"Parbleu!" swore the king, "I should never have believed it from anybody but you. Ha, ha, ha! The little she-wolf! She must be a beauty."

"Beauty is but a sou, Sire, in the treasure of sprightliness, wit, warmth and good nature which the girl, Giulietta, has to offer a man."

"Chancellor, I am tempted to wrap your pectoral cross in something fire-resistant to shield it from this conversation."

"Sire, long ago —"

"Yes, yes, I know. You were a married man before you were a churchman and you know all about women. That is what makes you so valuable. You understand what most celibates cannot, and you see where the common cleric is blind. Well, chancellor, what else about this little *Italienne?*"

Duprat manufactured a genealogy. Giulietta Leone, he said, was the orphaned impoverished last of a line of Italian nobility, "obscure but ancient," he assured the king.

After the glorious victory of Marignan the family had fallen upon evil days. Giulietta even stooped to do the marketing for the sisters of the convent to which she had retired in respectable poverty. While so engaged she had happened to see the Chevalier de Tonnerre in a market attempting to purchase a length of linen for the Mona Lisa. Giulietta, prompted by her noble nature, had become angry when she saw the merchant trying to take advantage of Henri, who was obviously a Frenchman, for she realized that the French came not as foes but as friends, to liberate Italy from the corrupt despots who preyed on their own people; and then Giulietta, like Veronica with the Veil, had offered one of her own garments to provide the linen.

"Garment?" queried the king, who was well versed in them.

"A petticoat, Sire," Duprat said, appropriately lowering his eyes in deference to the ecclesiastical garb he wore for the reception.

"Good girl. Good gallant girl!" said the king.

Without the petticoat she was ashamed to return to the convent, Duprat said, and Henri de Tonnerre had sheltered her among his suite. On the long trip to France she had fallen in love with the captain of the king's archers, one Armand, Sieur de Meung.

"I know of him," the king said, chuckling. "An excellent shot. A good eye for game."

"Sire, I am persuaded the girl is more than a game to him. They are deeply drawn to each other. One might say that the force which attracts them is irresistible. I saw the Sieur de Meung myself. There were tears in his eyes. I have agreed to marry them tonight, perhaps after the fireworks, if Your Majesty consents."

The king hesitated. "Wouldn't that be rather depressing, Duprat? So much solemnity after all the drinking and dancing?"

"The Italian girl is so beautiful," Duprat said, "so lively, so gay, so seductive, that it need not, nay, it cannot, be solemn." He warmed to his subject. "What an exquisite tableau, under the trees, near a fountain illuminated by torches and colored lanterns, with foreign dignitaries and ambassadors looking on! It will sanctify the evening. Beginning with the unveiling of the Italian masterpiece it will end with the union of a Frenchman and an Italian girl. How significant of Your Majesty's statecraft, your forceful but friendly conquest of Italy. How chivalrous, how benignant you will look in the eyes of the world. How solid, how permanent the victory of Marignan will appear."

"Yes," mused the king, "I suppose it would make an artistic end to the evening if you don't draw it out and make it too lugubrious. Marriages always depress me, like shackles."

"Your Majesty need never fear shackles!"

"And the visiting dignitaries will indeed draw the lesson you suggest; yes, yes, Duprat, I see. You are resourceful, farthinking. I wish I had a dozen of you."

"I wish I could fragment myself into a dozen parts, each part an apostle to serve Your Majesty," Duprat said smoothly.

"You honor me too much to compare me to Him," the king said, humbly, vastly pleased. Duprat bowed.

"With Giulietta so decorative," Duprat said — it seemed he had shed his cope and clerical hat — "I will make the marriage only so long as not to cheat the onlookers who will feast their eyes on her beauty, and as short as is compatible with the dignity of the sacrament, out of deference to the young couple's natural impatience."

The king laughed. "At heart you are a sybarite, Duprat. I am intrigued by this lass — as an instrument of Franco-Italian amity, of course."

"Of course, Your Majesty."

"But Henri de Tonnerre; I like that man; he should have some part of honor in the festivities, should he not?"

"It has occurred to me," Duprat said, smiling thinly, "that it would be fitting, since Giulietta Leone is an orphan without known relatives, for Henri de Tonnerre to stand *in loco parentis* and give the bride away."

❋
❋ ❋ 6 ❋ ❋

GRIM AS A HANGMAN and looking far older than his years Henri approached the chancellor-arch-bishop who stood, book in hand, mitered, coped and smiling an unctuous smile. Dusk was falling. The gardens of Fontainebleau were fragrant with the scent of flowers. Birds chirruped in the trees. The world was at peace, gay, and Nature was singing her evensong to provide sweet nuptial music for the Sieur de Meung and his bride.

Giulietta leaned lightly on Henri's arm. During the afternoon, while the Mona Lisa was unveiled before a distinguished and admiring group of guests, a bevy of dressmakers had descended upon her. Where they came from she could only conjecture. Things happened with amazing speed and crushing finality in France under the iron administration of Antoine Duprat. She had been folded into a costly wedding gown; deft fingers had fitted it swiftly to her figure. A jeweler had draped a rope of pearls around her neck. "From the king, madame," he had said. Then, silently, the gnomes had left her; she was dizzy with fatigue and long standing, but her peasant mind was clear. She sensed the powerful force behind her rapid marriage: the great chancellor-archbishop was clearing the name of Henri de Tonnerre, his close relative-to-be. She appraised herself in the full-length mirror. She had risen fast and far from the barefoot street urchin who had stolen chickens and rice to keep from starving in a dingy Italian town. "When you surrender yourself," her aunt had said, "it will be for princes." It had not turned out that way. It had been for Henri de Tonnerre, whom she might have loved but who now was giving her away to a husband whose face she had not even noticed. "I must pretend that I recognize the Sieur de Meung when we reach the altar," she cautioned herself. "I must look happy as a bride, and no one must know that I have been crying."

Her image said, "You will do, Giulietta Leone. You have only to look at yourself to know that you will do. These French are stupid at heart. They are easily dazzled. You will provide exactly the right touch of artistry to their artistic evening. Be as beautiful as you are. What have you to lose? Even your husband will be pleased, poor man. You are the scapegoat for the chancellor's sins, and Henri's, but so is the Sieur de Meung. He has a mistress he truly loves, within his shallow capacity, and now he must marry you." "I will make it up to the unfortunate man," Giulietta decided. Her mirror said, "A girl like you could easily soften *this* blow for any man; remember the princes, Giulietta. As for the captain of the king's archers, he is used to taking orders. Use him, as he is being used." And after that, Giulietta thought, she could go on to something better.

Standing erect, like a brave man about to be hanged

73

through no fault of his own, the Sieur de Meung saw his bride on Henri's arm approaching the portable altar behind which stood the powerful prelate who had decreed the marriage. "Your Eminence," he had protested, "I was scarcely aware of the Italian girl, except to hear what was common gossip throughout the troup. The Chevalier de Tonnerre picked her up at Marignan —"

"I hear differently," Duprat had admonished him severely. "I hear that you attempted repeatedly to enter her tent after the mission had crossed the French border."

The Sieur de Meung, wondering how he knew, had said weakly, "I may have had a drop too much one night, Your Eminence, and in my capacity as captain of the archers, making my usual inspection, I may have been somewhat too thorough in my duties and I may have entered the lady's tent to make sure she was safe —" his voice trailed off.

"In honor, Messire de Meung, there is only one solution."

Thus had the Sieur de Meung put away his mistress, his two-year-old bastard daughter, and arrived at the portable altar under the trees of Fontainebleau. He had never intended to marry anyone. He greatly preferred the carefree life of the guardhouse, drinking and rollicking among boon companions, serving his king, parading in his lily-embroidered tabard, lording it over innkeepers who bent double to serve him and peasants who quartered his men and treated him like the *haute noblesse* and never asked a sou in payment — and now came the heaviest hand in the realm to single him out for a life of dull respectability, thrusting him into a marriage bed and into the holy state of matrimony! "You, a paterfamilias, Armand de Meung!" he said to himself as Henri approached to deliver him his bride. "I never thought it would come to this. Ah well. Ah well. I must take the lady or lose my place. The chancellor threatened as much, and he never threatens idly."

But it struck him, as Henri and Giulietta drew near, that in this case the call of duty might not be burdensome. The bride was the most beautiful woman he had ever set eyes on. Was she smiling at him? Incredible! She was! He squared his shoulders, smoothed away his bristly red mustache like a man about to bite into a pheasant breast and smiled back. Soiled goods or no, she was his. The chancellor of the king's *épargne* had so decreed, and King Francis himself was looking on. The Sieur de Meung was suddenly a famous personage; everyone knew his name and was jealous of his good luck; his was the most fashionable wedding of the season. Shopkeepers would tip their hats and his credit would be boundless. What did it matter if the bride had spent twenty-one nights in the bed of his commander? Had the Sieur de Meung ever spent one, a single one, with a virgin? What did he expect? He thought back. No, try as he might, he could remember no such occasion. He would surely have remembered a virgin if there had been one in his life, unless he had been too drunk. Well, he'd get drunk tonight, that he would, and show this brazen petal-plucked foreign bride a thing or two! Henri de Tonnerre thought himself a great lover, did he? Faugh! What did Henri de Tonnerre know about love? He thought he was a man of the world, did he? Faugh! Henri de Tonnerre was as priggish as Duprat, that's what he was, only he just didn't know it. He knew for a fact, all the men did, that Tonnerre had never even contracted the Spanish disease that practically everybody picked up nowadays. A babe in the woods, that's what Henri de Tonnerre was and didn't know it. How drunk, how beautifully drunk the Sieur de Meung would get tonight and Madame de Meung, ha ha! she'd have cause to remember her husband.

But soft! Keep it out of your face. This is holy, ha, ha! The figure in the gold cope and the jeweled miter with a smile but no lips and eyes like a snake is opening the book. He is about to speak.

Henri whispered to Giulietta, "Adieu, Juliette."

Giulietta whispered, "It should have been you. It still can be."

"You will stand back now, chevalier," said the figure; and as Henri retreated into the shadows leaving Giulietta beside the Sieur de Meung, the figure intoned, "Armand, Sieur de Meung, will you have this woman —?"

That night Henri took horse for Montholon.

T HE SIEUR DE MEUNG lay snoring in their bed at the
late hour of seven o'clock in the morning, unshaven,
his breath sour with cheap wine. Madame de Meung, formerly Giulietta Leone, brewed him a pot of hot coffee lib-
erally spiked with brandy and brought it to the bedside.
Their only servant, a crippled veteran of the battle of
Marignan, was having one of his bad days and they were
alone. Juliette — she had grown accustomed to the French
version of her name by now — coaxed her husband back
to sobriety by the only means certain to suffice: a hair of
the dog that bit him always kept him going another day.
She looked at him calmly. How many days do you live at
one time, Juliette de Meung? One, live one day at a time;
tomorrow may change for the better. And the day after tomorrow may rocket you up to a position as high above this
as this is above your former state, like King Francis's fireworks that set fire to the sky on the night of your wedding.
Watch; wait, and hope for the unlikely. It had happened
before.

How like a rocket her wedding had been: all color and spectacle — and then the rocket explodes, darkness returns, darker by contrast than before, and the air is full of the stench of burnt-out powder. But it was exciting to recall the pyrotechnics which illuminated that memorable event and pleasant to enjoy the humdrum security of the life of the petty noblesse of France. She would never have to steal again — never chickens, anyhow — never go barefoot, never go hungry. "Many an Italian, even a noble Italian lady, is far worse off than I after the French crushed us," she reminded herself, raising the Sieur de Meung's head and holding the coffee cup to his lips. "Drink this, my dear," she said, cleverly injecting a tone of fondness into her voice, like the superb actress she had become. She loathed him. She loathed all men.

Her husband drained the fiery cup at a gulp.

"There's more," she said.

He said, "There has to be."

Her bruises had healed and the skin of her body was smooth again and seductive as on their wedding night, the night he had cruelly abused her to show her a thing or two. She had never complained or reproached him afterwards; she had bit her lip to keep back the cries, but she had not even whimpered at the time.

"Curse him!" the Sieur de Meung mumbled. He could not forgive Henri de Tonnerre for taking her first and so casually. "You don't still love that prig, do you, Juliette?" It was a constant question, constantly answered by now, answered always in the same way: I was a fool, my lord husband, and I have long since forgotten the Chevalier de Tonnerre.

"Good," said the Sieur de Meung, as the brandied coffee

warmed him and chased the demons out of his aching head. "I say *good*. Because he'll be bringing his bride to court tonight, and you'll see him again." He looked at her quizzically.

"I'll spit in his face."

He sat up in bed alarmed. His head was clearer now. Madame de Meung was quite capable of doing just that and causing a frightful scene in full court, before the king's very own eyes. *"Parbleu,* Juliette! You will lose me my place!"

"Then I shall merely treat him with the contempt he deserves," she said.

"Just avoid him," de Meung said. "I don't trust you when your temper's up."

To herself she smiled, but her outward expression was utter submission, wifely submission, the obedience a captain of the archers demanded in a subordinate.

"I shall avoid him as you command, my lord." It pleased her that her husband still was jealous. It was a weapon, a lever; it was money in the bank; it was a barn full of food to sustain the peasant while he planted next year's harvest, which might fail.

"Don't let him know you remember him."

"I never remember till you remind me."

"He wasn't much good, was he? He was a paltry lover. I know. You've told me." Her husband was pleading for reassurance; Juliette recognized the tone and prepared herself to comply, to please. She ran her tongue over her lips, leaving them wet and scarlet. "He never even beat me," she said.

"Ho, ho!" cried her husband, drawing her to him. It was now seven-thirty in the morning. "Ha, ha, ha!"

When it was over, looking the picture of the radiant bride and adoring wife, loathing him and all men — the sweaty carter who had buried her aunt would have been preferable; she could have railed at him when he was in drink, borne him a litter of peasant brats and saved his wages and taken care of him with dignity, instead of learning the art of pleasing swine! — when it was over she smoothed her hair and tidied her dress and said fondly, "You had better shave and eat a clove, *mon capitaine.* The king will want his guard to look smart tonight, and the chancellor will be at court."

"Aye, Juliette," de Meung said, drained and hungry. "There's talk of more war. Well, I always liked action, as you know." He emphasized the *as you know* with a leer.

She glanced at him and contrived a willing smile.

"I am a man of action," he said, wolfing down a platter of pigs' feet and cabbage.

"You certainly are," Giulietta said assuming a wonderfully convincing air of admiration. She hoped the nausea she felt did not mean a pregnancy. No, it could not possibly; but the revulsion was real and acute. She knew that de Meung still visited his mistress occasionally and gave her money, futher depleting the already meager de Meung income, expecting Juliette to manage the household expenses so that no tax collector from the king's *épargne* would come one day to the door and threaten that his taxes were in arrear. From the carter to the Sieur de Meung, from the Sieur de Meung to Henri de Tonnerre, perhaps even to King Francis, men seemed to be all alike. Bend, therefore, Juliette de Meung; bend like a willow. You have been called a willow; men like them plumper as a rule, but men like willows too, since they're like little girls, and even a bad man protects a little girl. Bend to the mad male tempest that roars over the world, redolent of blood and lust and sweat and wine. You have a weapon against the hairy baboons that rule you and all women. Use it; use them; forget you were born with a heart; forget your country is conquered; look out for yourself; look out for Giulietta Leone. Adapt; adjust. Flatter, please them, drain them. What is so limp and ridiculous as a shining knight with his armor off, his fighting body flaccid with spent pleasure, his loins woman-drained, his brain drowsy, off guard! Tomorrow he'll come grunting back for more, like a poisoned pig about to burst, but for the moment he is empty, like Sisera in the tent of Jael, who, while he rested his battle-weary head upon her lap, took a hammer and took a nail and smote the nail through his temples till it came out the other side of his head and went into the ground. What a long nail it must have been, mused Juliette de Meung, smiling. She had never seen such a nail. Yes, you have a weapon against the brutes. All women have. Women always have. Use it, the only weapon you have.

No one who viewed the festivities that night at Fontainebleau would have guessed that the kingdom of France was threatened with utter annihilation. Three mortal enemies lurked on three frontiers, with three spears poised to pierce her to the heart.

But King Francis gave a ball. His beard was scented and curled. His fingernails were pared and polished. He had chosen his rings with the care of a connoisseur, clear stones alternating with opaque and green never adjacent to blue. His large expressive hands flashed a symphony of good taste. His lips were all smiles; his tongue was all flattery to the ladies, while confident and vague to his clerical, financial and military men. If, behind his eyes, there glowed some vague apprehension it was not evident to the court.

But it was significant that the greatest men of France were all there, imperiously summoned in the king's name by the chancellor of the *épargne,* who was also there, inconspicuous as a shadow and as inseparable, speaking when the king faltered, silent when the king could speak on his own.

Present also, unabashed in woollen hose and a leather jacket, was the Chevalier Bayard, scorning to wear the slashed puffed sleeves that were all the rage and broadened the shoulders of lesser men, scorning the ornamental codpieces that some of the flashier courtiers affected. It was an English style, aping King Henry VIII, who required the support for a medical reason, the swelling of his diseased loins. The Chevalier Bayard was the last of the paladins of a France that was passing, a France epitomized in the old provincial gentry like the Montholons and the Tonnerres. He had never been worsted in battle by axe, mace, sword, spear or any of the knightly weapons. He viewed gunpowder and bullets with contempt — unchivalrous, newfangled, an invention of the canaille, below a gentleman's notice. One day, not too long hence, a bullet was going to kill him.

Present also was Admiral Bonnivet, personally brave but a deplorable tactician. His naval title was purely honorary. He fought his armies on land, and his only claim to fame was strategic retreats.

Present also was Claude, Count of the ancient house of

the Guises, fanatically brave and fanatically Catholic in a year when Catholics were staggering under the impact of the militant new Protestantism of Germany; a devoted impulsive Frenchman, erratic like all his clan.

Present also was the venerable General de la Trémouille, heavy with years and the laurels of a lifetime of battles won for France, still vigorous and doughty at seventy years of age.

Present also was Chancellor Duprat, who sensed more clearly than the king the terrible threat to France of a simultaneous triple invasion, fearing his own concomitant fall if it suceeded, a fall that would end with a hangman's rope around his neck and his feet dancing on air. Devotion to France competed with personal greed for glory and dread of personal death in his shriveled heart. His mien was grave and calm.

Present also were the ladies, whom Francis could not do without; and because of the ladies those other decorative hangers-on who made the court of the French king the most brilliant and spendthrift of Europe: maids of honor in fluttering lace, blackamoors in feathered turbans and Turkish sandals and painted toenails; guards of honor like the archers in tabards embroidered with gold that turned Duprat a bilious green and kept him sleepless at night devising new taxes to pay for such needless extravagance; musicians with costly instruments, a charge on the king's *épargne,* and Gargantuan appetites; grooms to care for six thousand horses that transported all these impedimenta wherever the king went; cooks to feed and wine stewards to quench the thirst of the court; saddlers, blacksmiths, jewelers, sempstresses, carters, pyrotechnicians to set off fireworks, plumbers to plumb the fountains, gardeners to crop the lawns and pluck any leaf that might have the effrontery to turn yellow while the king was in residence as the season wore into autumn without permission — all these were present, in person or on the chancellor's mental list of expenses. Well might his mien be grave.

Absent was Charles, Duc de Bourbon, Constable of France, commander in chief of all His Majesty's fighting forces on land and sea, the most notorious, most dangerous traitor ever to betray and bewilder King Francis. The King who charmed everyone else could not understand why Bourbon had left him.

Son of the petty noblesse, this great man had married above his station and received his title, Duc de Bourbon, through his wife. He had risen fast by reason of daring and natural ability. After Marignan, where he was largely responsible for the victory, King Francis had made him governor of Milan. In Italy he had an immense personal following. But his wife died without issue and the vast estates she had brought him, making him the wealthiest subject in Europe, had reverted to the Crown. He had conceived himself equal to a king; now he was diminished. Bursting with outrage and consumed with ambition this spirited genius rebelled in heart and hurt pride. He dared to bring suit before the Parliament of Paris against the Crown to recover his lost lands. He sustained an adverse judgment. Then he turned traitor.

Henry VIII of England, still wearing on his coat of arms the trifoliate lilies of France in perpetual claim for the French provinces lost at the close of the Hundred Years War, schemed with him, promising aid in an invasion, but gave none. The Emperor Charles Quint schemed with him, likewise promising aid. Charles Quint, for all his deep religious convictions, would have schemed with the devil himself to humble France. And in Italy the puppet Duke of Milan, where Bourbon had been governor, schemed with him, hoping to throw off the yoke of the French conqueror through the instrumentality of a French traitor.

The king had gone so far as to intervene personally, making a state visit to Château Bourbon at Moulins, in an effort to recall the constable to his sworn oath of fealty and duty to France. But Bourbon had remained chilly and aloof; his answers were noncommittal; he was barely polite. As soon as the king left he shut his gates in a sulk and instructed his servants to tell everyone, even a royal courier, that the Duc de Bourbon had gone hunting and it was not known exactly when the Duc de Bourbon would return.

Furious as a woman whose charms are scorned, the king then turned to the chancellor and demanded, "Hang me that man, Duprat!"

"Your Majesty, I cannot. Not yet."

"You hang everybody else. This man is a traitor. Hang him, I say, or I will."

"I earnestly hope that Your Majesty will not hastily commit any act so damaging to your popularity as that, Sire. The people hate to see the great ones hanged. It makes martyrs of them."

The king had had second thoughts. He had a compulsion to be adored. Duprat had always done his hanging for him.

"It would lose me friends, Duprat?"

"There is no doubt of it, Sire."

"But he insulted me!"

"He shall be punished, Sire. I promise."

"And he's dangerous."

"He would be more dangerous across the frontier. As long

as he remains on the soil of France we can watch him, and, to a degree, circumscribe his activity, intercepting his agents, keeping informed of his plans."

"What is he planning?"

"My latest information is that he plans to attack Marseille with an army of Imperial Austrians and renegade Italians as soon as the Emperor can raise them for him."

"Has the Emperor raised them?"

"The Emperor moves slowly, Sire. It will take some months before Bourbon becomes a menace to Marseille."

"I'd feel easier if he were dead," said the king. But he had no intention of making a martyr of him by a public hanging.

Duprat said, "He shall die. All Your Majesty's enemies shall die. I promise. Trust me."

Sometimes Duprat spoke in the comforting tone he had used when King Francis was only a little boy, sensitive and vain, when Duprat had been his tutor.

"I trust you," said the king.

But the tone that had comforted the child irked the man, the man grown to a king, the first French king ever to sign his decrees, "such is our pleasure," and have them immediately translated into the law of the land.

"Such is his pleasure, indeed!" Duprat scoffed silently. *Plaisir* had two meanings: *a gracious desire,* and as such a delicate means of conveying a command by an absolute monarch; but also ordinary *pleasure;* and often it seemed to Duprat that the latter was more important than the former to gay, good-hearted vacillating Francis the First.

"Of course I trust you," the king repeated, adding a silent apostrophe to the image of his chivalrous self that he kept perpetually before his mind's eye. "But I can think for myself, Antoine Duprat, and I have a plan to get rid of the Duc de Bourbon in a way that even your wily mind would never have invented! Oh, how you will praise your old pupil, Master Antoine, when I pull it off without consulting you! *Parbleu!* It will be epic."

No one could guess at the festivities that night that the security of France was threatened, but the king sensed an undercurrent of gloom, a reluctance to join in the entertainment. He sent word to the musicians to play faster and louder, but no one moved to dance and no one smiled. The military men clustered together in groups, speaking earnestly among themselves, excluding the ladies, who sat forlorn and beautiful along the walls. *Parbleu!* The whole evening was a failure. The Chevalier Bayard in his impossible leather and wool, smelling of horses, with a haircut two hundred years out of date, was addressing a circle of archers. Did the fellow never use scent? He was adjuring them to aim fair and true for France. Admiral Bonnivet was surrounded by naval dignitaries who seemed to be assuring him, to his astonishment, that Andrea Doria, a loyal Italian commander, could probably break the blockade of Marseille. But Marseille was not blockaded as far as the king knew. As far as the king knew there was peace everywhere in the world, and why all this concern for the future should interfere with the dancing he simply could not see.

In a gallery above the great hall reserved for the petty noblesse his eye was suddenly drawn like a lodestone seeking the Pole Star to a remarkably handsome woman, and he wondered where he had seen her before; and remembered. It was the Italian girl, the wife of his captain of archers!

Parbleu! Let her come down. An equerry refreshed his memory, de Meung, and he sent him to the gallery with word that if Madame de Meung would do him the honor of dancing with her sovereign, her sovereign would be greatly pleased. "Now that should loosen up the evening," Francis thought.

Watching the noble youth in his elegant silken hose embroidered with lilies and his doublet of cloth-of-gold, the king thought, "He will probably tell her my majesty commands her presence," which is just what the noble youth did, admiring His Majesty's choice.

Juliette received the unexpected summons to dance amid a chattering group of jealous ladies who instantly gossiped among themselves, "What *is* there about the Italians?" and commiserated with each other, "Probably he's only honoring her for political purposes."

Juliette blushed scarlet, turned pale at the possibilities, and instantly recovered a perfect composure.

"His Majesty wants me for something," she said to the ladies smiling her sweetest smile and, resting her hand lightly on the arm of the equerry, walked slowly down the staircase, while curious heads turned in her direction, and approached the king.

She curtsied in the deep Italian manner that was curiously more submissive and flattering than the French. It was also more feminine. In Madame de Meung it was infinitely alluring, and many an ambitious French lady, watching her enviously, wished she could manage such grace and determined to practice, though they whispered disapprovingly, "She's throwing herself at him. These brazen *Italiennes!*"

She looked up and smiled, "Yes, Sire?"

King Francis raised his hat, bowed graciously, extended a bejeweled hand and raised her from her curtsy.

"I was alarmed when you did not rise at once, Madame de Meung. I feared you might have turned your ankle. I forgot for the moment your country's customs are somewhat different from mine."

Her ankle! She could use that ankle. He had set his own trap.

"No, Your Majesty," she said, but she managed to bite her scarlet lower lip for a second as if she were in pain.

When King Francis danced everyone danced, and shortly the shining parquet floor of the great hall was filled with glittering couples treading the stately measures and intricate figures which comprised the latest, most fashionable dances to the latest most fashionable music. Queen Claude, who was sickly and tolerant of the king's vagaries, watched from her throne and smiled. Since he could not dance with her first — indeed she could not dance at all by reason of her illness — she was pleased that the king had chosen a decorative partner to lead off the ball. And the fact that Madame de Meung was an Italian was politically advantageous at a time when Milan was restive and gestures of amity towards Italy were necessary. Madame de Meung did not have to be *quite* so seductive, however, the queen thought with a pang. But *qu'importe?* King Francis was always incorrigible.

Among the dancers was Henri de Tonnerre with Marie, his bride of six months. With her he had taken up residence in one of the châteaux on one of the Tonnerre estates. It was heavy, dark and old-fashioned, like Château Montholon; the dowager duchess had visited them and felt quite at home playing cards with the old Comte, his father, both thoroughly approving the life of their young-sters, solid, traditional and no nonsense, and satisfied also with the union of the Montholon-Tonnerre estates that one day, probably not too long hence, would be doubly sealed if Marie had a child.

"If I know my daughter she'll have one at once," the dowager duchess said.

"If I know my son she'll have every opportunity," said old Tonnerre with a chuckle.

This was the way things ought to be done, they said; and they said things weren't done like that any more. Children had far too much to say about choosing their own spouses nowadays, and they did not respect their elders as they ought.

"Not as *we* did," said the Comte de Tonnerre.

"Not at *all,*" the dowager duchess agreed.

"And yet, *madame la duchesse,* we must try to keep up with the changing times," said old Tonnerre. "The Italian-ate fashions are deplorable, but strong."

"I concede no reason, Monsieur de Tonnerre, to cater to the lewd loose fashions set by the Italians," the dowager duchess said anxiously. She used the feminine *Italiennes,* Italian women. She had come to court for the first time in years, and so had Tonnerre, and she saw Madame de Meung dancing with the king. She had also seen, with a mother's keen eye, how Henri would turn his head away from time to time from blonde Marie to the dark and sultry Madame de Meung.

Old Tonnerre tugged at the lobe of his ear and said, "No doubt, no doubt. The times are unquestionably de-generate," but secretly he wished he were thirty years younger, dancing in King Francis's shoes, with Madame de

Meung's long lashes fluttering up at him. Since all was safe, since Giulietta Leone was now Madame de Meung, since Henri was sound at heart, he could afford to sympathize with his son's covert but hot glances in her direction.

Life on the quiet estates of Tonnerre with a wife who surfeited him with adoration was getting a little dull for the man who had fought at Marignan and brought the Mona Lisa home. Marie's beauty had stunned him, then raised him to a state of exultation just after his marriage. But now his mouth was sticky sweet with too much love and perfection. If only Marie had had one fault! If only there were something to do besides being respectable. If only there were a war, anything to provide some excitement. What can a man accomplish who eats honey all day and night and never a dash of pepper? How they peppered their food in Italy! Of course, he knew, they did it because the meat was sour and that was the only way to make it palatable. But a little pepper — had it ever poisoned a man? And it tingled on the tongue like danger. "Henri de Tonnerre," he said to himself, "you are growing dull as an ox. You are dying before you ever lived. The Mona Lisa smiled at me — no, that smile was a sneer — and told me I would die. But not before I live, not before I do, experience, feel, enjoy all there is in life!"

Marie said, "You look stern, Henri. Is something the matter?"

Henri said, "My dear, I have not even kissed the king's hand; he seems so preoccupied; I keep looking for a chance to approach him and offer my duty."

Marie smiled. "It's that Italian woman they're all talking about; she's kept everyone away from him, upset everything."

"I'll keep watching for my chance," Henri said.

"I'll watch too," said Marie.

Duprat viewed the evening with composure. Battles and intrigues torrented through his busy brain — there would be war, of course — but outwardly his demeanor was cheerful and confident. His plans were well laid; there were solid reasons for optimism. The war would be crushingly costly, but he had a new scheme to pay for it, involving neither taxes nor torture nor confiscation nor even an increase of personal unpopularity; nay, it would provide the chancellor of the *épargne* with a thumping new source of private income, it would add luster to the king's reputation and actually make the people happy. Never before had Antoine Duprat hit on a scheme that would do all this. Why hadn't he thought of it before?

As for the king, now dancing and flirting outrageously with the wife of Messire de Meung, it posed no threat to the security of the realm and, thank God, the former Giulietta Leone posed no threat to Marie. Henri was behaving himself with exemplary decorum. *Grand Dieu!* Why wouldn't a man, if he was married to an angel like Marie? "I will get him a place in the war where he won't be killed," Duprat murmured fondly, "for it is evident that Marie worships him."

During a lull in the music, when courtesy demanded that the king resume his place on his throne beside the queen, Madame de Meung did not retire to the background. Instead of returning to the gallery with the other ladies of the petty noblesse she hung on the king's arm until he was seated and then, unaccountably, rested her hand familiarly on the back of the throne.

"Well, madame," Francis said, looking up at her, frowning. "This is a little *too* casual, even for an Italian."

The queen raised her eyebrows, amused.

"Sire, I did indeed turn my ankle. It is torturing me. I cannot walk without assistance."

The king looked helplessly for Duprat, expecting him to come forward as he always did, expecting some smooth decision that would extricate him from the awkward social predicament. Courtiers and their ladies were trooping around the canopied dais to kiss hands. It was highly embarrassing that anyone, let alone a mere wife of a captain of archers, should stand so intimately close to the majesty of France. But Duprat was not to be seen. He was hidden in the shadows at the far end of the hall, totally absorbed in a complicated financial discussion with a swarthy Lombard banker whose genius for conducting crooked lotteries had brought him under the shadow of the scaffold and who, escaping to France, had entered the chancellor's service. "*Si,* Excellency, *si, si!*" he was saying. "In France I will keep it clean. Do I know how? But *si,* illustrious chancellor; if a man knows how to cheat at it, a man knows how to keep it clean!"

As the crowd of courtiers drew near, the king turned in desperation to the queen. "*Parbleu,* madame! What shall I do?"

Queen Claude said, "If Madame de Meung cannot walk, someone must carry her out and place her in a retiring room and summon a physician."

"But people will think I stepped on her toe! People are coming to kiss our hands! I would be laughed at if, the moment I finished a dance with a lady, she had to be carried from the hall and receive medical attention. Oh, where is that devil Duprat?"

"Then let the poor girl stand there, if she can, till they've kissed hands."

"What will people think?"

The queen smiled. She knew what people would think: that His Majesty's taste in mistresses was improving. "The people will think that their king is the first gentleman of the realm, as soon as Madame de Meung faints, which is nearly as certain as sunrise."

"*Peste!*" said the king. The tableau was too public for his taste. He sent the equerry to summon Duprat. Courtiers and their ladies made their reverences and kissed their majesties' hands. From the far end of the room the chancellor made his stately progress through the throng, frowning. He had in tow the Sieur de Meung who had become tipsy inspecting the wines at the catering tables. "I think, Messire de Meung," Duprat was whispering, "that you would do well to take your wife home at once. She is causing comment."

Henri and Marie approached the dais. The king sustained a sudden inspiration: Let Henri remove the girl from her conspicuous position! "This is the Chevalier de Tonnerre," he said amiably to the queen, "who brought the Mona Lisa home, you remember. Madame de Meung was in your suite, was she not, Henri? But of course she was. I'm afraid Madame de Meung feels a little faint. No doubt you will wish to escort her to a withdrawing room, where a doctor will attend her." It was a command.

Queen Claude unexpectedly spoke, smiling at Marie, "And you, my dear, stand here beside me!" For a moment

94

the two beautiful women stood beside the two thrones. Marie nearly swooned with the honor. Duprat, guiding the footsteps of the befuddled Sieur de Meung, coming closer to the dais, admired the queen's finesse: she had taken attention away from the *Italienne* by focusing it on Marie. "Divide and conquer," the chancellor murmured in Latin, to which the Sieur de Meung hiccuped, "What? Mass at this time of night?"

Giulietta sensed that the king was escaping her trap, and slumped gracefully to the floor, exposing silk-stockinged anatomy up to midthigh. Henri gathered her up and carried her, fainting and lovely, from the great hall while the queen continued to smile.

In an antechamber, where no one had the temerity to follow, he placed her on a couch. He had all but forgotten her; now memory returned full flood, her body, now again and so unexpectedly yielding and close, her warmth, her perfume; it was a heady moment. She stirred, regaining consciousness, it seemed. He kissed away her tears. "Giulietta! Giulietta mia!" he murmured. "Can it still be me?"

For answer she hissed and snapped at his lips with her teeth like an angry cat.

To the king, who entered just at that moment, it looked as if they were kissing. When Henri stood up there was a drop of fresh blood on his upper lip. He hastily wiped it away, but not before the king had seen it.

"Are you aware where you are?" the king said angrily.

Henri looked around. He saw the royal fleur-de-lys everywhere, embroidered on tapestries, carved on chairs, embossed on shelves of books. "I entered the first door I saw. I did not know it was Your Majesty's —"

"Study, chevalier."

Giulietta murmured as if she were only half conscious, "He tried to kiss me! He tried to —"

"Hush, madame," the king said, kneeling beside the couch. "Lie still. A physician has been summoned. To care for your ankle." King Francis fancied himself *un homme universel,* a man expert in all the sciences, in all the arts, the prevailing fashion among Italian gentlemen and aped the world over. He felt her pulse. He ran knowledgeable fingers over her ankle. It wasn't the one she had "turned," but she tensed her body provocatively and sighed, "That soothes the pain — a little — be careful." The king's hot nature responded. His temper flared jealously against Henri de Tonnerre. His scheme for terminating the existence of the Duc de Bourbon underwent a minor elaboration. He lusted after the little *Italienne* almost as much as he lusted for the death of the mighty traitor. Why should he not have both? Duprat always managed to get things both ways. But he must not tell Duprat what he had in mind. Henri was Duprat's protégé, married to his favorite kinswoman.

He stood up, all gracious smiles. "Greater men than the Chevalier de Tonnerre might well be tempted by such beauty, Madame de Meung. A woman, perhaps, would not pardon him; but I, who understand his temptation, I do." And to Henri he said sternly, "For shame, chevalier! You are fortunate to have stumbled into a private place where no spying eyes could witness your lapse. Now leave at once, and inform Her Majesty that I shall return in a moment. The physician will be here presently. Let the dancing continue." He slapped Henri good-naturedly on the shoulder.

When the physician arrived at the door a guard turned him away.

When the chancellor and de Meung arrived at the door

the guard said, "Sh-h-h! The physician is in attendance upon Madame de Meung. She must not be disturbed."

Five minutes later the king sat again in his throne, looking the perfect *homme universel,* the expert in everything.

When Marie spoke to her great-uncle Duprat later in the evening she said, "I was dizzy with the honor Her Majesty did me. Henri tells me the Italian woman required a physician. Is she seriously ill?"

"Madame de Meung is in experienced hands, Marie, and I think her illness will speedily mend."

"I don't like her very much," Marie said.

The chancellor glanced around.

"I wouldn't mention that to anybody if I were you, my dear. It might be dangerous."

"Why, uncle?"

He lowered his voice. "She is already the king's mistress. Shortly, I expect, she will become his *maîtresse en titre.*"

Marie laughed softly. "I am so glad."

"It is the king's affair, and it does not affect us," said Duprat.

"Great-uncle, for a moment I was afraid Henri was attracted to her."

"Good heavens, no, Marie!"

"What a jealous, suspicious, undutiful wife I have been in my mind."

"I said before and I say again," the chancellor told her with ringing determination, "you have not a care in the world. Trust old Uncle Duprat to see to that."

Madame de Meung remained officially under the care of the physician throughout the night. Next day she returned home in a royal litter, slung between four horses from the royal stables with royal fleur-de-lys plumes nodding above

97

their heads; and the Sieur de Meung received a visit from an equerry who stated that King Francis was pleased to present him with a purse, duly delivering it into his hand, to defray the medical expenses involved in Madame de Meung's unfortunate accident. "It must have been the high polish on the floor," the equerry said with a perfectly straight face.

"I hope that His Majesty does not conceive for one moment that I harbor the notion that the accident was His Majesty's fault!" de Meung hastened to explain in a whining voice, weighing the heavy purse. "Permit me to hope that Your Worship will convey to the king how deeply I feel the honor he has bestowed upon Madame de Meung and my humble self."

The equerry nodded and held out his hand as if to shake the Sieur de Meung's. The equerry's palm pointed up. De Meung, while he shook the proffered hand, slipped coins into it. They shone yellow. *Jésus!* The purse was full of gold!

For King Francis to covet one's wife was an honor; one did not beat or bruise her, lest His Majesty, who demanded perfection, be revolted at the blemishes. With such patronage, *such* patronage, one might look forward to a marquisate and a life that was one long holiday and get drunk and visit one's mistress at will.

But the Chevalier de Tonnerre, he thought glowering, was another matter entirely. The Sieur de Meung hated him with assassinate loathing, but he dared not show it and he dared not take out his venom on Giulietta, who now suddenly constituted his fortune and his future. He was moody and withdrawn for some days, but so ludicrously respectful towards her that she laughed. Men. First

98

they rape you, then they beat you, then they sell you — no, it was not a sale, it was rather a continuing rental — and then they are nice to you again. If she had known how, she would have poisoned her teeth when she bit Henri. She hoped Marie de Montholon had seen the gash. But Henri was clever. He would say he had got it shaving and Marie, blind with infatuation, would believe him. How naive, how abysmally stupid women could be when they love! Some of her hatred of men, concentrated in Henri, rubbed off on Marie like blood from a wound seeping into the bandage that encircles it. Encirclement, faugh! But that is my weapon against men. The pleasure Marie could afford the Chevalier de Tonnerre would be pale and unimaginative compared with Giulietta Leone's, bequeathed through uncounted generations of lusty Italian peasants, perfected by Henri the Frenchman, brutalized by the Sieur de Meung and now served up in a *potpourri,* spiced, hot and unforgettable, to drive a king to drink and bring him back begging for more! Ha, Giulietta Leone, Madame de Meung; last night, last night the king of France sweated between your breasts!

"Henri," said Marie, "what happened to your lip?"

"Oh that," he said, "I must have nicked myself with the razor."

"Henri, what do you think of secrets?"

"Secrets?"

"Secrets in general."

He glanced at her sharply. It so happened he had a secret of genuine importance, but he thought she referred to the cut on his lip.

"Secrets should be kept, Marie."

He felt guilty and irked and he looked stern. Was his

9 9

wife going to start nagging at him and getting jealous over a five-minute absence from a public ball, to which he had immediately returned? Oh, probably. The cut on his lip was a small matter if ever there was one; the true secret was a mission of vital importance to the realm, so secret and crucial that the king had forbidden him to mention it even to Duprat, exacting a solemn oath.

"My dear, I keep nothing from you except certain state matters."

"It is I who have the secret, my husband. There is no longer any doubt." She lowered her glance. Then she told him in a manner he could not but admire for its delicacy, laying her secret bare: "What would you say, mon cher chevalier de Tonnerre, if your wife were to tell you that next year she would present you with an heir?"

He picked her up and whirled her around in a transport of pride and joy, then fatuously sat her in a chair and propped up her feet and put a cushion at her back. "What am I doing to my progeny?" he cried.

"You're making him dizzy, you imbecile," Marie laughed breathlessly.

"Hang on, *petit Henri!*" Henri said, patting her still-smooth abdomen, grinning. "Oh, my poor Marie, I'm so terribly sorry. I might have hurt you. You must take very good care of yourself. You mustn't ride, you mustn't play tennis, you must walk slowly and carefully."

She laughed gaily. "I must, in effect, be in all things so lazy and slow that the babe will grow fat as an ox and split me in twain and then you will have no more Marie."

"Marie, don't even think such things."

"I can say them only because they won't happen."

He might be dead when his heir was born, he knew; and

the possibility was sobering. But he did not divulge his secret.

At Château Bourbon the commander in chief sat brooding, alone and unhappy. He was childless, his wife was dead and he was stigmatized with the reputation of "traitor." His estates were forfeit, his foreign colleagues and conspirators were untrustworthy. He did not conceive of himself as a traitor but a liberator. His blood was pure French, back through the Montpensiers, and beyond the Montpensiers pure Gallic and before the Gauls, the indigenous people of France, Caesar's foes whom Caesar praised, lost in the mists of antiquity. His dead wife, heiress of the Bourbons, had added stature to his ancient blood line. But then had come the lawsuit, which he lost, and the ancient blood of France was treated as a thing of no consequence. He felt himself cast aside and put upon. It shamed him to conspire with foreigners, but there was no one else to turn to. His own king had deserted him, motivated by the opportunism that was fashionable nowadays and so cynical that it turned the stomach. He envisioned a mightier France, fashioned after the old feudal policy; and let him but once come to power and he would throw out the foreigners. Meanwhile, perforce, he schemed with them. A king like Louis the Saint would have clasped him to his bosom and protected him to the death. A fop like Francis the First, shifty as a weathercock, discounted him. And Chancellor Duprat, perpetually on the watch for a confiscation that would increase the *épargne* (and incidentally buy new jewels for his miter and silver shoes for his mule) stole his estates, reducing him to beggary and thrusting him into the camp of the enemies of

France. So be it! More than one patriot had schemed with the enemies of one's homeland and then, having purged the *patrie* of iniquity, reconstituted it. But his temper, never equable, rebelled at such treatment; and his nature, always revengeful, could not forget his wrongs, no more than a man can forget the lice in his shirt that bite and irritate him and in time set a man to clawing at his own flesh if there is no one else to claw. The Constable of France felt himself persecuted.

After the death of his wife no woman was ever invited to Château Bourbon. He became a vegetarian and kept an astrologer. He harangued his retainers on the virtue of celibacy and drank only water and buttermilk. Meanwhile he brooded darkly, plotting the overthrow of King Francis.

Plotting against him in turn, King Francis, so opposite in every respect, said to Henri de Tonnerre, "If Bourbon succeeds, history will make him a saint. I depend on you, cousin, to assure that this madman does not succeed. You will bring him to me, alive if God wills, dead if there is no other way. Say nothing to my chancellor, who acts too slowly. And you will, of course, say nothing to anyone else, including close members of your family."

"I understand, Sire," Henri had promised.

"You swear?"

On holy relics of the saints Henri had sworn, deeply moved by the awesome solemnity of his trust.

"Good lad," said the king. Smiling had creased permanent wrinkles around King Francis's mouth — universally admired — and Henri could not see behind the eyes.

"You will take with you only the Sieur de Meung," the king said chuckling. "Mind he keeps sober and gag him if he chatters in taverns. I desire no violence; de Meung is a dead shot with silent weapons; he will know how to incapacitate, not kill. I want the Constable alive, not a martyr. You make martyrs of the great ones when you kill them."

"De Meung is a good man," Henri said.

After Henri the king summoned the Sieur de Meung to an unprecedented private audience. De Meung chewed a clove and turned pale with anxiety. Was the king tired of Giulietta already? Was he irked with her husband? Had he rendered her less desirable? But he searched his memory and he was certain he had neither beaten nor bruised nor even fatigued her since that night when she turned her ankle. In fact he had withdrawn from her bed and encouraged her to rest and pamper herself whenever she spent a night at home, so that she would be radiant and fresh when the king desired her again. What more could a loyal husband do?

"What have you done to displease His Majesty?" he reproached her. "You will ruin me! What stupidity have you committed?"

"I don't know what you are talking about," she said.

Wondering what would become of him, he presented himself at the door of the king's study and was admitted.

King Francis was seated at a table, writing something very small on a very small piece of paper. He looked up, but only his mouth smiled. His face was concentrated in thought, and to de Meung it looked stern. "He is writing my death warrant!" de Meung wailed inwardly. "Curse that Italian woman! I never wanted to marry her in the first place. She has ruined me!"

"Can you read, Messire de Meung?" the king said.

"Alas, Your Majesty, I cannot."

"Then I shall have to explain this to you," the king said, adding his signature to the paper with a flourish.

"If Madame de Meung has done aught to displease Your Majesty," de Meung began in a cringing voice, "it is owing to the fact that she is a foreigner and has not learned our ways; and no doubt with a little more time she will learn better manners; and if there is any way that I can instruct her in her duties Your Majesty has only to indicate wherein I may be of service, even to the whip."

The king's delicate stomach turned at the sight of the paltry little man, willing and anxious to bludgeon his wedded wife into adultery for personal gain; he understood him perfectly; better men than his captain of archers had shown similar anxiety to oblige when he had taken their wives and daughters. But it always sickened him.

"Pray, sit," said the king, pointing with his feather pen to a chair.

The Sieur de Meung breathed for the first time since he had entered the room. It was not, then, a sentence of death. He eased himself gingerly into the chair and sat on the edge, his back straight as a ramrod as if he were on parade.

The king folded the paper and placed it into a small oilskin envelope with a string attached so it could be worn around the neck. Then — for he deemed himself an expert in the stage also — he rested his chin for perhaps a full minute on interlaced fingers while his elbows rested on the table. He stared theatrically into the Sieur de Meung's shifty eyes. Jeweled finger rings shot flashes of fire through his scented beard. "I feel I can trust you, Messire de Meung," he said.

"That you can, Sire," de Meung said sturdily, exposing

pitted teeth in what he hoped was a smile. "Anywhere, anytime, about anything. Just tell me what I'm to do, even murder."

"You are a man of great loyalty and personal integrity," said the king.

"I hope so, Sire," said de Meung. To the king it was evident that the poor lout was sincere, and the king congratulated himself that he could engage men's loyalty while Duprat could only frighten them.

"My greatest vassal, the Duc de Bourbon, is tottering on the brink of treason," the king said.

"I'll kill him, Sire! I'll shoot him down! I will if it costs me my life. Let me get at him!"

The king nodded. "I appreciate your sentiments, Messire. The Chevalier de Tonnerre voiced the same."

"Who?"

"Henri de Tonnerre, your commander on the Mona Lisa mission."

"Oh, him." De Meung could not conceal his hatred and he scowled.

The king permitted himself an understanding frown in answer. "I think I know how you feel, and I share your sentiments."

"Oh, Sire, with you it's different."

"Naturally," said the king.

But all personal feelings must be put aside, the king said. He wished, for the good of France, to recall the Duc de Bourbon to his duty. He wished to be friends with him. He did not desire his death.

"Yes, it's better to have big people on your side than to fight them," de Meung said practically. The room was quiet, the fire crackled, de Meung was bursting with pride to be privy to high state secrets, sharing the king's confidence. He forgot Giulietta, he forgot his former fears. His king needed him. There was dignity in his voice as he asked, "How can the Sieur de Meung be of service to Your Majesty?"

"I have in mind to make one last appeal to the Duc de Bourbon," Francis said. "I have asked the Chevalier de Tonnerre to go to him at Moulins and, in all friendliness, to talk to him and try to wean him away from the Austrians, who plot the ruination of France. I have chosen you to accompany him on this delicate mission. Will you go?"

De Meung leapt from his chair and knelt and bathed the king's hand with tears. "Majesty!"

"I depend upon your good sense, my friend."

"Wouldn't it be better simply to poignard the Duc?" de Meung suggested in all sincerity. "What would I care what happened to me afterward so long as I rid you of this traitor?"

"I think not," Francis said with a faraway look in his eye. "No, I think not."

"Your Majesty is too gracious."

But the Chevalier de Tonnerre was young and impulsive, the king said. He had chosen de Meung to go with him as a sobering makeweight to counterbalance any wild and impractical notions Tonnerre might have. "You know how romantic he is," said the king.

Hatred, jealousy, loathing of Henri consumed the Sieur de Meung. "I will shoot *him* if he tries anything foolish!"

"I sincerely hope that will not be necessary," said the king, but he seemed to leave the possibility open. "The paramount consideration for France is that the Duc de

Bourbon return to his duty. I have written him a personal appeal in my own hand." He indicated the oilskin packet. "Wear this always and give it to him when no one is looking. I entrust it to you, not to Tonnerre, because Tonnerre, frankly, is not a diplomat. He would read it, he would think I was begging, and, in mistaken pride, he would destroy it. Yes, I am persuaded he would destroy it. But a king can afford to beg, Messire de Meung. Tonnerre would not understand that."

"I understand, Sire. Tonnerre is too big for his breeches. He thinks he can have everything he wants."

A sobered Sieur de Meung went home that night, full of devotion to his king that was deeper than Giulietta's, far deeper.

And it came to pass in an eventide that David arose from off his bed and walked upon the roof of the king's house: and from the roof he saw a woman washing herself; and the woman was very beautiful to look upon. And David sent and enquired after the woman. And one said, Is this not Bathsheba, the wife of Uriah the Hittite? And David sent messengers, and took her; and she came in unto him, and he lay with her.

Never since that time, Francis congratulated himself, had a king so neatly disposed of a rival in love; nay, he had surpassed even David, for he had disposed not of one but of two rivals, a husband and a lover.

On a day when the chancellor was at Sens immersed in state duties pertaining to the gathering war, working night and day with financial and military men, fervently praying to God for the salvation of France, on a day when the king

knew he would not be thinking of Henri, Henri and de
Meung rode out of Fountainebleau toward the south in the
direction of Moulins and Château Bourbon.

That night King Francis gave a ball to honor the new
Marquise de Meung. De Meung had got his marquisate;
Madame de Meung need no longer scutter up to the gallery of the petty noblesse. She could hold up her head
with the best of them now.

❋
❋ ❋ 8 ❋ ❋

O N THE BANKS of the river Allier in the duchy of
the Bourbonnais, near the mountains that separated
it from Imperial Germany, stood the squat square tower of
Château Bourbon, ducal seat of the brooding eccentric
Duc Charles de Bourbon, Constable of France, now medi-
tating defection to the enemy.

As Henri and de Meung approached the Duc's estates,
forfeit but not yet garrisoned by the king's troops, the
people showed signs of unfriendliness. Wine at the inns was
sour, service was sulky and slow. Their horses were brought
to them uncurried in the morning. De Meung complained
bitterly.

"Don't these peasants know who we are?" He was sporting a garish new coat with slashed sleeves and a violently
purple hat. "Can't they see I'm a marquis?"

"They see all too clearly, I'm afraid," Henri said thought-
fully. "Parisian gentry appear unpopular in these parts.
We'll have to moderate our dress, I suspect, to gain entry
into Château Bourbon."

"What! Throw my new coat away?"

"Or your life," Henri said.

"Not mine," said de Meung, glaring at him with ill-concealed hostility.

Henri wondered what was behind the glare, and was suddenly on his guard. It was natural, he supposed, that de Meung might harbor some remnant of resentment against him; but de Meung had boasted for hours on end about his elevation to the marquisate and chattered in tedious, even anatomical, detail about the favor his *marquise* had found with the king; so, Henri reasoned, his jealousy could not run deep.

Gravely and frankly Henri had explained to him the heavy charge King Francis had laid upon them: to bring back the Duc de Bourbon, dead or alive.

To this de Meung had suggested, "You are a very persuasive talker, chevalier. You will talk to him first, will you not?"

"I have considered attempting persuasion," Henri had replied. "But the king tried that and failed. No, we must take the Duc by guile, de Meung."

"That's not what the king told me," said de Meung; and instantly realized he had said too much. But the words were out and Henri had heard them.

"I was not aware that His Majesty had outlined our mission to both of us," he said.

"Oh, he just sketched in a suggestion or two," de Meung said hurriedly. "You're the commander, chevalier."

"His Majesty was thoughtful and gracious," Henri said, determined to probe deeper. But the bibulous marquis proved unexpectedly immune to wine that night, though Henri bought him three bottles in an effort to loosen his tongue. De Meung sulked and went to bed mumbling, "You're the commander. I just take orders. That's all I do."

Henri, increasingly aware of the unfriendly attitude of the people and uncertain of de Meung, could not help saying testily, "I confess I have had more pleasant traveling companions, *monsieur le marquis.*"

"So I seem to remember," de Meung said, and rolled over and snored.

Henri sighed. Tomorrow they would enter the Bourbonnais.

Geographical isolation alone would have rendered the Duc de Bourbon untypical of his age. Paris, bustling with the vanities and new fashions of the day, lay far to the north. To the south lay the commercial cities of the Mediterranean, full of a rich new breed of merchants, buying and selling for profit, as repugnant to the Duc as the courtiers and politicians of Paris. Over the eastern mountains lay the measureless reaches of the Empire, of which the Bourbonnais had recently been a part. For seven hundred years, ever since Charlemagne, French kings had done homage to the Holy Roman Emperor, sometimes with tongue in cheek, sometimes sincere, sometimes for some of the provinces of France, sometimes for all. But the present French king was one of the tongue-in-cheek "subjects" of the Empire, and the present Emperor, Charles Quint, was mortally hostile to him.

In the face of ever-mounting consciousness of nationalism felt by the rest of the people of France, nobles, clergy, bourgeois and peasants, the people of the Bourbonnais, a border territory, had held to their ancient feudal way of life, separate and remote. Here, in this feudal backwater, the

Duc de Bourbon took hold of the clock of History and tugged with all his might to stop it, and, if he could, to set it back. Personal tragedy had aggravated the vagaries of his temperament. In his own mind he was not a traitor but a Messiah, bringing not peace but a sword, conspiring with the enemies of France only to save France. Of two feudal masters, one's king and the Emperor, a choice common in the old days and still open to the feudal-minded, the Emperor had the more ancient claim on the Duc.

But though Bourbon could justify his choice, his staunch French blood rebelled at the stigma of traitor; so, for a while, he wavered, taking no action. At this time, the king, with wisdom and statecraft, might still have saved him for France and written a brilliant page in the annals of his reign. But within the week King Francis, through his levity and folly, would push him irrevocably over the line and into the camp of the enemy; but not before devotion and daring had brought the harebrained scheme to abduct the mighty vassal within a hair's-breadth of success.

There were two inns in Moulins, one named Louis the Saint and brilliant with lights.

"Ah!" said de Meung, expectantly. "Here the wine will be good."

"Not for the likes of us," Henri said, aping a craftsman's patois. "This place is for gentry."

De Meung grumbled. They were riding a rough cart attached to two heavy draught horses. It jolted and rattled. The commodious interior was full of tools: shovels, picks, long brushes of the kind used by chimney sweeps but stiffer by reason of the heavier work they had to perform; there were suction devices and long steel "snakes" that could be thrust into drains to remove obstructions. There was a barrel of lime, for cleaning purposes, and a hogshead of aromatic pine oil to sweeten the air after the team of master plumbers had finished their work.

Henri had wanted to burn their good clothes, but de Meung set up such a howl at losing his brand-new coat that Henri had compromised, "Oh, all right, hide it in the hay." It was a bale of fodder that thrifty craftsmen might reasonably carry with them in their cart and that might, just might, serve to conceal the body of the Duc de Bourbon later on.

"I'd have liked to stop here overnight," said de Meung, looking wistfully at Louis the Saint. Inside were gentlemen at laden tables, feasting and laughing; some were smoking pipes. Liveried servants served them and an attractive barmaid made the rounds with long-necked bottles of wine. It was a well-known stopping place for noble travelers and rich merchants on their way to the cities of the south.

"You would be sure to be recognized," Henri said gravely, glancing sidewise at him. "The captain of the king's archers was already prominent. How much more conspicuous must be the Marquis de Meung."

"No doubt, no doubt," de Meung said, complacent, appeased. "I suppose you cannot hide quality, chevalier, even in craftsman's rags."

"You certainly can't," Henri said.

"But I never thought the king would send me storming a castle through the drains."

"It's been done before," Henri said. "Ask any engineer. But we won't 'storm' Château Bourbon and we won't enter through the drains, though they'll provide an escape if my guess is right."

Very old castles, like Château Bourbon, often had running water and excellent sewers, constructed during the ages when the art of the Romans, with their passion for baths, still lingered on in France. Later had come castles with extremely primitive facilities. Now again, with rebirth of Roman and Greek inspiration, people were gaining an interest in classical cleanliness. Henri was certain that Château Bourbon spanned the two ages. Under its ancient walls must surely lie a way out, once one got in.

The other inn in Moulins was Le Rat Mort, The Dead Rat. Its windows were small and the light behind them was guttering and yellow, as from cheap tallow candles.

"Is this the place you take me, a marquis?" de Meung said.

"It was recommended by the man who sold me the wagon," Henri said, himself a bit dubious.

On closer inspection the windows were clean, no fetid smell came from the stables in the rear, and, most heartening of all, a thick column of smoke, savory with the odor of roasting sheep, rose from the chimney. The proprietor was a saving man but not a sloven, he spread his gratuitous stable refuse on his garden, a typical thrifty Bourbonnais.

The proprietor was approaching.

"Note that his apron is clean," Henri whispered. "I entreat you, hold your tongue while I test him. We are better off than you think."

"*Canaille!*" muttered de Meung, eying the stocky figure.

"Be quiet," Henri said.

"Oh, you're the commander. Go ahead. Get our throats slit by this peasant."

The peasant gave them good evening, appraising the well-stocked wagon.

"Me and my apprentice," Henri said, "we'd like to put up for the night." He made no attempt to speak like a native of the district, knowing it was impossible. He spoke like a simple workman from another province.

"You would be from the north," said the proprietor, as if northerners somehow were suspect.

Henri attacked.

"Your hostelry bears a forbidding name, proprietor," he said, frowning. "Perhaps I shall camp in the fields. The Dead Rat. Faugh!"

The proprietor saw a patron slipping away. Outlander or no, revenue was revenue and there were empty rooms in his inn. The wagon was substantial, the horses well fed; and the craftsman spoke with authority. He would not ask credit; there was solid prosperity here.

He called a stable boy, who came running. The first thing always is to immobilize the horses while you impress the prospective patron, so he does not drive away and camp, as this one threatened, in the fields.

"*Maître*," he said, giving Henri the title of "master" in his craft, "Le Rat Mort is a jewel of a hostelry. *Parbleu!* When I took the place over, the rats were *vives* and vicious. They nibbled at the toes of the guests. God's truth! It was called at that time by another name, which I will not dignify by repeating. It was infested with rodents. But I, Hercule Pajou, I slew the vermin with poison and traps. Now my inn is as clean as a palace, cleaner than some I could mention. Proudly I display my sign *rat mort* in signification that my valued patrons may sleep in safety, on clean straw, between blankets where no life but their own is in evidence, with fire on the hearth for a nominal charge in the morning, meat for breakfast. Everything."

"Very well, Pajou, we will stay and not camp in the fields," Henri said.

"Oh, *maître*," said Pajou, "to go farther tonight would be suicide; the fogs, the swamps, the miasma, the cold, the wolves —"

"I have already said we would stay," Henri said laughing. "You need not deprecate your delightful province. Swamps are my business."

"The *maître* is a plumber?" said the innkeeper.

"The best," Henri said gaily, "and looking for business. Everything up north that was cleanable, I've cleaned. Armand, give that good lad with the horses a copper."

De Meung dug in his purse and found among the gold and silver pieces a copper sou.

"Here," he said. The boy caught it in midflight and grinned.

"Mind that you curry them sleek as a —"

The youngster finished the simile, graphically.

"He is very young," said the innkeeper apologetically. "My son. In time he will learn manners."

"That's how good horses ought to be curried, that smooth," Henri said smiling.

"I hope you will stay a long time," Pajou said.

"As long as work holds out."

"Perhaps I can be of assistance in recommending customers."

"That would be greatly appreciated," Henri said.

They dined on roast mutton, and the wine was so good that de Meung momentarily thawed. "I'd never have thought you could pass for a plumber," he said, almost respectfully.

"*Monsieur le marquis*," Henri said, "I am beginning to like you."

That reminded de Meung that he detested the Chevalier de Tonnerre and he froze up again. His detestation grew when Henri got them work in the neighborhood, which they dutifully performed, so that de Meung could not stand his own smell. "I was not cut out for this sort of thing," he complained.

"That is why we must study to perfect ourselves in this somewhat mysterious craft," Henri said, "since, patently, we must not bungle the job with the Duc de Bourbon."

The secret of Henri's success was the hogshead of costly pine oil, a fillip beyond the reach of a real plumber, which made his reputation and was grudgingly conceded by their patrons as something new to the Bourbonnais and highly desirable even if it did come from an outlander.

"How are chances at the Château?" Henri asked the innkeeper one night.

"Ought to be good," Pajou said. "They've never been touched within the memory of living man. They're that big."

"Then they certainly require attention by now," Henri said.

"It would take weeks," Pajou said.

"I'd not mind, and the pay would be good."

"Oh, the Duc," Pajou said, "he spends money like water. Yes, the pay would be good, but the Duc never sees tradesmen. Besides, nothing ever gets clogged in the Château. Drains are too big, I guess."

"Doesn't he mind the odor? Drains stink when they're not cleaned for so long."

"The Duc lives in another world," Pajou said. But he wanted to keep his prompt-paying guests. "I know the Duc's major-domo," he said, tentatively.

"Do you know him well?"

"He is a cousin of sorts."

Henri hesitated between a gold and a silver bribe. On balance, it had better be silver. Gold would excite suspicion.

"No doubt your good cousin has many financial obligations," Henri said, his hand straying towards his purse. His education in the power of money had advanced by giant strides since leaving Paris. His understanding of old Duprat had grown. Anything could be bought with money, a bride or the key to the gate of Château Bourbon. What a vast and unchivalrous world existed outside the field of battle, where only honor and life counted! How simple it was to cleave to a code: cling to honor, lose your life. One did not even have to think. But how queerly, how lowly lived the multitudes of this world, to whom a silver franc was a week's sustenance. Poor things. Without their francs they might murder or starve. What lay between the two extremes, the King Francises for whom only the code counted and the innkeepers Pajou? Much, he suspected; men like the chancellor of the king's *épargne*. He wished he knew him better. He wished Duprat had been party to the king's mad scheme to abduct the Duc de Bourbon; there would have been a better chance of success. Marie was Duprat's blood relative. He felt drawn to her, her cool good sense. He would have liked to be able to say to himself, "Henri de Tonnerre, you will live to see your son christened." Instead he was haggling with Pajou. It is difficult at times to live up to the image of the *homme universel* that your shaving mirror reflects. But one tries.

"No doubt the Duc de Bourbon's major-domo must maintain a certain standard of living," he said to Pajou.

"And a very large family as well," Pajou agreed. "Very expensive, as you know."

"I do not know yet," Henri smiled, "though there are signs."

"I congratulate you, *maître*," said Pajou.

Under his fingers Henri felt three fat silver francs in his purse and extracted them and tendered them to the innkeeper. "My friend," he said, "I would count it a kindness if you would recommend my services to your cousin, the major-domo. He will keep me in mind if you give him these two silver francs, which are the fruit of honest toil."

"Two?" said de Meung. "That's three!"

Henri and the innkeeper looked at him scathingly.

"Your apprentice is somewhat shortsighted," Pajou said.

"He functions well underground," Henri said.

Pajou said, *"Maître,* for two silver francs my cousin the major-domo will think about nothing but the rehabilitation of Château Bourbon's drains for a fortnight!"

"He can count on me," Henri said, "and meanwhile I and my apprentice shall continue to enjoy your excellent fare and courteous hospitality."

"Maître, I hope it will be many weeks."

Henri knew he would succeed or fail before the passage of another week. "If I am so fortunate as to be employed by the Duc," he said earnestly, "other gentry hereabouts will hear of me. With a recommendation like your cousin's, the Duc's major-domo, I might find work for a year. Who knows?"

At the postern gate of Château Bourbon, opening on the rear court that served both as a mustering ground for the Duc's bodyguard and a feeding ground for the chickens, two craftsmen appeared in a sturdy wagon and were admitted by the Duc's major-domo. The Duc, with larger considerations weighing heavily on his mind and with no chatelaine to assist him, left the management of his château entirely to his major-domo, from the stocking of the larder to the hiring of masons and, naturally, plumbers. From the tradesmen and the artisans, from all who passed through the postern gate, the major-domo exacted a private little tax of his own. Then, when they were paid, they signed receipts for a little more than they had received. In this manner the major-domo had already supplied a four-hundred-franc dowry for one of his daughters, now happily married, and would shortly have enough for another, who was already fifteen and in danger of being a spinster. Little Louise was far prettier than her raw-boned elder sister, but feather-witted and flirtatious. The sturdy sons-in-law whom the major-domo envisaged wanted soldier wives with practical good sense, and shied away from Louise, who never could think of one thing long enough to get anything done and was given to short-lived intense attachments.

The Duc never hesitated to authorize repairs to such things as the stonework and ironwork of his castle, but he said to his major-domo, "A plumber? I was not aware that anything was amiss."

The major-domo enumerated a dozen deficiencies after three centuries of neglect.

"Oh, very well," said the Duc, and authorized the work, shrugging.

To Henri the major-domo said shortly, "I have arranged

sleeping quarters for you and your man over the stables."

"Where?" demanded de Meung.

"They are commodious and convenient," the major-domo said. "Did you expect an apartment in the château?"

"My man refers to the loss of time involved in such distant quarters. Our work will not be in the stables, but in the kitchens, the wells, the conduits adjacent to the moat, the Duc's bath."

"Who told you the Duc had a bath?"

"Well, doesn't he? In the newer châteaux there are none, but in one this old there must be. If there is not work here I am wasting my time, and your cousin Pajou deceived me."

The major-domo liked a man who knew his job.

"The Duc has a bath," he admitted.

He also liked his two silver francs and looked forward to more.

"You may lodge over the main kitchen if you prefer," he said, "though I'll have to displace some of the servants, and they'll grumble."

"Perhaps they will put up with the inconvenience if you give them these from me. Remind them that it will be only for a short while." He gave the major-domo a jingling handful of copper coins that amounted perhaps to a franc. The money dropped into the dark recesses of the major-domo's purse, never again, Henri was sure, to see the light of day.

"They will not be inconvenienced, *maître*," he said amiably, "even if your stay should be longer."

"Only long enough to finish the job," Henri said.

The major-domo looked at the two craftsmen sharply. Something about them did not quite ring true. Henri's face was too aristocratic and there was a hint of the military about de Meung. But next day he rummaged in the wagon and found nothing suspect: the tools were not new; they were well worn and well cared for and they were the right kind. There was even a large bale of fodder for the horses. Probably Henri and his man were merely examples of the new type of worker that was permeating society these days, better spoken, better educated in their craft, lacking the traditional feudal subserviency of recent reigns — why, they even doffed their caps as if they were afraid of taking cold in the head and their bows lacked the comfortable groveling quality of the peasant who knew his place. But they were competent, ambitious and swift. A disturbing age, this reign of the First Francis, thought the major-domo.

He set his daughter Louise to spy on them: she found them sedulously evacuating a small kitchen drain clogged with the grease of centuries. "It leads to a dry-well in the court," Henri said.

Louise giggled. How could a "well" be "dry"?

"Now the cooks won't have to dump their slops into the moat," Henri said. "This was designed to keep the moat clean."

Louise was impressed. "Nobody ever knew that before," she said. "Everybody'll be glad; you'll make their work easier. Is this how it's done up north?"

"This is how it ought to be done everywhere," Henri said; and he gave her a long tedious dissertation on the lore of drains, starting with the magnificently engineered Cloaca Maxima in Rome, as if drains were the passion of his life.

"There must be hundreds of these things about the place," Louise said dimpling. "I know some of them. I'll show you where they are."

She gave her father a glowing report. "He is terribly efficient, Father."

"What did he talk about?"

"Nothing but silly old drains. It was boring, but I listened. He made everything so interesting."

Her father eyed her sharply.

"Did he continue working while he was talking about these drains?"

"Oh yes, all the time. He has skillful big strong hands. His teeth are so white and he smells like a forest of pines."

Her father sighed. Louise would be forming another of her lightning crushes on handsome young men. High time the girl was married and settled down. But it was encouraging that Henri worked while he talked, and that his talk was boring. Only such a man would have the patience to put up with her. And it struck him that the dowry an itinerant plumber could demand would be nominal.

"You shouldn't have told him there were hundreds of drains, Louise. There are many, but not that many."

"I wanted him to stay."

"I rather like him myself," the major-domo said, and his thoughts ran in the same direction. He could always set Henri to work on the subterranean passageway that ran to the river, long since abandoned and full of debris. "He and his helper seem good steady men, Louise; a little uppity, perhaps."

"I wouldn't care if he was," she said.

In addition to Louise and her married sister the major-domo had four other girls of assorted ages to marry off. "I hope she lights on this one," he muttered half aloud.

"What did you say, Father?"

"Nothing, child. Nothing at all."

Next day the major-domo said sternly to Henri, "Your helper is making eyes at one of the maids down the hall from your room. When I assigned you these quarters I anticipated no such laxity. You are fortunate the Duc hasn't heard of it; you should know by now how he feels about such matters. His conduct has shocked my daughter, Louise, a decent well-brought-up young woman."

"I'll speak to my man," Henri said.

De Meung was continuing to cause him trouble, slipping out at night to drink with one of the maidservants, a middle-aged widow who was delighted with the attention and knew how to steal from the Duc's ample wine cellar. "The Duc never touches it," she said. De Meung said, "We ought not to let it go to waste." "Just be sure you don't talk in your sleep!" Henri had cautioned him.

And next day he reported to the major-domo, "I have spoken to my man and he'll behave himself from now on. My helper would long since be a master himself, but for his weakness for women and wine. But he never misses a day's work."

"He should settle down and marry," the major-domo said. "Nothing steadies a man like a good wife and the responsibilities of a home. Don't you agree?"

Henri sensed a trap. He had told Pajou there were signs that he might become a father.

"Major-domo," he said, with the air of a man in the confessional, "you will find very few itinerant craftsmen fortunate enough to be happily married and father of *legitimate* offspring, though some of us set ourselves that goal for the future."

"I see," said the major-domo. No doubt the handsome young man whom Louise found so attractive had run away

from a liaison up north. Well, maybe he had learned his lesson. "Perhaps that is why some masters still travel like
journeymen, eh, *maître* Henri?"

"Unquestionably, major-domo," Henri said, feeling like
Peter denying the Lord.

The major-domo nodded understandingly. "Such a man
would not want to travel, or run away, for the rest of his
life I should think. Would he not, after making his mistake
and repenting, want to settle down and marry some decent
well-brought-up girl?"

"Such a man would assuredly desire a more settled way of
life, I am certain," Henri said. He could tell from the
major-domo's face that the answer was acceptable.

"Well, just keep that apprentice of your busy and sober,
and I'll see what can be done to keep you in work."

"There's the Duc's bath," Henri suggested.

"The Duc wouldn't like all the scraping and pounding."

"I assure you, major-domo, the Duc won't even know
we're there. We'll be quiet as mice, and then one day the
Duc will awaken and behold! his amenity will be shining
like marble and sweet-smelling as a cathedral! My reputation in the Bourbonnais will be made."

The major-domo chuckled. Henri's color had risen. His
face was animated.

"Louise told me you were dedicated to your craft, *maître*
Henri. Well, there is nothing wrong in that."

Henri was speculating that the drains of the Duc's bath
must lead somewhere out of the castle walls.

"Mistress Louise is a charming, intelligent young woman,"
Henri said.

"Louise will make some honest man the best wife in the
province," the major-domo said. "An excellent cook, a good

housekeeper, healthy, strong and obedient. She will give him many children, *maître* Henri, legitimate children," he added with a touch of reproach.

"Any man would be lucky to find such a helpmeet," Henri said. "And the Duc's bath, major-domo?"

"Oh that. I wouldn't bother with that. It has functioned for centuries."

"The water supply?"

"In times past it was pumped from a well in the court to a tank a floor above the Duc's apartments. But the pump disintegrated a hundred years ago and the pumphouse is used as a chicken roost now. He bathes in a bucket of water a man carries up to the bath."

"And the waste water?"

"The man dumps it down the drain."

"How big is the drain?"

"Well, once the man got drunk and dropped the bucket and had to climb down after it."

"Poor fellow," Henri said. "Is he still there?"

"The Duc, as you know, abhors wine and excess. Fearing the Duc would punish him, the man, scared to death, wandered about underground and found his way out through an exit in the foundations. Or such is the story."

"Is the man still in your employ?"

"Certainly not," the major-domo said.

"That's too bad," Henri said. "I'd have liked to talk to him. He could have traced for me the drains to be cleared, and I could have saved the Duc time and money."

"Don't worry about that, *maître* Henri. Louise knows all the old tunnels. When my children were young they used to play in them. You know how children are when they're young. No? Well, one day you'll know. They're quite charming when they're young. They will disappear for hours and come up unexpectedly out of the ground, all laughing and hungry, with dirty hands and faces, behind some old iron grill work, maybe in the chicken house, almost anywhere, totally innocent that they'd scared their mother and me out of our wits. Once when Louise was ten she popped up behind the altar of the chapel."

"The whole complex system ought to be charted and cleaned," Henri said emphatically.

"No doubt, no doubt, *maître* Henri," the major-domo agreed. "It would take years."

"It would be a labor of love," Henri said.

"It would also provide you with well-nigh permanent employment, would it not, *maître?*" the major-domo said, his voice heavy with understanding.

"Is that a reprehensible ambition, major-domo?"

"Not at all, young man, not at all. It can be arranged. I follow you. I shall arrange it. I myself am somewhat vague about the meanderings of the subterranean passages of Château Bourbon. But I shall try to ask Louise to recall from her childhood memories — mind you, she isn't a child any more — where they lead. Louise can be of great help; greater than I."

"If she remembers," Henri said.

"I will see to it that she remembers. You can draw a picture of the passages on a piece of paper —"

"That is called a 'plot' or 'chart,' " Henri said. "I'll write in full directions, where they start and where they lead."

"You can *write, maître* Henri?" Good heavens! The plumber was a clerk! If he got into trouble he could claim benefit of clergy and be tried in an ecclesiastical court. A treasure!

"A little," Henri said.

"Don't write anything in the Duc's chart," the major-domo said. "Just draw pictures and make your X. The Duc is very old-fashioned. He'd distrust a clerkly plumber."

"Very well," Henri said.

"And then when you've drawn your chart I shall present it to him and request his authorization for the work. My dear *maître* — I almost called you 'my dear son' — do you realize that this could lead to a career that would last for a lifetime? Permanent work for the rest of your life? With industry on your part, and a word of recommendation from me, you could attach yourself to the staff of Château Bourbon forever?" The major-domo grinned conspiratorially.

"You remind me," Henri smiled, "that I owe something for lodging and fare to your cousin Pajou at Le Rat Mort, who still keeps my rooms for me though I have not occupied them for a week. It is he who set me on the road to this good fortune. I conceive that he ought to be recompensed — at least half price."

"I will take care of cousin Pajou," the major-domo said. "Don't give it a thought. I know for a fact that he rented that room as soon as you and your man took occupancy of the quarters over the kitchen."

"He did?"

The major-domo shrugged. "Some merchant or other from Paris, who has stayed on. Pajou's place is always full of merchants. I'll give him quarter pay, and cousin Pajou will be glad to get it."

"I am fated to be perpetually in your debt," Henri said. "And now to my drawings, major-domo. I shall be swift."

"I will send Louise to you," the major-domo said. "There is plenty of time."

"He is very ambitious," the major-domo said to his daughter. "God's truth, Louise, I never saw a man in such a hurry. He is not at all Bourbonnais. He strives to excel. An aggressive man, Louise. He will make his place in the world. I find him acceptable, even if he is a northerner."

"So do I," his daughter said.

"Be distant and ladylike in the big sewer," her father said. "He can write."

"Distant?" she smiled. *"Oui, mon père."*

"This sort can be caught by a lady," he said severely.

And mentally he muttered, *"Chère bébé!* You poor queer little thing. Nothing was ever with you like with the others. You didn't walk till you were three. So slow in so much, so far in advance of your age in all that pertains to a man. The man I found you with in the Duc's bath that day; the man who fell and broke his neck; I was asked today if he were still in my employ! I know where his body lies. But here is a good man, Louise, patient, dedicated to his craft. He will care for you. I could get him for a hundred francs dowry, since he is hiding from some indiscretion up north; but for him I will endow you equally with your saner sisters, if you can contrive to snare him. I promise that *he* will not fall and break his neck, no matter what you do — in fact, the sooner you do it the better."

Something of this showed in his face.

"Distant," she promised, dimpling. "Like a lady."

"I do not mean that you should be *too* distant, Louise. I mean to imply that *maître* Henri is thorough and painstaking, and you must try to oblige him. He is drawing a picture of the old tunnels where you used to play when you were little. Follow him, therefore, when he takes the lead, even if he leads you into passageways you do not know; and do what he says. I would go myself except that I do not know the tunnels as you do. You understand me, child?"

"I will do what he says," she said.

Louise came to him that evening, bearing in her hand a small lighted lantern. "I expected you earlier in the day," Henri said. He had wasted an entire seven hours of daylight, pacing his room, impatiently waiting for her. Probably she had forgotten.

He pointed to the Marquis de Meung, placidly snoring on his couch with an empty brandy bottle on the floor, dropped when his hand could no longer hold it. "And there is my man," he said. "I had nothing for him to do today, so he found his own amusement."

Louise smiled, shrugged. She had done up her childish pigtails in a tangled pyramid on the top of her head in an attempt to ape the fashionable coiffure of a Parisian lady. Thereupon she had placed a silver snood which she had found in an old clothes press belonging to the dead Duchess of Bourbon. She had stolen a razor from the Duc's barber and shaved her forehead so as to give herself the abnormally high hair-line so coveted by Italian and Parisian beauties. She looked like what she was, a precocious child, intensely self-aware, terribly in a hurry and trying to give the appearance of a woman of fashion.

"A year," Henri mused, "and she'll have it all naturally; she won't have to play-act; she'll be lovely in her own right. Strange little girl."

"I had many chores to do today," Louise said. "I couldn't come earlier. Anyhow, what does it matter whether you inspect the tunnels by day or by night? It's always night in the tunnels. Are you afraid of the dark?"

"Oh, very well," he said.

Together they walked down dusty stairs of stone, long unused and covered with moisture. Dust had filtered from the ancient stones of the foundations; it clung to the steps in a queer half-mud, half-solid state, slippery underfoot and offensive to the nose. Scattered like peppercorns over a pudding were the droppings of generations of bats. "You'd better hang onto my arm," he said. Her arm slipped into the crook of his and held tight.

As his eyes became accustomed to the gloom he saw in the guttering light of the lantern a pillared dungeon with a low-vaulted roof of superbly fitted masonry. "They didn't use mortar in those days," he said. The stillness of the place caused him instinctively to lower his voice, but still the last words echoed back, ". . . in those days, days, days," softer and softer till the echo died away, lost in some distant winding passageway that could trap and destroy all sound.

"Don't be frightened," he said. She seemed to be holding more tightly to his arm than the danger of falling warranted.

Louise laughed gaily, and the cheery echo came rippling back. It was a pleasanter sound than his whisper, which, distorted by distance, had returned like an ominous croak. "I'm not frightened," she said.

"A place like this struck me as likely to frighten a little girl alone."

"I'm not alone, I'm not a little girl, and I know this place," she said. Her tone was full of a red-lipped pout that he could not see but he knew was there, and it was warm and delightful.

"It is good to have a competent guide," he said, giving her arm a gentle squeeze. "Watch your step here, Louise. It's wetter underfoot." They were approaching the most

131

distant of the tunnels that led from the dungeon. Doubtless this was the winding one that engendered, then destroyed, the echoes. Henri speculated that it was also the one he was seeking, the one that led beyond the walls.

Henri's squeeze, though scarcely paternal, was not like a lover's either; but it caused a sudden reaction in Louise as if it had been an invitation to intimacy. Her body stiffened, then relaxed and molded itself against his. Her arm slipped out of his and encircled his waist. Swift as one of the lizards that scuttled in and out of the crannies of the dungeon she slithered from his side to his front. The words, "My dear, you're effectually blocking my passage," rose to his lips; his stride forward had brought him squarely and strongly against her lithe and pliant young body. He would likely have voiced the words, but her hands slipped up his back and pressed against the nape of his neck and brought his face down to hers; and, as surely as she had blocked his stride, so now she blocked his speech, pressing her lips against his. The lantern dropped. The darkness was complete. The silence was absolute except for the distant murmur of lapping water and the quick close breathing of the girl, which he could hear as well as feel; her breath in his face was heady and sweet and hot. All his senses were involved.

"I'm afraid I dropped the lantern," he said. It was not the observation of an *homme universel* and he felt strangely inadequate.

"Don't go in there," she said. "Stay here. Don't go in there."

"Louise, I've got to go into all these old tunnels. I told you, I have to make a chart of them."

He would rather have stayed. He mused, "If I were a true *homme universel*, confound it, I'd take her now, and what would be the harm, or even if there were monumental harm? She's ripe for the plucking; it would be a delicious adventure, and I'd probably stop her from throwing herself away on some groom later on; and in ten minutes I'd be about my exploring. Poor little emotional beast. Maybe this is how they couple in the Bourbonnais. It has its intriguing aspects."

"There's a dead man in there," she said.

Sobered, he answered, "Louise, there are dead men everywhere. I must go in anyhow."

Her father had said, "Where he leads, go!"

"I won't go till you kiss me," she said.

"Tut, tut," he said. "I'll kiss you on the way back, if you show me where this confounded passageway leads."

He bent over and picked up the lantern, but had nothing to light it with. An *homme universel* would have equipped himself with a flint and steel. He swore.

She kicked him savagely on the shin.

"I won't go till you kiss me," she said.

Angered at himself and her he locked her in his arms and kissed her so long and hard she could not breathe; dizzy, she slumped against him and, when at length he relented and released her, she melted against him and sobbed, "I'm sorry I kicked you."

"You've an admirable aim in the dark," he said testily. "Hold onto my hand now and we'll go back and light that damned lantern and start all over again." His shin smarted and he was annoyed at himself for letting the girl divert him.

"You're angry with me."

"No, child, but next time we'll attend to business. Agreed?"

He was leading her, groping his way back, steadying himself against the wall.

"Agreed," she said. Her body hurt, from neck to hips, with the fury of his embrace. But he had embraced her.

"We won't have to go all the way back," she said. "There's a quicker way of lighting the lantern. I'll show you. I know the way."

"Back through the big tunnel?"

"No, there's nothing there but a pool of water. The river end is under water, flooded. Father thinks the river level is higher than it was in the old days. I've heard stories that men used to be able to walk in and out of the castle once, but it must have been hundreds of years ago."

"You can't walk in and out that way any more?"

"Not any more."

"I shall mark it on my chart as a dead end," Henri said, frowning. Patently one could not use the big tunnel as an avenue of abduction for the Duc. "I need not explore it."

"It's horrid anyhow."

She had come to a low opening in the wall.

"Crouch down or you'll bump your head," she said.

A current of air, sweet with old incense, struck against his face. Far ahead he could see a dim flickering light.

"Why is it horrid?"

"That's where the dead man is, rotten and unburied. The man Father found me with. We weren't doing anything, but the man fell and broke his neck, Father says. Maybe he did. I don't care. After a while I didn't like him any more. Father said he hid the man's body in the tunnel so as not to worry the Duc. I saw it there once. It was horrid."

The light ahead was closer now, and the odor of incense was stronger. Henri remembered a chance remark of the major-domo's.

"The chapel?" he asked.

"Yes," she said in a low voice. "The crypt beneath the altar. Be very quiet. I think there's someone there."

After the Stygian darkness Henri could see a little now in the dim illumination that came from the end of the tunnel. It flickered, as from a candle, and cast a grid-shaped shadow on the floor of the passageway beneath.

"There *never* are people there!" she whispered in his ear. "I'm afraid. Let us go back."

"Sh-h-h!"

There were two voices, and one was the voice of de Meung.

"It's the Duc! He's talking to someone. We'll be caught. Come back!"

He pressed his finger against her mouth and took the lead. "I will go a little closer," he said. "Don't talk."

Crouching, he led her forward, walking on tiptoe. She followed in his shadow, and as silently.

The voice of de Meung came whining, ingratiating. "The Chevalier de Tonnerre was specifically instructed to treat with you, my lord Duc. The king told me so. Instead he keeps up his silly disguise and subjects me to countless indignities, me a marquis!"

The Duc de Bourbon heartily detested all traitors but himself, whom he did not class as a traitor, and particularly self-seeking traitors, faithless to their masters, like de Meung.

"Indeed," came his voice to Henri, heavy with scorn. "And Francis sent you to spy on him, eh? Very like him.

And perhaps you planned to carry out this little abduction of my person yourself in case Tonnerre failed!"

"My lord Duc, your abduction was entirely the chevalier's idea, not the king's, not mine. Here, sir; here is a letter in the king's own hand. I think it's a letter. I saw him writing it."

There was a silence. In his mind's eye Henri saw the yellow packet changing hands. "I thought it was a talisman he wore around his neck! Fool, fool, fool that I was!"

Suddenly the sound of laughter struck Henri's ears. It was throaty and bestial and charged with fury. It ended with a scream of pain and a labored entreaty, "Don't! Don't, my lord Duc! Oh God, oh my God!" Then there was a choking sound and then there was silence.

Louise pressed against Henri in terror. "I never heard the Duc laugh before!"

"Quiet, child; something terrible is happening up there. Be quiet and listen."

"No, I'm afraid. I'm going to get out of here!" She tried to pull him away but he stood firm.

"Hush, Louise!"

She broke from him and fled; he could hear the swift soft patter of her footsteps fade away in the darkness behind him.

In the crypt above, the Duc spoke again. A lonely man, tortured by the schism in his soul, torn between his divided loyalties, he sometimes talked to himself. At no time had he ever talked to himself so bitterly as now. He was the only man left alive in the room. His words were the funeral oration of the Marquis de Meung, who lay dead on the grating, stabbed through the throat.

"You drunken clod, you traitorous abomination! You

miserable instrument of a weakling monarch! Frail clay, frail image of failing France! You are better dead. Oh, I would that all your kind might lie as you do now, powerless to work the doom on my motherland which I see approaching as surely as the fires of Purgatory. But I thank you, clay, for teaching me this lesson, that there is no faith in King Francis, and now I know what I must do."

The Duc was a massive man, six feet tall and strong as a bull. At Marignan in the thick of battle he had fought with a mace. Last of the generation of mighty strikers, he gloried in the ancient weapon and deplored its derogation into a purely decorative symbol of command, the marshal's baton. Nor was he, even in the heart of his stronghold, ever without his dagger, which he had just used on de Meung.

Now he reached down and wrenched up the grating and, spurning with his foot the limp body, rolled it over and thrust it into the hole. It fell almost at Henri's feet, as the grating crashed down.

"Clay, sleep with clay! Your burial is better than that of most of your kind, in a crypt below a crypt, beneath two altars! Faugh!" He spat through the grating. Then he washed his hands in holy water from the font beside the altar and the pink drops fell on the body. And then the light went out above the grating and Henri heard the Duc's firm righteous step fade away. The Duc had left the crypt.

Henri listened to de Meung's heart, but it had stopped beating; and bent his cheek to de Meung's nostrils, but there was no breath.

"Adieu, poor marquis," he muttered. "I have nothing to bury you with. I will slay the monster who slew you!" It was an oath of vendetta to the dead, and Henri spoke it full voice.

Then he reached up and, with an effort, dislodged the heavy grating and clambered up through the hole into the pitch-black chapel.

He was instantly pinioned to the floor by a dozen powerful hands. Lights flashed in his face. The Duc de Bourbon stood in the center of a group of men-at-arms.

"I thought I heard rats in my cellar," he said.

❋
❋ ❋ 9 ❋ ❋

OUTSIDE THE GATES of Château Montholon a
military trumpet sounded an imperious note. Marie
looked out of her casement window and saw a large company of armed and mounted men, and for a moment she
wondered whether the castle were under siege. Rumors of
war had penetrated even to the peaceful countryside.

Since the departure of Henri for the south she had taken
up quarters with her mother in the rooms she had occupied
as a child. "Soon I'll be readying the nursery again," the
dowager duchess had said fondly. "I have saved your little
cradle all these years, Marie."

Marie would rather have remained in her new home on
the Tonnerre estates, but neither Uncle Duprat nor her
mother would hear of it. "In these times, child? And in
your condition?"

Marie had shrugged and smiled. "I do not really care
where I stay, ma mère, while Henri is away." She had not
heard from him; it seemed an age since he had departed.

The duchess had said, with the forthrightness that was

considered out of date, too direct for the polite discourse that Francis the First had made fashionable, "Read your calendar, Marie; you can read. And look at your waistline. You have not let out your dresses. When you start straining at the seams and feel the little one kicking within you it will be soon enough to worry about the passage of time. Why! When I was your age your father was away at his wars for years at a time."

"Didn't you miss him, too?"

"I'm sure I must have," her mother said vaguely. "But it was a long time ago, and he always came back."

Marie hoped Henri would.

"Of course he will, child."

She went to the window and looked over Marie's shoulder, irked that anyone should blow a horn under her walls. Then she chuckled and summoned her captain.

"Lower the bridge," she commanded, "and tell the major-domo to sprinkle something aromatic in the hall. Quickly!" There had been cabbage and fish for dinner that day.

To Marie she said, "It's your great-uncle, dear. He's on a horse again. I wonder what it means."

The chancellor spurred his charger across the draw-bridge, which clattered down to afford him passage over the moat, which he noted with approval was full. He approved also of the duchess's men-at-arms, who stood sentry on the walls. Montholon was ready for any emergency.

Following him came his guard with fleur-de-lys pennants snapping in the brisk spring breeze. A single square-shaped banner with a cross encircled by a golden crown of thorns identified the cavalcade as ecclesiastical in character, led by the premier prelate of France. All else in their appearance was military and formidable.

Despite the duchess's valiant attempt to sweeten the air for her uncle's sensitive nose Duprat sniffed at the lingering odor of cabbage and carp and held to his nostrils a handkerchief heavily impregnated with oil of cloves.

"Are you trying to suffocate me, Agathe?" he said sternly. She knew him very well and she loved his little foible. *"Mon oncle,"* she said smiling, "it is Lent. Welcome to Montholon. You nearly frightened the life out of Marie. She thought you were an enemy army."

"I dispense you forthwith from the rigors of Lent," he said. "Cabbage and carp! My poor Agathe, you cannot have sinned to *that* extent. We shall have chickens during my stay."

"I have already ordered them killed, and I dare say the feathers are flying by now," the duchess said laughing.

He kissed her on the forehead. "This is the only house in France where I am at peace," he sighed. "It is good to see you again, my niece."

Marie advanced to kiss his ring, but he raised her and planted a sound avuncular kiss on both her cheeks. "Child, you are radiant. For you I pronounce dispensation from fasting altogether through Lent this year. My grandnephew must feed fat before you usher him into this world, and it seems to my celibate eye that you are looking a little peaked."

Then, bethinking himself, he said, "Nay, I extend my dispensation to all Montholon, lest I work a hardship on your mother and tempt her people into sin, since once they see the meat in the pots they will eat it on the sly, as who would not." He winked slyly at Marie, who thought she had never seen him in such an expansive mood; but her mother, who knew him better, sensed trouble. Danger always exhilarated Antoine Duprat and stimulated him to action.

"When will Henri return, Uncle Duprat? I have not heard from him. Is he all right?"

He patted her shoulder. "Of course he's all right, Marie." But he was voicing a faith, not a conviction, and the duchess saw the doubt behind his eyes.

He said to her, "Agathe, prepare a comfortable private room for Mario Campi, one of my suite, an Italian person, a financier. I set great store by him. He will want a fire and a quart of sour wine with mountains of eggplant and cheese."

"Instead of a good chicken supper?"

"Good heavens, no; now; in addition to a good chicken supper."

"I shall arrange it, uncle."

"At the moment, this monster of a man is the most important creature in Christendom," Duprat said soberly.

"He isn't to me," Marie said.

Duprat nodded. "I know, dear; I know. I will tell you all I dare divulge. The king conceived a daring plan to get rid of one of his most dangerous enemies. It was not without merit, but wildly impracticable. King Francis, as everyone knows, is prone to envision the end but woefully neglectful of the means. He did not consult me and I learned of his scheme too late to stop it. Henri, who in some respects is almost as impractical as the king, though more admirable, had already departed. With better planning and worthier aides your husband might have succeeded, and France would be in less danger today. But for reasons of his own the king burdened him with a stupid drunken companion who, as it turned out, was treacherous as well. Do not gasp and look frightened, Marie. I know for a fact that Henri is alive and well treated.

"As soon as I learned of the king's action I dispatched an agent with urgent orders and ample authority for Henri's immediate recall. My agent reported that Henri could not be reached. He was already far advanced in his mission. With great daring and considerable skill he had insinuated himself into the very heart of the enemy's castle. I adjured my agent to watch over him from a distance, and he sent me daily reports of Henri's activities. For some days it appeared that the king's mad scheme might actually work. Francis has always been fortunate in his servants. But then the drunken aide turned traitor and betrayed his master. In doing so he met his own death, which was amply deserved. But he also divulged Henri's identity. Your husband had had to adopt a mean disguise, Marie. Subterfuge is necessary on diplomatic missions nowadays. The king's enemy, as soon as he realized that he had in his power so highly placed a personage as Henri de Tonnerre — Henri's relation to me, no doubt, played some part — did not slay him, as he had slain his companion, but placed him in strict protective custody, so strict, I may say, that I have not been able to penetrate it. He demands, Madame de Tonnerre, no less than fifty thousand livres, in gold, as your husband's ransom." The chancellor was visibly shaken.

Marie looked at him.

"Do not plead with me with your eyes, child!" he said. "I'll buy him back. He's worth it. France needs men who can do what he did, with wit and courage and precious little else. I would buy him back if only for use in my own organization. As a matter of fact, I would buy him back if only for you, even if he weren't of any use at all. But do not expect him too soon, Marie. The negotiations are still in the initiatory stage and may be protracted. And naturally I must buy him back as cheaply as possible. Next year, and the next, France will need every ounce of gold that I can wring from her. I must not squander a sou. That is why Mario Campi is with me.

"And that is all I can tell you now. Take very great care, Marie, and you too, Agathe, not to mention this to a soul."

Marie said, "I thank God he is safe, even if he is a prisoner."

Later she said to her mother, "Great-uncle Duprat seems to think Henri will tamely languish in prison till he is ransomed."

"There is no disgrace in that," her mother said. "Kings have done the same."

"But I know my husband better than great-uncle Duprat, and it wouldn't be like him to wait for someone to 'buy him back.' He'd resent a price on his head." She smiled. "He would think it too small, among other things."

"Young men nowadays have an exaggerated opinion of themselves," her mother sighed. "They're always in a hurry. But you know Henri very well, Marie."

"Henri will get so angry that he'll manage to escape on his own."

"That would be foolhardy and unchivalrous," the dowager duchess replied sternly. "He should give his parole, like any other gentleman in captivity, and not try to escape but wait to be ransomed. That is the proper way."

"I don't think the parole carries quite the weight that it used to, *maman*," Marie said smiling.

"That's perfectly awful," her mother said, clucking her

tongue. "I hope the boy does nothing foolish; he probably will, though."

"I don't care what he does, so long as he comes safely home."

"That's exactly the point. Traditional protocol is well established in these matters. Even the Turks hold their prominent captives to ransom. They come back sleek and fat and clothed in silk trousers. For your sake Henri should guide himself by the path that assures his safe return."

"Will you tell me something, *ma mère?*"

"Certainly, child."

"Uncle Duprat was so vague. But this enemy of the king's — it is the Duc de Bourbon, is it not?"

"Hush, Marie. Of course it is. But we must not let on that we know. The chancellor does not name him because he hopes he can still win him back for France. There isn't a ghost of a chance, as everybody knows. But Uncle Duprat never gives up. He knows and we know that war is coming, but as long as he can stave it off, France has more time to prepare. Be very polite to this Mario Campi, therefore, whom we entertain tonight."

"I don't much like Italians," Marie said.

"Who does? But this one will finance the war, Heaven and Antoine Duprat only know how."

In deference to Campi the dowager duchess waited supper till the late hour of five o'clock in the afternoon. The table was covered with a large damask tablecloth that completely hid its surface and hung down over the edge like an altar frontal. At each place there was an individual porcelain dish and beside it a knife, fork and spoon. How people complicated their lives nowadays, she thought! The simplest things were made ceremonial and difficult, and all for show. Oh well. It was only for an evening, and she knew how to handle the absurd new paraphernalia.

Yet Mario Campi devoured three chickens and a pork pie without once having to wipe his fingers. Nor did he need to wipe his mouth with a napkin, though an alert servant, bemused at the shimmering table setting, stood ready behind him with a napkin ready, prepared to rush to the rescue if needed. Campi's thick beard, gleaming with oil and delicately scented, was as clean at the end of the meal as it had been when he first sat down. The rim of his goblet, which he held up repeatedly to be refilled, shone like a new-cleaned jewel. How in the world, wondered the duchess, can a man eat so much so fast and so delicately? And all the while, though his mouth was full, he talked; but one would have thought his mouth was empty, so clearly did he enunciate. Of course, he had a dreadful Italian accent; but he spoke with a clarity and precision that rivaled the king, who still said *"j'avons,"* like Duprat, Marie and all the old country gentry.

"Si!" said Mario Campi and *si* was *yes* in French as well as Italian. "Society is a pyramid, like the pyramids of Egypt. Big at the bottom, minuscule at the top. Some men are so built, and all women. The temptation to digress is formidable — the incomparable geometry of love. I do not digress. At the bottom of the social pyramid is the little man, the peasant, the unlettered creature of the soil; and at the top, your gorgeous King Francis. But without the peasant the king is a disembodied pinnacle. Without support he can do nothing on his own. Alone he can only gaze at the stars, and the stars are cold; they disavow him, and

he falls impotent into the desert sands. The tree grows out of the earth, the flower has roots in the soil. There are mushrooms that draw their sustenance from excrement. There are water lilies that open their floreate petals to the orb of the sun and congratulate themselves, 'How beautiful am I!' but their roots are embedded in mud, good mud, rich vital mud, swarming with the life-power. Does the flower know? No! There are cities in my homeland that once a volcano covered with ashes, but now we dig them up and rediscover the beauty that was Italy, its strength, its power. All from the bottom seeping up to the top. But here in feudal France you conceive that the power seeps down from the top to the bottom. No, no! The leaf does not support the tree; the flower does not sustain the stem; the tail does not wag the dog. There is but one source of wealth, my friends, the poor man's poverty. Tithe it. What do the rich really own? Tax all the nobles, tax them till they scream, tax them till they rebel, tax them a quarter of their holdings; what filters into the treasure casques of the chancellor of the king's *épargne?* A trifle. A nothing. A tenth of a tenth of what he requires. The king is bankrupt. Do you know the origin of that dismal term? Certain bankers in my country, when they found themselves shorn of funds, unable to discharge their obligations, before they jumped into the canals and ended their stupid lives, would come into the Exchange, and there the *banca* on which they were wont to sit as they transacted business was *rotta,* namely, smashed to pieces; and they were denied entry into the assembly. What remained but suicide? Some defenestrated themselves. But this need not be.

"The vitality of the flower, of the tree, of the king of France, all comes from the soil. And who are the soil? Who but Jacques Bonhomme, the peasant? And how to persuade Jacques Bonhomme to part with his hard-earned coppers? Release him from his bondage. Let him dream. Give him a chance, no matter how long, to clasp the moon to his sweaty bosom. Say to him, 'Jacques Bonhomme, here is a sporting chance. Engage in a sport, like your betters, who chase the boar over your laboriously plowed fields and ruin them. You too can bag a trophy like your betters. You can be as rich as they. For a sou you can win a hundred thousand livres, and live like a prince and endow your daughters like princesses.

" 'All that is required is to buy a ticket in the national lottery. You can buy as many tickets as you like, as you have sous, and increase your chances. The odds are long against you, but so is the weather. Can you ever be sure of your harvest, Jacques Bonhomme? Drought, rain, floods, hail, the smut, the wilt' — good heavens, I do not even know the names of the agricultural hazards but Jacques Bonhomme does — 'all are against you. Is this worse? Here is a hazard no more dangerous than the weather, and the reward, if you win, will be a lifetime of luxury and ease.' "

He paused to drain a goblet of wine, then held it out to be refilled.

"Signor Campi has proposed a national lottery based on the Italian model that has proven such a sure source of revenue in his country," Duprat explained, "and I have accepted it. I have no doubt it will benefit the king's *épargne*."

Campi said with satisfaction, "The printing presses are hot night and day with the vehemence of the millions of lottery tickets now being struck off. I have some in my pocket to show you."

They were flimsy little things. They went round the table and each one examined them.

"Can it be," mused Marie, "that each of these little pieces of paper represents a hundred thousand livres?"

"*Si!*" said Mario Campi. "The beauty of it!"

"Not each ticket, Marie," Duprat said. "Only one will win. The others will be worthless. But nothing is lost but a sou if you lose, and if you win, the reward is beyond your wildest dreams."

"Perhaps you will wish to keep some of these sample tickets," Campi suggested. "Who knows? One might be the winning number."

Duprat reached out and gathered them into his hand. "I'll take them," he said. "My family do not gamble."

"*Ohimé!*" sighed Campi. "How strait-laced is the chancellor of your king's *épargne!* In Italy it would have been so easy to do a little favor for a friend."

"That is why you are in France," Duprat said. "Here the national lottery will be conducted in accordance with strict rules. The tickets will all be placed in a big revolving wire cage and thoroughly mixed. A public figure of unquestioned integrity will be nominated to make the draw. Perhaps I shall nominate him myself, if I can find an honest man. Blindfold, before public witnesses, he will draw out a ticket at hazard, and someone, anyone who has purchased a chance, from Marseille to Boulogne, from Bordeaux to Dijon, whoever it may be, he will find himself rich. I will invite him to Paris. The king himself will present him with his winnings. Overnight he will become a figure of national envy. Everyone will rush to buy tickets for the next lottery, which I shall announce at once, and in this manner, without one word of grumbling, funds will pour into my *épargne* to finance whatever the future holds for France."

"*Si,*" said Campi. "There will be, naturally, certain administrative expenses, *non è vero, Illustrissimo?*"

"He that reapeth receiveth wages," Duprat sighed, and in this concession, taken from Saint John, Campi saw his fortune made and the chancellor's augmented, for it was inconceivable that Duprat should not take a percentage of the gross of the national lottery.

Duprat did not tarry at Montholon. That busy restless man had much else on his mind. He stopped but a moment, out of love, to comfort Marie, telling her all he dared in the delicate state of negotiations with the Duc de Bourbon, assuring her that Henri was alive. It was all the comfort he could give. It was all the time he could spare.

Refreshed — the sweet child always refreshed him — he pressed on to Fontainebleau with Mario Campi, with his manifold burdens and vaulting ambitions, his obdurate patriotism and his glittering cavalcade, full of determination to confront King Francis, if need be in his perfumed boudoir, and sound a Jeremiah note of doom in his ears, from which these days hung two beautiful ruby earrings: it was said that the Italian woman had bitten one one night and the king had covered the tooth marks with jewelry. Many young courtiers instantly copied the fashion without knowing how it originated, not having the benefit of the chancellor's confidential reports. "What is in store for a France where men cut their hair because a king gets a scalp wound in battle, and wear rubies in their ears because a king's mistress bites him in bed?"

To Duprat's diplomatic, financial and ecclesiastical responsibilities, which he took very seriously, were now added a host of military responsibilities also, since the army looked to him as the only source of their pay. The king never gave a thought to so trivial a matter. The army also looked to Duprat for guidance. The military chain of command led up through the captains and generals directly to the chancellor of the *épargne,* without whom, desperate and hungry, the French army, the best disciplined in Christendom, would have degenerated into ragged marauding bands of plunderers, as had happened again and again in the annals of neglected armies when no one was strong at the top. Duprat was aware that a clergyman who assumes the command of an army is a person split in twain, placed in an anomalous position, suspect by his peers and distrusted by his subordinates, perhaps even suspect by God. But there was always the precedent of the doughty Archbishop Turpin of Reims, equally at home on a warhorse or on his knees, wearing celibate wool or a cavalier's steel as his duties demanded, the prelate who fought in Charlemagne's wars and won battles while Charlemagne dallied with women, Charlemagne, that tempest of a man, so much like Francis if Francis had been born in a cruder age! And one of the women — the legends that made him eight feet high could not suppress the scandal — was his sister. Francis, to his credit, had not sunk to such depths. Who better than I, the chancellor mused, in this queer transitional age, between the known past and the unknown future, in a present fraught with disgustabilities like Mario Campi and the Duc de Bourbon, sees enough to do my job? If any there were, Duprat had no doubt that the good Lord would single him out and set him about the business, and Antoine Duprat could go back to chanting a daily Mass at the archiepiscopal palace of Sens. Till God did, he would answer as best he could whatever challenge his duties imposed, none of which he had asked for; and he would take with clear conscience the hire of which, said Saint Luke, the laborer is worthy.

The Duc de Bourbon knew, Antoine Duprat knew, the king did not know, that the province of the Bourbonnais was surrounded on all sides by a formidable French army loyal to Duprat, poised to strike the instant the chancellor gave the nod. For Marie, and for reasons of state, Duprat held his fire. It was better for his grand-niece that her husband be not slain in a moment of panic. It was better for France that the mighty traitor of Bourbon be coaxed back to the king's side. So, while the future of France and the fate of his beloved grand-niece hung in the balance, the one his duty, the other the single soft beat of his highly practical heart, the chancellor of France's *épargne* spurred on to Fontainebleau to confer with King Francis, who was in solemn conference that day with his tailor.

The tailor was an Italian refugee. Something in the ethos of the conquered convinced the king that the Italians were better tailors than the French. And in truth they were loose and daring. Nothing so liberates the arts as disaster in battle. Since Marignan the conquered Italians had painted better pictures, graven better statues and sewn better suits than could be found anywhere else in the world. This, he was quick to concede, was not to say that a national defeat was not in itself deplorable; but it did demonstrate a most wonderful measure of a nation's recuperative powers. Perhaps not only a nation's; perhaps all of mankind's. Prostrate Greece begat Rome; prostrate Rome begat the Empire; the Empire in its dotage begat

France. Perhaps the history of man was foreshadowed in the mystical vision of Ezekiel, a wheel in the midst of a wheel. The Hebrew of the Scripture was obscure; the Greek was, as usual, amphibolic. But Duprat knew for a fact that, in the watchmaker's craft, wheels within wheels made good mechanical sense, the one bequeathing its life-power to the other, which turned faster and faster and faster. Fast and loose, but vital, King Francis was. It was good to serve such a man. It was exasperating to be his prime minister.

"Crimson slashes in the sleeves, Your Majesty," cried the little tailor, dancing excitedly round the king, who surveyed himself in the full-length glass and watched the new suit take shape. "My God, what magnificent shoulders! Such shoulders have I seen only on the statues of antiquity. It is said there were giants in those days, never to be duplicated, and the statues of the gods memorialized them, stupefying all subsequent generations of men, who were dwarfs, misshapen monstrosities in comparison. But under my needle, under my chalk, here before my eyes I behold the old gods alive again in the perfect majesty of France! Would its majesty deign to present itself in profile?"

The tailor swiveled the king on his heels. King Francis submitted obediently, though no one but his barber and, of course, Juliette, who was present, ever dared touch his person.

The paean of sartorial hyperbole torrented on. Francis listened as earnestly as if the subject were some grave matter of state.

"What a beautiful flat belly! Lean as a hound's! I knew it was perfection, but I could not believe my eyes, and I said to my eyes, 'No, perfection is impossible, even in King

Francis,' and I made the belt two inches too long. Lord, I believe; help thou my disbelief. Now I am punished for my sin."

Huh, click, plop.

There was a sound of muscular exertion from the tailor, the sound of a sharp metallic operation as a tailor's punch gouged a hole in the belt, and the little noise of a circlet of leather falling to the floor.

"Now the belt will fit my king!" the tailor cried, and circled Francis's waist with a zone of exquisitely tooled and gilded leather four inches high, set with jewels and carrying an ornamental dagger.

"I never go armed in court," Francis said frowning.

"But, Majesty, in Italy it is the very latest style."

"In France, I think not," Francis said.

"Of course not!" said the tailor. "It was the fault of my stupid apprentice. He is new to France, Your Majesty. Here."

Skillfully the tailor detached the scabbard. From a pile of ribbons, feathers and bows on the table he selected a Nuremberg "egg," a mechanical timepiece or "watch" about the size of a baby's fist. "Here is an even later style. One has only to glance at the hand, which moves though the eye cannot detect its motion, to know what time it is. It is wound with a little gold key, which is attached to the case. Listen to it tick!"

Francis listened, vastly pleased with the remarkable little invention. He could hear the mechanism inside.

"Adorable," he said. "Is it not adorable, Juliette?"

Juliette smiled brightly.

"It tells the time with amazing precision," the tailor said. "One can correct any little inaccuracy by the sundial, but the watch is never wrong by more than two hours a day. A miracle! *Vois,* Sire, as the French say, *là!*" and he patted the king's thigh where the watch hung sparkling. "Now you are better than the Holy Roman Emperor."

"Of course I am," Francis said.

"He dotes on clocks and watches. He has hundreds of them."

"He does?" Francis said, displeased. "Hundreds?"

"But the clocks of the Holy Roman Emperor are wrong by *three* hours a day, and he hires a special craftsman who does nothing but repair them."

"Hear him, Juliette? The Emperor's clocks are wrong by *three* hours a day. I win again."

"And now we must choose for Your Majesty the feathers in its cap, mustn't we?" the tailor said, tentatively fingering a pile of fluffy plumes plucked from ostriches, aigrettes, pheasants, birds of paradise and, he assured the king, rocs from Ethiopia.

Juliette said, "This one is lovely," and picked a tail feather from a fighting cock, iridescent with shimmering hues of purple and red.

"Perfect!" the king cried, "and with it I honor you in the mourning violet of France!" When death occurred in the French royal family, those of blood royal mourned in purple, lesser people in black. "It never occurred to me. My dear Juliette, I will wear the cock's tail for you alone, in memory of your cherished marquis."

"You honor me too much," Juliette said, who didn't give a hoot about her cherished marquis.

"I wish I could with propriety decree a week's formal mourning," the king said. "I know how you must regret that good man, your husband."

He was so genuinely sincere; Juliette warmed toward him; all that was silly and paltry in her lover paled in the face of his compassionate, but mistaken, understanding of what he felt she thought and what she could not feel; and all of the love that she might have had for the Marquis de Meung, pent up and now released by death — *versé* was the word — was now "dumped" on the boyish, curly-cropped head of King Francis, who stood before the mirror soliciting her approval. "My dear one!" she breathed.

"Eh? What?" said the king.

"An excellent choice," said the tailor. In his nimble fingers the fighting cock's tail feather affixed itself to the royal cap of soft pliable hunter's velours, in a forest shade of green.

"It is not enough," said Juliette.

"Beg pardon?" the tailor said, looking quickly from her to the king for a cue. "Please? More? What? The trefoil?"

"The king always wears the fleur-de-lys of France," Juliette said.

"I took it for granted you'd know," Francis said to him.

The tailor's hands flew. "Was it thought I had forgotten? *Voici!*" and he held up two snow-white ostrich plumes, plucked when the birdlings must have been less than two weeks out of the shell. "*Vois-lalala!*" he cried, as he pinned them, one on either side of the cock's feather, to the king's cap. "Here, Sire, in Trinitarian perfection! Try it on!"

The king pulled on his cap and looked inquiringly at his mistress. "Well, madame, what do you think?"

"If you were any more wonderful I should suffocate with desire," she said.

"Then I shall take off this finery forthwith," he grinned. "Come, Juliette."

He strode out through the door, preceding her, in the direction of their private apartment. He heard a vicious slap, as of a lady's palm on a tailor's cheek. He turned his head. "What was that?"

The flush on the tailor's face was reddening where Juliette's hand had struck him; one cheek was paling with fury, the other was pink with pain.

"I must have dropped my scissors, Sire," the tailor said, groping at the floor to hide his confusion. His countrywoman had seen straight through him.

"Be more careful next time," said the king.

Juliette said, "*Caro mio,* I cannot abide that horrid little man."

"I thought him most pleasant," the king said. "Come, Juliette. I want you."

A simpering equerry whom Duprat would willingly have strangled informed the chancellor at the closed door of the royal apartments that His Majesty could not be disturbed.

"Convey to His Majesty his chancellor's humble duty," Duprat said scowling like an angry Jove at the youth, "and tell him I have just ordered the occupation of the Bourbonnais. Do you hear me, you pasty-faced cod-pieced oaf? What is your name? Who is your father? How did you get your place? Mind you don't lose it. Match your stockings! Sky-blue and pea-green is too much. Off with you! Or I'll nominate you for the Sistine Choir in Rome."

"I am Jules de Pantoise, Your Eminence. My father died at Marignan. *Par grâce, pas les castrati!* Not the Sistine Choir!" He skittered off. As the door opened and shut, a draught of frangipani and red jasmine assailed the sensitive nostrils of Antoine Duprat. *"Hélas, doulce France!"* he breathed. "Where will this end?"

Not till evening did the king grant him audience.

"My dear chancellor!" he greeted him. "Welcome to Fontainebleau! I was composing a poem; I did not wish to be distracted. After the poem I wound my new watch. What a wonderful world we live in, chancellor! Time is a precious commodity; the watch convinced me of that:

> "Tick by tick the hours fly,
> Under the sun's all-seeing eye,
> Round the bend is eternity —

"Those are the first three lines. Rhyme me a word with *eternity*, chancellor. At that point my watch ran down."

Duprat smiled at the king's effusiveness. It was impossible to be angry with him. *"Majesty* rhymes with *eternity*, Sire."

"Why, so it does. I should have thought of it. One never sees clear what is close, does one. What a precious fellow you are. Majesty, eternity. That is lovely. Tomorrow I shall write another line — after my hunt. There's a boar the size of an ox, they tell me, that big, Duprat! He killed a peasant yesterday. He hid in a bramble bush all day, and just as the poor man had finished his plowing he came roaring out and gored him to death. Then ate him. The field looked like Marignan. Will you help me hunt the beast down? Four in the morning. Then I must have my portrait painted, right after breakfast as soon as the light is right. Then we shall talk, chancellor. You always have something to talk about. What is it this time?"

Hunting had formerly been a passion with Duprat, and he was in a mood to stick a boar. How often in his younger

158

days had he ridden, pike in fist, the wind in his face and a warhorse under him, confronting the hideous creatures who seldom fled and often charged, till the pike pinned the mighty pig to the ground! And then the hunting breakfasts, when the enemy was roasted and eaten! How deeply he sympathized with the king. They were glorious memories, perilously close to the exultation of the Mass. But like gluttony and lust, he had subdued his passion for hunting; and all that remained of the hungers of his youth, which had been in their time as multifarious as those which now bedeviled King Francis, now concentrated their elements into one: the hunger for gold. All powers eventually equated themselves into gold, which one could use both for good or for ill. The chancellor of the king's *épargne* hoped that on Judgment Day the balance against his soul would not all be debit.

"You taught me to hunt," King Francis said. "You taught me to read and to pray, everything. Come, join us! At four o'clock. And then if you must we shall talk, for I see words thick in your mouth as bees."

"At four o'clock I shall be in my chapel," Duprat said, "praying for Your Majesty's success in the Bourbonnais."

"Eh? What? The Bourbonnais?"

"Where the great traitor of Bourbon has just slain with his own hand your servant, the Marquis de Meung."

"Oh yes. Poor Juliette. She hides her suffering admirably. A jewel of a girl, Duprat. I thank you for bringing her to my attention."

The king's manner was defensive. He sensed that his chancellor knew more about the death of the Marquis de Meung than he did. He looked like a guilty child, caught in some prank that had not come off.

Duprat pressed his advantage. "In Your Majesty's name I have ordered Your Majesty's forces to occupy the province," he said. "The occupation started today. There is no resistance; the people submit voluntarily; the Duc de Bourbon is in flight. The army he hoped to raise against Your Majesty never materialized. They do not follow him; they follow you, their king."

"That is good," the king said soberly. "You have done well, as always, Duprat. And now we have had our talk, have we not? And you will join me in the pig sticking?"

"Does it not interest Your Majesty to know whither the Duc de Bourbon has fled?" Duprat said. "Is it of no consequence that he is at this moment crossing the border into Italy, where legions of the conquered are flocking to his standard?"

"Is it war, chancellor?"

"Or that he holds to ransom your friend, the Chevalier de Tonnerre?"

"Nay, then it is war," the king said.

And the king added, "Why! This is better than pig sticking! *Aux armes, n'est-ce-pas?*"

"France is already in arms."

"What do I do now, Duprat?"

"The first thing to do," Duprat said, "is to replenish the treasury. It costs a great deal to fight a war. Have I Your Majesty's permission?"

"More taxes, Duprat? One day you will end up in the gutter with a knife in your back, and I shall be most unpopular."

"No, Sire, no more taxes. A national lottery, after the Italian model."

King Francis nodded, smiled. He did not understand, but

he was willing to authorize anything after the Italian model. A new fiscal device was added to the chancellor's bag of tricks that day, ample to ransom a king, more than ample to ransom Henri de Tonnerre. Duprat was satisfied with his day's work, and next morning, delaying his Mass, he joined the hunt and cheered loudly when Francis skewered the boar, a particularly nasty specimen.

"*Caro mio,*" said Juliette, alarmed at the huge carcass, "he might have skewered you!"

"You should have heard the chancellor yell!" King Francis said, laughing heartily. "He lost twenty years and twenty pounds, and status in the sight of God. I actually think he was jealous that he didn't make the kill!"

"You take dreadful chances," she said, "and you're all sweaty."

"Good heavens yes, and I must sit for my portrait. I'll have to take a bath."

There was so much to do and to enjoy.

On the border of Italy Henri de Tonnerre chafed at his shackles.

❋ ❋ ❋ 10 ❋ ❋

A T THE INN of Le Rat Mort in Moulins townspeople
were arriving and departing in haste. The easygoing
provincial atmosphere, where a man could spend an hour
over a glass of wine, was gone. Every time the door
opened there was silence; everyone looked up, and the
newcomer would be asked when the soldiers would arrive.
Was it true that the northerners were all bearded ruffians
who would steal their cattle and ravish their women? Was
it true that the Duc de Bourbon had suddenly decamped
in the night and disappeared for foreign parts unknown?

Innkeeper Pajou whispered from table to table, "There
is no doubt about it; the Duc has fled; I have it from an
absolutely trustworthy source."

"From your cousin, the major-domo?"

"Yes," Pajou admitted in a tense voice. It was clear from
the attitude of the clientele that they felt the Duc had
deserted them. But Pajou knew how often the Duc had
attempted to rally them to his standard. One and all they
had elected to stay with their families and farms. "The

Duc departed virtually alone," Pajou said. "A few men-at-arms, a few old retainers accompanied him."

At the inn that night the northern merchants and travelers were treated with unprecedented courtesy. The bows of the host were low, the wine was his best.

In a corner an undistinguished little man whom no one had ever noticed though he had stopped at Le Rat Mort longer than most travelers remarked to Pajou in a voice intended to carry, "Reassure your good patrons, maître Pajou, that King Francis's soldiers are Frenchmen like themselves. They are terrible only towards the king's enemies. What is there to fear? Moulins is as French as Paris."

Some looked askance at the man with the harsh northern accent, some nodded distantly; but no one answered him.

"I have seen the king's soldiers often in Paris," the man said. "Most of them are good family men with many children and little farms in the country, to which they will retire when they get old. They are not ruffians. They are hard-working men whose business is to defend France against enemies from abroad and keep order at home where there is unrest." It was a somewhat rosy account of King Francis's armed forces, most of whom were mercenaries, but the clientele of Le Rat Mort knew no better and hoped it was true.

"We understand, *monsieur*," Pajou said. He sensed a sudden air of authority in the inconspicuous little merchant. "We are all for King Francis here. When the soldiers come put in a good word for me." He called the merchant Monsieur de Niel, stressing the "de."

Niel laughed. "I am plain Louis Niel, maître Pajou. I

cannot claim the noble particle. But I have traveled widely and I know whereof I speak."

" 'Noble particle,' " someone whispered. "He is a clerk."

"Maybe he is the king!" someone answered in awe, and indeed stranger things had happened in France. In early times the *haute noblesse,* rough and ill-spoken as their subjects, often wandered unrecognized in the poorest districts of their towns. As recently as the eleventh Louis a king had been known to disguise himself and frequent the slums of Paris to hear how the common man was talking about his laws, and to change the laws if the talk was too critical. As for the present king, Francis's amorous escapades were so well known that no good Bourbonnais would have thought it strange if he had showed up in disguise at Le Rat Mort enamored of one of the barmaids.

There was general laughter. "Him? The king? Francis is six feet high and built like a bull."

"I am afraid I cannot qualify, my friend," said merchant Niel, "but I am grateful for your compliment." He ordered a bottle of wine for the man. He could have ordered a barrel for every man in the room. He had with him twenty thousand livres in gold for Henri's ransom. But merchants were not noted for their liberality; he knew he would be suspect by the thrifty Bourbonnais if he ordered drinks all around.

A number of glasses were raised to him and the scattered smiles grew more friendly.

A man in the livery of the Duc's guard burst in, downed a glass at a gulp and departed almost as swiftly as he had come. But he had time, before he left, to throw out answers to a volley of questions: Yes, most of the Duc's guard had elected to stay behind, despite the Duc's pleading.

Who wanted to go adventuring into Italy? Yes, he too was worried about his family; he had a wife and daughter; he was going home and lock the door and bar the shutters and stay with them. No, he had seen no soldiers yet but they were reported closing in.

"In this man," thought merchant Niel, "I behold the true *homme universel,* far purer in type than Henri de Tonnerre, for this man is more cynical. Antoine Duprat has calculated justly, as always, and the royal satyr-in-rubies will have an easy time of it when he occupies the Bourbonnais."

"My cousin, the Duc's major-domo, he went with the Duc?" Pajou asked.

"Sure, he went," the man said. "He had to look after the Duc's buttermilk, I suppose."

"And little Louise?"

"Who's she?"

"The major-domo's daughter. And the major-domo's wife, what of her?"

"The Duc took very little baggage," the man said. "He looked as if he wanted to travel fast. Don't think he took any women at all. What'd he do with women anyway? He took a plumber of some sort, they say. This plumber's assistant had been stealing wine from the Duc's cellars and corrupting one of the maids. Duc hates that sort of thing. Probably the plumber'll be hanged. Too bad. Everybody liked him. Good night, *mes amis.* Better lock your doors tomorrow."

Louis Niel, the merchant, said silently to his glass, "Ah ha! So the Duc is making for Italy and taking his hostage with him! I do not think this is going to be easy."

But the chancellor would ruin him if he did not get

Henri back alive, and confiscate his estate if he should be careless enough to be captured, or die and lose the twenty thousand livres in the process.

He deliberated whether to wait for the soldiers, who would supply him with a bodyguard, or forge ahead on his own. There were drawbacks and dangers to either course of action. It was tempting to wait for the soldiers, but by that time the Duc might be over the border. Duprat was a hard master; his terrible shadow stretched from Paris to Moulins, demanding instant action. Niel made his decision: he must follow the fugitive road wherever it led, and he must start now.

But many roads led to Italy. It was unlikely that any of the Duc's men who remained behind would know which one he had taken. The major-domo's family would know, however, and might be induced to talk. "Even Duprat will concede that a small gratuity to the wife will constitute a legitimate expense of travel," Niel thought.

Casually he said to Pajou, "I should imagine the daughter and wife of your cousin, the major-domo, will be ill at ease now that the Duc has left the château without protection."

"The mother will bear up," Pajou said, rubbing his chin. "But little Louise is a giddy girl, given to fancy and wild imaginings. She will be terribly frightened. Frankly, all of us are a little on edge."

"I shall be glad to reassure her personally that there is nothing to fear," Niel suggested.

"My dear monsieur Niel, you are too gracious! I bless the day some angel directed your footsteps to my humble abode. A word from you, monsieur, will quiet the fears of a very distraught and high-strung — but otherwise very delightful — young woman. Monsieur Niel, you are a true chevalier!" He lowered his voice to a whisper. "Your presence at the château will also serve to calm the anxieties of those who remain, the servants, the grooms, the cooks and maids and all the silly women who might panic. What a deplorable welcome if a score of hysterical females should raise the bridge and refuse entrance to King Francis's men! Yet Château Bourbon is so strong that it could hold out for a week. Monsieur Niel, let us go at once to the château! And I beg you, put in a good word for poor Pajou and Le Rat Mort when the soldiers come."

"I will indeed," Niel said. "The moment I see them."

At Château Bourbon all was confusion and disorder. Wild rumors were flying: the Duc had murdered one of the king's agents; the king was sending a fierce army to punish the entire province; they would make their headquarters at the château; everyone in it would be slain. Each hour more of the Duc's household packed up whatever possessions they could pile on a cart and fled. Some had no other home and had lived and worked within the walls for years. As for Henri, word ran that he had been a royal prince in disguise, else why had the Duc not slain him too?

"There is some truth in the rumor that the plumbers were highly placed emissaries of the king," Niel said, "but they came on a peaceful mission. As for the brutality of the king's soldiers, who will arrive at any moment, there is no truth whatsoever in that. Since when does the first gentleman of France war against Frenchmen, his loyal subjects? No, no, my friends. Calm yourselves. The Duc would have done far better to remain at Bourbon and greet the army of his sovereign, which nominally he himself still commands as Constable of France and commander in chief. Instead he has fled, like a man with a terrible burden of guilt on his soul. But we of the north know that the king desires only peace in his realm and will welcome him back to his duty even now. *Parbleu!* What would it do to business if civil war were to come at the same time that France is threatened from without? I am only a merchant, my friends, a common person like yourselves; but I know I speak for all men of my class. Whither has the Duc betaken himself? There may still be time to reason with him."

Louise looked at her mother, who said dubiously, "He is not really a bad man, just gloomy and strange. I have watched him for weeks, withdrawing more and more into himself. He has never been the same since the duchess died and he lost his suit before the parliament of Paris. She brought him his title — they left him that at least — but the dowry she brought him, vast holdings of land — that they took away and gave to the queen."

Louise began to cry. "I hated Henri for a while, but I cannot bear the thought that he is in danger."

"You were a fool to hate him," her mother said frowning. "Couldn't you see he was a gentleman under his craftsman's garb? What a dense creature you are! You could have made a brilliant marriage."

"Henri will try to reason with the Duc," Niel said. "Henri is a close friend of the king and will assure him of Francis's clemency."

"A close friend of the king?" the mother murmured. "He goes to court? He sees the great ones of France?"

"Assuredly, madame. He knows many of them intimately," Niel said. He had touched on the mother's greed and was winning her confidence. "I may tell you in confidence that Henri is a belted chevalier, a man who fought bravely at the king's side at Marignan, and that he is a particular favorite, indeed a close relative, of the chancellor of the *épargne*."

There was a pause as the awesome disclosure seeped into the mother's comprehension.

She turned on Louise, her eyes snapping, "Louise, I could beat you! You silly girl! To have let him slip!"

"I didn't like him any more."

"What of it? Maybe it will please you to hear that the Duc shackled him hand and foot. How do you like to hear that? Have you any notion how gyves and shackles bind?"

"I did not know he had shackled him. How horrible!"

"Well, young lady, now you see why I must answer this good man's question concerning the whereabouts of the Duc."

"Yes, mother, I see."

Looking steadily at Niel, the mother said, "The Duc is at Trévoux, monsieur. I break my pledged word to my husband to tell you this."

"You will not regret it, madame."

"I didn't know he was shackled," Louise murmured.

The mother had been appraising Louis Niel, the merchant: he was not really old, not really unattractive. He protested that he was a common man, but who knew who anybody was in these troublesome days? He spoke with authority; he was patently rich and he moved in the highest circles. Suppose he actually was a commoner. If a belted chevalier could not be snagged for Louise, why not a rich merchant?

"Monsieur is married?" she asked. "Madame Niel must be lonely whenever monsieur is away on his commercial travels."

"Alas, madame," Niel said, "I have never had time to fall in love."

"What a narrow view," Louise said smiling. "Most men have time for nothing else." Louis Niel had suddenly caught her fancy and presented a challenge.

"Will monsieur stay the night?" the mother said amiably. "The good Lord knows there is plenty of room. You could occupy the Duc's apartments if you wish."

"No, madame, I shall have to depart at once for Trévoux."

"*Ma mère,*" said Louise, "the roads are dark, but I know the way."

"There would be danger, child."

"Not from me," Niel said with such disarming candor that Louise and her mother laughed.

"What an ungallant remark," Louise said.

"But I could indeed use a guide."

The mother sighed, "Louise will do as she pleases no matter what I say, no matter how it looks. She always does. God speed you, sir, and keep you in His care, my daughter."

Trévoux was a wretched little town, capital of one of the Duc's estates, forfeit since his famous lawsuit but not as yet occupied by the king's troops. Trévoux lay in the "principality," as it was registered in the king's roster of fiefs, of Dombes; and the Duc was thus "Prince of Dombes," among his many other titles. Easternmost of his prop-

erties, it was a marshy malarial region, sparsely inhabited
by a population of poverty-stricken peasants, shepherds
and a strange race of swamp fishermen who built their huts
on stilts on the insect-infested shores of the stagnant bogs.
They were ignorant in the extreme. So cut off from the
world were they that many old people believed that Louis
XI was still king of France. Virtually no one, except in the
town of Trévoux, had ever heard of gunpowder or seen
a musket. Dombes lay on the border of the Empire, and
from Trévoux ran an ancient road to Italy. Here in this
backward borderland the Duc still hoped to raise a force
of fighting men to accompany him in his flight to the
standard of Charles Quint, the Holy Roman Emperor.

Vain delusion! A man could as easily coax the sluggish
catfish out of the swamps or transport the myriads of mos-
quitoes to another locality. Like the fish and the insects
the inhabitants seemed to have lived in this inhospitable
region since the world began.

At the castle of Trévoux, a small structure with vegetation growing out of the cracks in the walls, the draw-
bridge chains had rusted through and a ragged boy sat
dangling his legs over the edge, fishing out of the moat below.

"You there!" cried the Duc. "Fetch me the master of the
place!"

The lad looked up at the travel-stained group of mounted
men, crossed himself and raced into the castle.

Shortly a slatternly woman wiping her hands on her
apron appeared. Behind her vast hips the little boy peeked
at the strangers, sucking his thumb, staring.

Bobbing like a cork the woman advised the Duc, "The
Sieur de Trévoux has went fishing, m'sieu, but come in,

whoever you are." She beamed amiably and waddled toward the open gate. "This way; mind that plank there; it falls out if you step on it."

"When will the Sieur de Trévoux return from his fishing?" the Duc asked.

"Who knows? Maybe a week, maybe ten days. Oh there now! I told you to watch out for that plank!"

Henri, with shackles on his wrists, could not direct his mount with precision, and the beast had stumbled on the rotten plank.

"*Peste!*" Henri swore audibly. The woman looked frightened and muttered in unintelligible patois some ancient provincial incantation against the plague.

An elderly steward emerged from the gate with a skin of wine under his arm and a battered pewter cup in his hand. Apparently it was the custom of the countryside to welcome travelers with the local restorative. The Duc's men drained it readily enough, the cup passing from hand to hand, but the Duc himself said, "Thank you, no," and reproved his men with an icy stare.

"Is there something wrong with the wine, monsieur?" the steward asked, offended.

It was sour and warm and redolent of the skin container, but it was strong as a bull.

"I never drink wine," the Duc said.

A slow light began to dawn behind the dull old eyes of the steward. "It is my lord of Bourbon!" he breathed. "I never saw your lordship, but the whole world knows your abstemious habits. Welcome to Trévoux."

"Put up my men and send me the Sieur de Trévoux, my good fellow."

"At once, at once, *monseigneur*. I will fetch him myself. I know where he is fishing."

"How long will it take?"

"A day to go, a day to return, not an hour more."

"Have you no one else to send?" The steward looked feeble and unfit to undertake a fast ride of two days.

"No one who knows the swamps as I do, *monseigneur*."

"Where are all the young men of the district?"

They were about their usual business, the steward said, tending their flocks, fishing the swamps, where else would they be?

"No one guards the castle?"

"Why? Against whom?" asked the steward. "Never in my time, *monseigneur*."

The Duc sighed, dejected. How many men of military age could be found in this godforsaken land? Far too few. How long would it take to assemble them? Far too long. How many would rally to his banner? Probably only a handful. The Duc de Bourbon felt his heart sink. If the men of his own castle deserted him, what fidelity could he expect from these primitives who scarcely knew his name? They would remain with the catfish, the smoky huts in this dreary place, out-of-time and other-worldly, where they seemed part of the soil from which no power on earth could remove them. How to translate the sodden clod from its stagnation, how teach it that over the Italian mountains lay hope for a better France? The clods had lain and vegetated a thousand years in Dombes, content to be nothing else.

"I and my suite shall remain only the night," the Duc said. "Then I shall press on."

"But, *monseigneur,* the Sieur de Trévoux cannot possibly return by tomorrow morning. He will be desolated not to have the honor of entertaining your lordship. So sudden a visitation! So quickly gone! You never came before. Why do you depart so soon?"

"See to my men," the Duc said, not deigning to answer. The note of sadness carried clear and registered strong in the peasant mentality of the steward, who knew when a beast was in pain.

"Yes, *monseigneur.*"

The Duc and his suite passed over the bridge.

"And what shall I do with the chained one?" the steward asked.

"He is my guest," said the Duc.

Perhaps it was some curious custom of the outlanders, the steward thought.

Goats' milk and catfish, even in Lent, was not Henri's notion of honorable captivity. He was having supper at a small table with the Duc, while lesser members of the suite gorged themselves, out of hearing, in the damp great hall of Château Trévoux.

As a matter of practical transportation of his hostage the Duc had ordered Henri's ankle shackles struck off; one cannot ride a horse with feet chained together. Their removal had brought blessed relief from the pain of the bruise on his shin where Louise had kicked him. The iron collar there had been exasperating and he had feared the swelling and sloughing of the skin that often occurred in small wounds that were constantly irritated. A Doctor Paré was said to cure them with poultices of beaten egg and moist bandages in Paris, but who could command the services of a Doctor Paré in Dombes? and all other doctors poured boiling oil on them. It was an uncomfortable thought.

"I gave you my parole," Henri said irritably, "but you shackled me anyhow."

He had assumed that the Duc, of all people, feudal to the core, would honor a man's parole.

"I do not trust the word of you new men," Bourbon said.

Once Henri had submitted to shackles his conscience was clear. "Maybe you shouldn't," he said to himself, but he did not say it aloud. His parole no longer bound him.

"Eat," said the Duc wearily. "There is no help here for me and tomorrow I shall carry you into Italy. Duprat will ransom a man like you. And if he does not I shall persuade you to join me. You, who give your parole so casually, you new men who cannot be trusted, you will quickly sense which side will win and comport yourselves in accordance with that which advantages you."

There was some truth in the Duc's sad and cynical statement, but it also worked in reverse; and the Duc, blinded by his own wrongs, could not see that his own guard had left him for the very reason he condemned, namely, they sensed that the king would win.

"Your lordship has the courage of strong convictions, which is an admirable characteristic," Henri said, "but your lordship was the first to desert the highest of all rulers save God: King Francis."

"You are a brave and foolish man to say that to my face," the Duc said. "But I fancy you would be less brave if you did not know I need your ransom and cannot kill you. You are a commodity, Henri de Tonnerre. I propose to keep your value intact. But I'll shoot you dead if you try to escape."

"Not a dagger in my neck, *monseigneur?* That's how you treated my poor companion."

"Your companion was a traitor," said the Duc. "He deserved nothing better. And he was not the protégé of Antoine Duprat."

The chains that fettered Henri's wrists clanked as he ate his supper. To raise a spoonful of food to his mouth he was forced to lift both hands. No one of the Duc's entourage, supping at the lower tables, thought it odd that the Duc should eat at the same table with his eminent hostage or that that hostage should be chained.

"You will not take it amiss if I eat somewhat slowly," Henri said. "I am not used to chains at supper." It was as close as he could bring himself to complain at the indignity.

"I gave away the key," the Duc said, "I did not wish to succumb to the temptation to unfetter you. I too shall eat slowly so that your awkwardness will not be noticed."

Henri nodded and forced a smile. "I am going to have to kill you after all," he thought. "I shall be sorry." But the conviction was growing in him that the Duc de Bourbon, the mighty warrior of Marignan, the Constable of France, was mad.

At four o'clock in the morning with a tatterdemalion suite of provincials the Sieur de Trévoux strode into his castle, all muddy and smelling of fish. His sport had been interrupted. He had hastened home. He had had startling news. His purse was heavy with gold, a gratuity, as it would be set down for Duprat's eagle eye, from the merchant, Louis Niel.

While he and his men were placidly fishing a small group of riders from Moulins, led by a man in the garb of a well-to-do merchant, had come upon them. The merchant's hat was rich velvet, comprised of many folds, for Louis Niel was changing his skin, adopting a dress more in keeping with the dignity of his high mission. The merchant's saddle-bags were heavy. With him were some members of the Duc's personal guard whom he had bought over to his side, and a young woman whose position was anomalous but who, he told Trévoux, had furnished confidential information of the route that the Duc de Bourbon had taken. Often the truth is the best. "Her father is the Duc's major-domo," Niel said. "She knew where the Duc is. *In your château,* Messire de Trévoux! You are sheltering a traitor."

"I didn't know I was sheltering anybody," the Sieur de Trévoux said. "I have been away from my seat for some time. The Duc de Bourbon! *Heu!* That great man!"

"Not so great any more, messire, unless you make him so."

He sketched the Duc's flight and traitorous plotting against the sovereignty of France.

"Maybe he'll win?" suggested the Sieur de Trévoux craftily. France to him was as foreign and faraway as Italy or the Empire. He knew nothing of international politics and cared little who won so long as Trévoux was undisturbed. Louis Niel knew that to such a man an appeal to patriotism would be futile. A more personal argument was required.

"I do not think he'll win. But whoever wins, you cannot shelter one of the belligerents without making your city a battlefield. The Duc de Bourbon will attract the king's army as honey attracts a swarm of bees; and you, messire de Trévoux, will get stung, your château blasted, your people slaughtered."

"The king's army?"

It had already marched into the Bourbonnais and taken possession of Moulins. The Duc's formidable castle had surrendered without firing a shot.

"Moulins is invested?"

"Messire, Moulins is occupied. What chance has Trévoux?"

"I want no trouble in my district," said Trévoux. "I will speed my uninvited exalted guest on his way the moment we return."

"You would do better to keep him captive till the army arrive and deliver him to King Francis. I have no doubt His Majesty will make it worth your while."

Trévoux seemed to agree, nodding slowly. "But how do I know His Majesty will reward me for delivering the traitor?" How, indeed, could he be certain King Francis would win, he wondered. He saw himself caught squarely in the middle.

"This," Niel said, "will serve as an earnest of greater payment to come when you deliver the Duc's person to the king's authorities." Five hundred livres changed hands and clanked into the Sieur de Trévoux's fishing creel.

"The Duc's stay will be longer than he imagines," Trévoux said amiably. But Niel had negotiated in costly commodities all his life with sharper men than the Sieur de Trévoux and knew by instinct when a man will default on his bargain.

"I shall wish to see him before you jail him, messire. The Duc has with him a hostage whom the king, and

178

particularly the chancellor of the *épargne,* is most anxious to free. The rescue of the Chevalier de Tonnerre will be almost as profitable to you as the delivery of the Duc."

Heu! Heu! Chevaliers, ducs and secret negotiators with saddlebags full of gold! A formidable array of guests for Château Trévoux, and a peaceful man would do well to get rid of them all as speedily as possible. Perhaps, thought the Sieur de Trévoux, all of them could be appeased with proper management. But it would have to be done cautiously, or one or the other would overrun Dombes and he would be the first to be hanged.

At four o'clock in the morning the Duc was roused from his sleep by a hand on his shoulder and a strange voice that said, "Welcome to Dombes, *monseigneur.* I am your host, the Sieur de Trévoux. Your lordship is in great danger here. The king's army has occupied Moulins and I can protect you only a little while, a matter of hours, before they arrive at Trévoux."

The Duc looked up into the shifty eyes of the man, dressed like a brigand, and thought, "Dear God, this one too is faithless."

In the room adjoining, the door open, Henri listened.

"You will give me a moment to dress," said the Duc. The Sieur de Trévoux had sat down on a stool by the bedside and gave every indication of staying the rest of the night.

"But of course, *monseigneur,"* Trévoux said, rising awkwardly and walking towards the door.

"And be good enough to send me my major-domo."

Heu! The great one dressed in privacy and required a servant to hand him his clothes like a king!

"Yes, *monseigneur,"* Trévoux said.

The major-domo appeared in his nightcap and only half awake, unaware that the Sieur de Trévoux had returned. As he helped the Duc dress he was met with a torrent of whispered orders that made his spine crawl with fear. He made a move towards Henri's room to shut the door.

"No, let him hear," said the Duc.

"He will kill you!"

"With his chains? Not before I can kill him, I think."

"Shall I not kill him first, your lordship?"

"His corpse will not bring me fifty thousand livres. No, I must let him live unless he does something foolish, which is likely. The rascal would rob me by dying."

He ordered the major-domo to pass the word to his men to dress and arm themselves without lights and without making a sound. "Moulins is fallen to the king, and the king's army are even now approaching Trévoux. May God drown them in the bogs as He overwhelmed the hosts of Pharaoh! When the men are dressed let them hide themselves in the stables, going out one by one like scouts; and then, at the signal of a pistol shot, which I shall fire, we will leave this desolate place and cross over into Italy. Have I money with me, major-domo?"

"Of course, *monseigneur*. Much."

"Give this peasant host of mine a thumping gratuity. For his 'hospitality,' lest he extend it. It is fortunate he cannot raise his rotten drawbridge. Oh, the venality, the wretchedness of my vassals!"

"How big a gratuity, my lord?"

"How do I know? Enough to make him want more. You are used to bargaining with peasants."

"Whatever you give a man he always wants more," the major-domo said. "I shall go about the business at once."

"Be swift!" said the Duc.

Shortly the Sieur de Trévoux found himself enriched by some hundred additional gold livres, which he added to Louis Niel's and hid under his straw mattress. It would not be changed for a week, and by that time he would have discovered some safer place to hide it, out of sight of his loyal retainers who might want their share. "I never thought to net so much on a fishing trip!" he marveled. But how big must be the war that was coming, for the great ones to scatter their gold with such liberal hands!

At this point Niel entered the room. The Sieur de Trévoux looked up guiltily from his mattress. His hand was full of the Duc's gold.

"I did not hear you knock, monsieur Niel. I am placing your princely present in a secure place for fear one of the Duc's traitors will find it and rob me."

"A wise precaution," Niel said, noting the hiding place. "And now I must hold you to your promise to detain the Duc till he can be handed over to the king."

"Certainly, monsieur. I will place a guard at his door immediately."

"Let no one enter, however. I wish to speak to him privately."

"Let me carry your saddlebags," the Sieur de Trévoux said, eying them covetously.

"I think not, messire," Niel said, hitching them higher on his belt. They clinked invitingly.

Sticking into the belt the Sieur de Trévoux saw a brace of pistols.

"Merchants must equip themselves with curious impedimenta nowadays," Niel said significantly. "Would you be good enough to give me a lighted candle, messire?"

"The Duc has one burning in his room."

"All the more reason for me to have one too."

The Sieur de Trévoux gave him a candle. "Monsieur Niel, monsieur Niel, I want no murder in my house!"

"Neither do I, especially my own."

Belted and spurred for travel the Duc sat on the stool beside his bed, examining the priming of his pistol. It was time for the shot that would assemble his men who by now must be ready beside their horses in the stables. Suddenly Louis Niel entered.

"How . . . did you . . . get here?" the Duc demanded.

"The chancellor was gracious enough to delegate me to watch over Henri de Tonnerre," Niel said quietly. "I am a merchant on a commercial venture. I spent a dreary time at Le Rat Mort in your delightful capital, *monseigneur*."

"And they actually took you for a merchant?"

In Louis Niel the Duc recognized Louis de Niel-Nemours, the sinister head of the chancellor's vast and secret organization of agents.

"I am really a merchant of sorts, sir. I have come to treat with you for the ransom of Henri de Tonnerre."

"The chancellor must think highly of him to send *you!*"

"Very."

"I demand my stipulated price of fifty thousand livres," said the Duc.

"I deem your lordship in a very poor position to demand anything."

"And I deem my lordship in a somewhat better position than you think, monsieur de Niel-Nemours."

Both men were surreptitiously approaching their lighted

candles to the priming of their pistols; each saw the other's movement.

"You are aware that your candle will blow out if you make any sudden motion with it," Niel-Nemours said.

"I am not unacquainted with firearms," the Duc answered. "Henri de Tonnerre is in the next room."

"I know that."

"He is chained."

"I know that too."

"Give me my fifty thousand livres and you can have him."

"My dear Duc, quite impossible. I do not have it with me. I have had all I could do to lug twenty thousand over your fishy muddy territories. I could not carry fifty. It would load a mule."

"An ass can carry a mule's load."

Niel-Nemours smiled. He was content to string out the negotiations. The longer he talked the closer would come the king's army.

"You cannot insult me, *monseigneur*. I will give you what I have, twenty thousand — minus, I must say, some few hundreds I have expended in corrupting certain members of your loyal guard, to say nothing of our host, the Sieur de Trévoux!"

The Duc de Bourbon ground his teeth and swore, "Gold, gold, gold, and the faithlessness of men!"

"Yes, my lord Duc, beginning with yourself."

The Duc's candle edged towards his pistol. So did the other.

Their voices had risen and Henri could hear them dimly through the heavy door. He sweated and strained at his shackles, which clanked. The Duc heard them.

"My rat is restless," he said unpleasantly. "Which do you

think I will shoot, monsieur de Niel-Nemours, him or you when he opens the door? I cannot shoot you both. A merchant ought to know."

"If Henri de Tonnerre has any sense in his head at all," Niel-Nemours said loudly, *"he will not open that door!"*

Henri paused. The iron clanking ceased.

"Behold the valor of the king's chevaliers!" the Duc sneered. "The rat is silent."

"Stay where you are, chevalier!" Niel-Nemours cried. "He is trying to shame you into exposing yourself!"

It was not a voice that Henri knew, nor had he ever set eyes on Duprat's shadowy and immensely powerful lieutenant. But it sounded like the voice of a friend. "Who are you?" Henri cried.

"Stay where you are!"

Other ears had heard the loud voices. The Duc's majordomo pushed aside the guard at the door and burst in.

"Are you all right, my lord Duc?" Then he saw the two pistols, and one was leveled at the heart of his master.

"Traitor!" he shouted at Niel-Nemours, drawing his dagger and throwing himself upon the stranger.

Niel-Nemours touched the flame of the candle to the venthole of his pistol. The priming flared and the weapon barked. The major-domo fell to the floor, holding his belly hard with both hands.

A general of the Duc de Bourbon's experience knew that a bullet in the bowels is mortal, often very quickly if it strikes ones of the larger organs there. "Alas, my friend!" he cried. Then his pistol too fired: Henri, hearing the first shot, had pushed open the door and was rushing upon him, cursing, his heavy fetters upraised to crush his head.

When the Duc's bullet struck him he spun round like a scarecrow in the wind, his arms flailing, and fell with an "Ugh!" of pain to the floor and lay still.

The Duc rose and knelt at the body of the rapidly dying major-domo, oblivious of his personal safety. "Poor faithful clay," he muttered, "already I see the worms in thee. Were there more like thee I were not the avenger I now will be from this day forward, till Francis or I shall die!"

"I think your aim was a little off," said Niel-Nemours. "I see no blood on Tonnerre. Your bullet struck his manacle; his fall has merely stunned him."

The Duc leapt forward, dagger drawn.

"I have another pistol," said Niel-Nemours, the candle very close to the weapon, his voice calm as a sepulchre, his hand very steady.

The Duc halted, mouthing such curses as seldom had been uttered in the little room, which now began to fill with people. Henri groaned and sat up, disoriented, trying to focus his eyes upon the confusion. The force of the bullet had deformed the iron manacle on his right wrist and his hand clawed out at an unnatural angle. Then he saw the Duc and stood up and raised his chains again to strike.

"Better not," warned Niel-Nemours. "The king will prefer him alive."

The Duc's men had assembled in the courtyard at the first shot, which they took to be the prearranged signal. But hearing a second, they bolted towards the castle, fearing their lord was in trouble.

Louise pushed through the crowds in the halls and ran into the room and saw her father on the floor. His hands were streaming red now, his face was ashy pale and glazed with the sweat of the moribund.

"Monster!" she screamed, and beat her fists against Henri's chest.

"Stand aside, woman!" Niel-Nemours commanded.

"Monster! Monster! Monster!"

"I will shoot you too if you do not stand aside."

"You killed him? You?"

"He would have killed Henri had I not."

Louise began to sob violently and cradled her father's head in her arms, rocking and crooning like a mother with a child, "Oh papa, papa, papa, don't go away."

"Why, it's little Louise," said the major-domo, his mind wandering. "What are you crying for, Louise? I've candy in my purse. I'll give it to you and you'll stop crying."

He moved his hand laboriously toward his purse.

"I'm sticky with something," he said.

His purse opened. Money and a key rolled out.

"I am going to be sick today," he said. Then his eyes closed, and slowly half-opened and he stared out on a world of which he was no longer a part.

Now the Duc's men crowded in. The Duc's eyes took fire and he smiled, as he had at Marignan when the tide of battle turned in his favor. "Kill me that man with the pistol," he shouted, "and truss up my hostage! To Italy!"

But Niel-Nemours's men were also shouldering into the room. They were former members of the Duc's guard; they had shared the same quarters and drunk together for years; some were relatives; all were friends; now they were divided.

"Shame! Shame!" they cried, and for a moment there was hesitation and uncertainty.

Now came the Sieur de Trévoux with his motley suite of local men. "Not in my house! Not in my house!" he shouted.

There were too many against him now. The general in the Duc counseled compromise.

"I will take your twenty thousand and leave you my hostage provided you allow me and my men to depart," he said to Niel-Nemours.

"Agreed!"

He tossed his heavy saddlebags to the Duc.

"Pick them up," the Duc ordered a man close to him, scorning to touch them.

The man fumbled at the flaps to see what was inside.

"You needn't count it," Niel-Nemours said scathingly. "It is all gold and all there."

"It is gold," said the Sieur de Trévoux, desperately trying to please and oblige.

"Ha! You know? How do you know? I am not surprised," the Duc said dolefully. "Venality! Venality! Turncoats! Traitors!"

Then he ordered his men, "Come!"

They edged towards the door, backs to the wall, facing their former companions with drawn arms.

In the courtyard as they mounted their horses the Sieur de Trévoux waved his hand and cried, "Adieu, adieu, *monseigneur!* God speed you!"

The Duc de Bourbon cursed him. "I shall return and hang you!"

But the Duc had not yet quite done with the "hospitality" of his host. On the drawbridge, skulking in the shadows, one of Trévoux's men rushed up with a long razor-sharp knife, an instrument used locally to gut fish, and slashed at the saddlebags. One slit open. Gold sprinkled out from the gash and traced a yellow spoor in the gathering drawn behind the thundering hoofs. Peasants would sift in the dust for some days on the road that led to Italy searching for the shining coins. "It will keep them occupied," thought Niel-Nemours contentedly. He was satisfied with the results of his mission.

In a soberly balanced account which he sent to Duprat by courier he stated:

Your Eminence: I have ransomed Henri de Tonnerre, expending only 20,000 livres; but of this 3000 has been recovered from the purse of the Duc de Bourbon's major-domo, and another 2000 can be recovered from the Sieur de Trévoux, lord of this place, who can produce no tax receipts to show payments into the *épargne*. The king's soldiers arrived this morning, and I at once instituted suit in your name to collect the aforesaid taxes, sitting myself as judge. I have no doubt that the verdict will be favorable. Henri de Tonnerre refuses treatment for a bone bruise where a bullet from the Duc's pistol struck the manacle with which the Duc had chained him, and is riding up to Paris. As for the Duc himself, the rascal made good his escape before the soldiers arrived. I had him followed. He is now in Italy. Shall I institute criminal action against the Sieur de Trévoux, who made no effort to stop him? I do not recommend this course of action, the populace of this frontier district being shifty and lukewarm in loyalty to the king and deeming it unwise to alienate the local lord. I await your further instructions.

> Faithfully,
> LOUIS DE NIEL-NEMOURS

✳
✳ ✳ **11** ✳ ✳

KING FRANCIS was busy as a butterfly these days, flitting from project to project. His chancellor warned him that war was very close now, and the king, highly stimulated by the prospect of battle and absolutely without a sense of personal fear, nay, welcoming the chance to repeat his prodigies at Marignan, made preparations in all things that seemed to him important in the conduct of a war.

"You are quite sure it's coming, Duprat?" he asked, his eyes shining.

"Quite sure, Your Majesty."

"Why then, I must hurry, mustn't I?"

"We must all hurry, Sire."

"There is so much to do, especially here at the heart of things, for the heart of a nation at war must be sound."

"Such is the central theme in my whole career, which Your Majesty graciously permits me to pursue in Your Majesty's service."

The king now took up residence in the Louvre, to be at the heart of things. But the castle, built by his ancestors of a rougher age, cramped and stifled him and depressed his mood. Architecturally it was defensive. The First Gentleman of France neither lived nor thought defensively. He engaged hordes of workmen to fill in the moat, and on the new-made ground, fertilized by two hundred years of decomposed trash, he brought in scores of gardeners to plant flowers. He hired masons to chip at the slit-windows and knock out the bars, and glaziers to set in sheets of glass to let in the light and a view of the gardens. The portcullis of King Philip Augustus was demolished, and in its place was substituted an oaken doorway with carved figures of cherubs and the gods and goddesses of ancient Rome. The stables were enlarged to shelter three thousand horses of courtly chevaliers who flocked to Paris to attend him and sue for commands. A hall was hung with beige damask to supply a background for his ever-increasing art collection. One large room resounded with the noise of hammers and was strong with the fresh odor of sawn oak, for the king was putting up shelves for his books.

Painters and drapers decorated the royal apartments, one for Queen Claude, far away in another wing, one for himself. Adjoining the king's was an exquisite little hideaway with a common door. This was for Juliette. Here the king spent many hours choosing just the right shades of tapestries, carpets and bed linens, and he heard with enchantment that there was an alchemist who, by impregnating candles with a secret aromatic substance, could make them give off a warm peach-colored light and smell like a summer rose. He engaged a German horologist, who put a clock on the mantelpiece; it tinkled prettily on the hour.

"We must not waste a minute in the national crisis," he said to Juliette. "Soon I must leave you and go to the war."

He spent long hours being fitted for a new suit of armor.

"I wish you would have it made smoother and tougher," Juliette said.

"But Juliette, they can't make pleats in thick steel! How would I look without pleats? A hundred years out of date."

So the king's armor was fluted and pleated like a high-fashion court doublet, inlaid with gold in the slashings.

"Spearpoints will lodge in the creases," Juliette said. "Swords will cut right through it; it is too thin to protect you. Oh my dear, my dear, you take terrible chances!"

"What are these arms for, pray?" he laughed, extending them. "To keep my enemies away, *madame la marquise*." Then they encircled her. "But not my friends."

She pressed her face against his cheek.

"Tears, Juliette?"

"I wish you were not going. Stay here, and give commands. Kings don't fight any more."

"What an extraordinary notion," Francis said. "What is a king for? I have a chancellor to give the commands."

So King Francis prepared for war.

Antoine Duprat had also moved into the Louvre, exchanging his splendid archiepiscopal palace for a suite of whitewashed rooms of almost monastic simplicity.

Couriers were arriving from all parts of Europe in rapid relays and hastily departing. Among the scores of dispatches he received that day was only one that warmed his heart and made him smile, the one from Niel-Nemours that stated that Henri was safe. The others dealt with heads of state: England, to win her over or at least assure her neutrality; with a score of Italian princes, some of whom had to be threatened, some of whom could be bribed. In view of the bribes and the cost of the king's exotic preparations for war it was well that money was pouring into the *épargne*. The lottery was proving a huge success.

Marie had come to Paris to meet Henri the moment he arrived. Her love for her husband strengthened Duprat in his heavy and cynical duties: faith was not dead, nor decency nor all the old virtues so long as there were women like her in France and men like Henri de Tonnerre.

"If I am prejudiced in their favor," said an exculpatory small voice in his mind, for he knew he was violently prejudiced, "there is Scriptural precedent to justify me."

Abraham had bargained with God for the sparing of Sodom, which Duprat equated with all that was rotten in France. "What a chancellor of the *épargne* Father Abraham would have made!" Would God destroy Sodom if fifty righteous could be found in the city? And God said No. Forty-five? No. Then, scaling down the Good Lord's price, Abraham, wonderful Jew, obtained a reprieve if forty, then twenty, then ten righteous could be found: and the Good Lord said, "I will not destroy it for the ten's sake." And even when ten could not be found God saved the family of Lot. Assuredly, in France, there were more, far more than ten righteous, so Antoine Duprat knew in his heart that France would be spared.

Henri rode up from Trévoux greatly troubled in spirit and in some bodily pain. The key that spilled out of the major-domo's purse fit his manacles and he had removed them, but his right wrist had swelled up the size of a puppy and his hand was now useless. Niel-Nemours stayed behind to institute suit against the Sieur de Trévoux, saying, "I'll leave him something, not much," and ordered an escort detached from the king's soldiers to accompany Henri on his journey north. "There will be highwaymen on the roads, chevalier. There always are in times like these."

At Moulins, now heavily garrisoned by Francis's troops, a guard of his own men from Tonnerre joined him. "The chancellor sent us," they said when he asked how they knew his whereabouts. "He knows," said the captain of the guard, "where every man sleeps every night in France."

Some of the younger men-at-arms tried to hide smiles and one of them blushed.

"Perhaps not our handsome Mortier here," the captain said smiling. "He kept slipping off to Château Bourbon, some wild little baggage named Louise."

"I hope he watched his shins," Henri muttered. They thought he was in a fever. His face was pale and drawn.

"Your hand looks bad, chevalier."

"It is nothing."

It was puffy and whitish, and he could not move it without experiencing a dull deep-seated pain, but his mind was too full of the failure of his mission to pay much attention. "It wasn't de Meung's fault that he was stupid and got himself murdered. But I swore to slay the Duc, and I didn't. An *homme universel* would have schemed his way out of my predicament."

It irked him that his fighting arm was immobilized. He longed for the king's forgiveness and he longed to be at his side again in battle. "It is not enough to do one's best," he thought angrily.

And he longed to see Marie.

He was uncommunicative and he rode his guard till they

feared for the horses, and him. "You are pushing yourself too hard," the captain cautioned. "There are doctors in the cities we pass. Stop a day, and let one look at your wrist." But Henri would not stop.

Paris was full of marching men and hurrying horsemen and flashing arms and shouted military commands, but the palace of the Louvre was strung with colored lanterns, illuminated as for a festival.

"King Francis has found a new *amie,* a most beautiful girl," ran the gossip, gleefully and admiringly repeated from tongue to tongue. In the eyes of his subjects the First Gentleman of France could do no wrong. In their envious daydreams they shared his pleasures with him, every man a king. "The Queen Mother is furious and Queen Claude is sick abed. Is he not wonderful, *un homme, plus que ça, un roi universel?*"

In his stern and comfortless apartment Duprat received Henri, rising, extending both arms and crying, "My dear chevalier, welcome, welcome home!"

A sober slow-spoken surgeon of solidly orthodox learning and considerable reputation answered Duprat's urgent call. One look at Henri's wrist and Duprat had said, "You should have had this looked at, Henri."

"It didn't hurt much," Henri said.

"The beginning of corruption never does."

"I was in a hurry to embrace my wife and see the king."

"I know what Marie did when she saw you: she wept. I know too that you have not yet seen the king. Now you will see my doctor, young man. It is not my intention that you widow my grand-niece. She loves you too much, and so do I."

The surgeon wore a robe that reached to his ankles. It was richly edged with costly fur. He carried a walking stick in the old style, high as his armpits, topped with a silver carving of the caduceus, symbol of Hermes, the god-physician. With him came his apprentice, who alone performed operations and touched the patients until in time he too would graduate beyond the menial chores of his art, wear the long robe and collect fees in private practice.

"Examine here," said the surgeon, touching Henri's swollen flesh with the tip of his staff. In such a manner also the great man would point to the organs to be cut when an operation was performed by the apprentice.

"What is it we see?" the surgeon asked.

"*Maître*, the flesh is white under the pressure of your staff. The blood returns sluggishly after the pressure is removed."

"Good," said the master. "Where also do we observe such symptoms?"

"In a man with a dropsy."

"Good again," said the surgeon. "And the treatment?"

"The hand must be amputated."

"Precisely," the surgeon agreed. "Does Your Eminence have a chamber handy and a sturdy chair into which the patient can be strapped while the operation is being performed? It will not take long. Once the stump is cauterized I shall be on my way again within the hour."

Duprat glanced from Henri, whose face was purple with rage, to the assistant, who was fumbling with a leather bag of instruments, and then to the wise old face of the surgeon, whose expression was serene and absolutely confident. Duprat had enormous respect for the master's opinion.

"You propose to lop off my hand?" Henri growled. "Just

195

like that? No thank you, sir. I'll keep it a while if you don't mind."

"Are you not being somewhat hasty, *monsieur le chirurgien?*" Duprat asked. "I see no wound, far less corruption of the flesh. Is it not, perhaps, merely a sprain?"

To a lesser person the surgeon would have given a scathing reply and stalked out of the room. But the chancellor of the *épargne* was not a man whom one lightly antagonized. But even to Duprat his manner was severe.

"For fifty years I have practiced the healing art, Your Eminence. *You* see no wound; *you* see no corruption of the flesh! You invade my province, sir. I see below the unbroken surface of the skin; I see the bones, and I see them fractured."

Duprat listened, grim-faced. He too had suspected a broken bone.

"I see the shards of bone struggling to free themselves, working their way upwards, tormenting the flesh and seeking the surface. Look at the patient's eyes; already they are feverish with humoral imbalance. Look at his cheeks; already the hectic spots appear. In a week, in ten days, the shattered chips of bone will begin to corrupt the flesh, eating their way out, till they break through, and then the corruption will spread throughout the patient's body. And then there will be no need of my healing art, for the hand will burst and stink and the patient will die of a generalized gangrene."

"You paint a pretty picture," Henri said, shaken but still angry.

The surgeon did not listen to him. In a conciliatory tone he addressed Duprat. "Since Your Eminence has somewhat invaded my province I make so bold as to intrude slightly on yours." Then he said ominously, "If thy hand offend thee, cut it off!"

"Surely there is no harm in waiting a day," Duprat said.

"It will not affect your fee," Henri said. Duprat frowned at the sarcasm in Henri's voice.

"I am sorry for you, chevalier," the surgeon said calmly. "Now, alas, you will go to the quacks. They always do, Your Eminence," he said, glancing at Duprat, "like sinners smitten in conscience, afraid of the confessional, consulting the soothsayers and necromancers. As for my fee, there is none. All I have ever asked of God and my art is an opportunity to help. I charge no fee when my help is refused. Come!" he said to his apprentice, who was crestfallen and disappointed. He was expert at amputations and the hand of the Chevalier de Tonnerre, preserved in alcohol and neatly labeled with the name of its owner, would have served as a valuable advertisement.

The surgeon made his adieux. "Your Eminence, chevalier, I hold myself in readiness to be of help whenever I am needed, as assuredly I shall be." He kissed the chancellor's ring, smiled without bitterness at Henri and withdrew in dignity and silence.

Duprat rubbed his chin and shook his head, undecided. "He's the best surgeon in Paris, Henri," he said dubiously. "When a man doesn't charge a fee you can trust him. He didn't upbraid you for your insolence."

"It is my hand, sir!"

"There's a disinterest about him that I like. Ah well. You must decide for yourself. But do not go to the quacks, Henri!"

A brilliant assembly of guests, the *haute noblesse* of France, bearing ancient names and boasting the blood of Crusaders, thronged the Louvre that night. All the great officers of state, high prelates, marshals of the army, admirals of the navy, and noble young commanders with their ladies. Duprat, who disapproved of women at court, muttered to himself, "The corpse of King Philip Augustus must be blushing in its grave at the sight of the Louvre he built being turned into a ballroom. And on a night like this, when the future of France trembles in the balance! This should be a time for grave councils, for massive financial and military preparations. It should be a time for prayer. King Francis makes it a time for dancing."

But he had to concede that the ladies were decorative, and that their beauty was more stimulating to young men on the eve of battle than graybeard counselors and fiscal budgets.

"At least the Queen Mother still wears her crown!" Duprat noted. In these changing times royalty tended to wear them less and less for ordinary occasions. But *she* would never change. It nestled in her snow-white hair like a garment on a body, as naturally, as easily, as functional. She was the king's mother, who had chosen Duprat as tutor for Francis when he was a boy and when she was Regent for him. When the king went to war no doubt she would act as Regent again. Tonight she was displeased; and the jewels in her crown shot fire like her eyes. But her face was under iron control and she smiled from time to time on those she trusted and wished to honor, gauging the smile to her estimate of the recipient's worth. The chancellor of the *épargne* received the most cordial smile of all.

Queen Claude, however, who sat on the dais beside the

Queen Mother under the canopy, wore a velvet headdress, as if she cared nothing for her crown. Or as if it had been taken from her. Or as if a mistress wore it invisibly, with all its distinction, and always would. Or perhaps, thought Duprat, the poor lady wore the headdress only to keep her head warm on her doctor's advice. It was brave of her to appear at all in her weak state. "No doubt the Queen Mother ordered her out of the sickbed," Duprat thought. Queen Claude took no interest in the festivities. She had long since passed beyond jealousy and now, to his eye, she was even beyond amusement at her husband's flagrant and public amours. "I think she will welcome death when it comes," thought the chancellor, "and I think it will come soon." Then Francis, abroad, basking in the glory of the victories he would win, would decree a long period of state mourning and not give the matter a second thought.

Duprat kissed the two queens' hands, Queen Claude's cold as ice, the Queen Mother's strong as a man's. "Who is that gross dark person with you?" the Queen Mother asked.

"Madame, that is Mario Campi, director of the national lottery."

"You may present him later. I'm afraid we shall need men like him, chancellor."

"Madame, he will burst with pride."

"Judging from his rotundity he is well on the way to bursting already. What is the news of the Duc de Bourbon, chancellor?"

"I regret to report that the traitor is having some success in raising an army in Italy. Italy has never forgiven us for Marignan. He will attack soon in the south."

"Francis will not wait to be attacked," the Queen Mother said fondly. "My son was born to attack. Before he saw the light of day he battered at the door of this world demanding to have his own way; his first cry, the peers tell me — I was a little faint and did not hear it clearly — sounded like a war cry."

"It is said to have been lusty and healthy, madame."

"I approve of his plan to attack over the mountains into Italy, chancellor. Do not you also?"

Duprat bowed. He did not.

"Madame, my duty is to pray, and to pay."

"He will do as he pleases when honor calls, you know. He always does. I see in your face you do not agree. But he won in Italy before. He will again."

"Pray and pay, madame."

"An aggressive war is over sooner than a defensive war, chancellor." The Queen Mother was slipping into the role of the mother queen, and Duprat sensed her anxiety for her son and her need of comfort.

"Your son will return, madame; and France will be safe. Look how his people love him! That is something I cannot buy for him. It is an art, God-given."

From the dais the Queen Mother looked down on the glittering throng of guests, among whom the king, having not yet taken his seat under the canopy in the throne that rose an inch higher than Queen Claude's, two inches higher than the Queen Mother's, was mingling democratically, slapping backs in good fellowship though no one dared to touch him. And wherever the king paused in his circulating among his guests an admiring buzzing circle formed round him of young cavaliers and their ladies.

"Listen to their voices, madame! The ring is sincerity. Sincerity cannot be feigned, madame, not to my ear; nor fidelity, nor love."

He had used the wrong word. The Queen Mother's face darkened.

"Some love him too much, and the wrong way."

"But he is young, madame; and these little friendships never last long. Witness the Marquise de Meung."

The Queen Mother did not answer. Duprat did not wish to leave her on this note. "Once he is away with his army, among men, breasting the enemy, he will forget his amusements."

"He need not have chosen the Heilly girl!" the Queen Mother said. "A brazen shameless chit, one of my maids of honor!" The effrontery of Francis in picking a mistress from her own suite of ladies particularly incensed the Queen Mother. "I could stomach Juliette because she was an Italian and the king's notice of her was good for French policy in Milan. But Anne de Pisseleu d'Heilly is French and serves no useful purpose. I do not feel sorry for Juliette; she deserves what she's getting. But her doleful countenance is gaining sympathy for her and hurting the king's prestige among his soft-hearted cavaliers."

Duprat did feel sorry for Juliette. She was being snubbed by everyone, relegated to the background. Little Anne de Pisseleu d'Heilly, by contrast, was the object of flattery and attention by a constant stream of courtiers who clustered round her, elbowing their way to a position close to her, currying her favor, preening themselves if they managed to receive one of her radiantly beautiful smiles. On the outskirts, scarcely noticed by the king, Juliette contemplated the scene, and thought, "Put not your trust in princes."

This was a softer Juliette, more mature and understanding than the Giulietta Leone who, after Henri, had sworn to torture her next lover. She had grown to love the king, and now he had cast her aside; and far, far from torturing, she yearned only to love and be loved by him, and he was going to war. The thought of his death was a sharp physical pain in her own body.

"Stand guard here at home," the Queen Mother said to Duprat, "and prepare a safe, a *safe* France to which he may return after his expedition into Italy."

Duprat had been waiting for a chance to tell her how thoroughly he had prepared the defense of the frontiers. "Madame, the north is secure; I have disposed strong forces against the Germans; in that sector some fighting already has broken out but the Germans are repulsed with heavy losses. Likewise in Provence I have built formidable defenses around Marseille and provisioned the city for a long siege."

"Always defensive, Duprat?"

One never said No to the Queen Mother.

"More than that, madame. Admiral Andrea Doria is preparing to run the blockade which will surely be thrown around the port the moment it is invested by land. The cost has been great, but success is always costly."

"The king is fortunate in his servants," the Queen Mother said smiling. "You may now present your lottery director, chancellor."

Mario Campi had hovered about the dais like an animated mountain, his black eyes darting from Duprat to the two queens, waiting for a glance from his master. Duprat raised an eyebrow; the director was instantly at his side. To be presented! It was a moment of triumph. Despite his bulk he knelt and kissed hands with the grace of a ballet dancer.

"Tell me something about your proposals," the Queen Mother said. A Savoyarde, she spoke Italian with a perfect accent, and spoke it now to honor him. Campi's emotional nature responded as to a caress and his hard eyes momentarily misted over. *"Madonna!"* he murmured.

Thought Duprat, It is easy to see where King Francis inherited his charm. If only he had inherited her ability! But if he had, what need would there be for a Duprat, and Duprat would never have been chancellor of the *épargne*, the richest, most powerful subject in Europe today — or if not today, tomorrow; for Duprat planned to tithe the lottery into his own purse.

It was a proposal, Campi said, whereby the treasury of France would never be empty, like the barrel of meal in the Bible, which wasted not and the cruse of oil that never could fail; and as sinless in origin, since not a sou would come from increase of taxes. It was a means of tapping the measureless wealth of the masses, a wealth hitherto hoarded and beyond reach. It would serve to unite the millions of little French men and French women in love and in hope to their king, whom they never might see nor hear speak but who would now enter into their personal lives and out of his pure benignity grant to each one an ineffable dream, nay, more than a dream, a practical possibility of becoming a millionaire overnight. Such was the nature of the national lottery, madame.

When the Queen Mother smiled Campi was quick to sense that he had pleased her and should say no more. Shortly she extended her hand and dismissed him.

Queen Claude, bored and fatigued, said, "Madame, I will retire now."

She rose; the king, watching, breathed a sigh of relief that the corpse at the feast was about to remove itself and handed her gracefully down from her throne and then turned her over to her ladies, who escorted her from the hall, he bowing splendidly, the guests parting to let her through. Then there was a burst of joyous music, the orchestras struck up a dance tune, a fountain of wine of Champagne began to play and everyone danced till dawn.

No one danced with the Marquise de Meung, who took her place among some widows on a bench against the wall. Heads turned but not one of them spoke to her. Some were old and deaf and genuinely could not hear when she greeted them; others were suddenly smitten blind and did not see when she smiled at them. A month ago they had courted her and sought the king's ear through her.

Juliette loathed her successor but she did not blame the king. Little Anne was radiantly beautiful and precociously witty and agreeable to talk with. So young; so lovely; dear Francis, no wonder! He cannot help it, she knew. No more could a bee help buzzing in a garden where every flower was open, tasting the honey from each flower in turn. She wondered how long this one would keep him. She wondered how quickly she could leave the hall without angering the king. She still occupied the hideaway he had decorated for her, though he never opened the door now. If she left too soon he would be irked and throw her out and install Anne in her place. She did not think she could stand that. But neither would her pride permit her to remain all night in a crowd where no one spoke to her. The chancellor, like all the others, was keeping a safe distance. But then, Duprat had never approved of her. His only concern was the king, to get her safely married so that the king would suffer somewhat less of a scandal. Well, she was still a marquise. Nobody could take that from her; and she had a right to sit where she was sitting, as long as she could bear the indignity of rejection on every side. Once Bayard passed close and smiled at her, *le chevalier sans peur et sans reproche,* in his neck-length haircut and leather doublet. But Bayard was so other-worldly and pure in heart that he smiled at everyone. Juliette felt like the Magdalene, only less successful.

Among the crowd she saw Henri de Tonnerre. She would have welcomed a word even from him. But he was with that confoundedly angelic wife of his, who, they said, was going to have a child. "I could still have him if I wanted him," she thought. But she wanted only what she could not have, not any more, not ever again: Francis.

She noted without interest that Henri had not kissed the queens' hands. He was not dancing and he held his right hand hidden in his doublet. She scarcely wondered why till the king approached him. Over the music she could not hear what they said, but she could see that the king was extraordinarily cordial.

"Henri!" he was saying. "I have not seen you since your return. Why did you not ask for an audience? How did it go? You were after the Duc, were you not?"

Henri was never sure when the king was joking and when he was making the most of his notorious forgetfulness and pretending to be oblivious of the past, so that he would not have to face the consequences of his deplorable decisions, such as sending two men to kidnap the Duc de Bourbon. A reply as facile as the king's query was required.

"I presented myself at the first opportunity, Sire. My mission ended in failure."

"Failure? Because Bourbon got away? Not at all, *mon ami.* I am delighted. For now we have a chance to add another laurel to our crown when we beat him on his own ground.

I am glad he got away. Aren't you too, madame?" he asked Marie, raising his hat. King Francis, who alone might go covered indoors, would raise his hat to a charwoman. It rendered him immensely popular.

"I was sad when my husband was sad, but if my king is glad so am I," she said.

"I will write that down," said the king, looking into the middle distance where no doubt the muses were. "Henri, you've a jewel of a wife, since not only in beauty but also in wit she sparkles, absolutely sparkles! Treasure her, chevalier. By God, I see you have done so!" He was smiling broadly at the swelling of her pregnancy, which was now noticeable. "Another Tonnerre, eh? My congratulations. It is better to create friends for a king, which few can do, than to kill the king's enemies, which anybody can do. I think I shall write that down too. A theme for a poem, wouldn't you think?"

Marie laughed, and so did the king; and everyone within hearing followed the lead. When King Francis was gay everyone was gay. For some days the mot went the rounds as a profound royal epigram.

The king, pleased with his wit, raised his hat again to Marie, preparing to pass among other guests, and extended his hand to Henri, a mark of favor. Henri withdrew his swollen hand from his doublet, winced when the king pressed it cordially in a strong handclasp.

"Here, here!" Francis said, looking down. "What is this?"

"It's a little swollen where the Duc took a shot at one of my manacles, Sire."

"Have you had it looked at? It looks bad."

"The chancellor's surgeon was good enough to suggest treatment."

"O-of!" said the king. "That old sawbones."

"He wants to amputate," Marie said.

"He does, does he? Tut, tut, child. Nobody's going to amputate my Tonnerres, not so much as a hair, let alone a whole hand. Come to me tomorrow, Henri. I know a doctor who'll fix you up in no time, plenty of time to join me in Italy."

"It wouldn't be one of the quacks, would it, Henri?" Marie asked when the king had left them.

"I don't know, Marie," Henri said.

Next day he sought audience with the king, who was in his study with a young man of vaguely professional aspect. Yet if the man was a surgeon he gave no evidence of it. Neither the long robe nor the physician's staff was in evidence; and the youngster he had with him, who carried his instruments, looked like a peasant just off the farm.

"Now we will examine that wrist of yours, Henri," said Francis, scowling in concentration. "Here, let me palp it." Poet, musician, warrior, monarch, King Francis deemed himself expert in everything.

"Badly swollen, Henri, badly," he pronounced as his diagnosis. "A good purge, eh, Doctor Paré? This is Ambroise Paré, Henri, an excellent man."

"A good purge never hurts anybody," the doctor said, "except when the bowels are inflamed. Never cured much either except when the patient has overindulged, and I don't think this one has."

"Maître Ambroise has a scurrilous tongue," said the king, laughing. "That's why I like him. His colleagues maintain that medically he's a heretic. But there's magic in his hands."

"If Your Majesty would deign to stop crushing the bones of the wrist," Paré said, "I shall try to be of assistance."

"Hear him, Henri? He doesn't care how he talks to me. One would think I was a carter." But the king stopped playing the surgeon and turned the patient over to Paré. "Save me that hand, maître Ambroise," he admonished. "I shall need it."

"Does this hurt?" Paré asked, giving a twist to Henri's swollen wrist that caused him excruciating pain.

"A bit," Henri conceded, pale as a fish.

"It should have hurt like the fires of Hell," Paré said, "and if it didn't, there's bigger trouble than I think. Did it hurt?"

"If you were an enemy I'd bash in your skull for what you just did!" Henri said, sweating.

"Good. Good honest lad."

"What is amiss with the wrist?" Francis said.

"Hush, please. I am listening. In a moment I shall tell you."

With that he lifted a knee and planted it squarely against Henri's chest and wrenched with all his might, at the same time clamping an educated hand on the swollen wrist, seeking out the bony structure beneath and manipulating the bones blind with his powerful fingers, till a sound was heard like the snap of a chicken neck being twisted, muffled by flesh. The doctor muttered "Good!" and held on, calling to his assistant. "Bring me the glove with the spring in it!"

To Henri he said, "I am sorry, chevalier. I had to do that. I know how it hurt."

"Did it?" the king asked Henri.

Henri could not answer. He had never experienced such pain. Paré bathed his forehead with a handkerchief soaked in brandy. "Lean back, chevalier, to keep the traction taut," he commanded; his hand still pulled. "You won't want to, but you must do so." His face was kindly, but keen and observant.

Henri leaned back and gritted his teeth.

"Sometimes I have to tie them," the doctor said. "You make it easy for me, *monsieur le chevalier*."

"I wish I could say the same for you."

"Excellent," Paré said, grinning. "He does not even faint."

It would have been less painful to lop it off, Henri thought for a fleeting moment.

The assistant — perhaps he was an apprentice, if so unorthodox a surgeon was permitted to train one — approached with a thing that looked like a mechanical hand, made of steel and leather and springs. Paré slipped it into Henri's hand and adjusted it; it stretched the hand from fingertips to a point below the wrist. It was more than a splint, such as man had used for broken bones since the beginning of history: it was a splint with springs. Slowly the pain began to diminish.

"Now, if God wills, you will be all right," Paré said.

"What did you do?" said the king.

"Majesty," said the doctor, "the body is a complex mechanism, capable of infinite pleasure."

"I know that," said the king.

"And infinite pain. It is easily set awry. The beautiful bones in Henri's wrist, which God made to supplement and complement each other, each performing its appointed task, alas, in the Chevalier de Tonnerre, all was scrambled, out of place, one bone rubbing on top of the other, abrading. Had they so remained the chevalier would have had a crippled hand for the rest of his life, as immobile as in a paralytic. I pulled everything apart, separating the bones that would have fused one into another. If the chevalier wears the mechanical hand, with the springs that keep the bones where they should be, he'll be good as new in a week from now."

"I shall watch his progress," the king said, "and if it turns out as you say I will reward you. I need this man."

"I only attend them," Paré said, more seriously than was his wont. "God cures them. Now I must take leave of Your Majesty."

The king raised his eyebrows. No one left the presence without formal dismissal.

"A charwoman is giving birth in a garret a few streets away. They've given her up because the midwife fears a breech presentation. Feet coming first. They say she'll die. It's a pity not to try to save her. I shall leave now, Your Majesty, and see if they let me in. *Au revoir.*"

And with that, whistling a dance tune, Paré took his leave, his assistant following in his wake.

Henri thought the surgeon had very bad manners.

But his wrist most certainly felt better.

King Francis had now completed all preparations for war according to his lights. He had dined and wined the thousands of loyal chevaliers who had spurred into Paris from all corners of the kingdom, looking to him to make the decision whithersoever they should go and whatsoever they should do for the common weal of the realm as he saw fit to define it, even to the extinction of their individual lives. Francis felt a certain glow, a delicious spiritual uplifting.

Greater love hath no man than this, he remembered from Duprat's tutoring in his youth, than to lay down his life for his friend. "I am the first of the thousand kings of France to rule *du bon plaisir*. I need only command and all France obeys." He was deeply moved.

There had not been a thousand kings or anywhere near, but Francis was poor at figures. He deemed himself touched by a star, humbly infallible. "If they trust me so," thought he, "I am worthy of the trust, and the genius of France is centered in me like rivers of water seeking the common sea." It was a holy mission, God-delegated. He sustained not the slightest suspicion that he had ever made a mistake, neither in his present preparations for war, nor his life with Queen Claude, nor in his shifting choice of mistresses: for patently he stood above the rules that applied to the common run of mortals.

Mountaineers in the Alps, whither he was bound, might have supplied an explanation, had he required one. When a man is very very high, breathing a rarefied atmosphere, his mind is prone to delusions of grandeur; he sees the world very small, as from a great distance, below his feet, so small that it seems easy to control, like insects in a carpet; and he cannot escape an Olympian sense of omnipotent power. So, godlike, had ruled the Pharoahs, and it must be conceded that they had wrought wonders; so lived the French king, in thought and deed. His subjects worshiped him. He accepted their worship as his due and felt deeply the reciprocal duty of protecting them out of the plenitude of his power.

Music, good music, was an important factor in the universality of his accomplishments. From the Queen Mother, with her sensitive Italian ear, he had inherited a capacity for musical enjoyment. With his generous good nature he wished to share that pleasure with others less fortunate: with the isolated, like the Dowager Duchess of Montholon, or the old-fashioned, like the Chevalier Bayard, who was tone deaf to all save cathedral chants or the battle song of steel; Francis felt it his duty to educate them up to a greater appreciation of the marvelous melodies now being composed by the modern Italian composers, singing and sensuous, to the accompaniment of ingenious new instruments scientifically designed to produce new and purer sounds. Hence came the great orchestras he sponsored, the new dance tunes that echoed through the Louvre during the recent festivities and surrounded the king wherever he went with an aura of lilting melody that enhanced his natural charm.

That all might be in order before he left he scanned the list of country houses he had ordered erected during his absence — airy châteaux that would constitute the architectural glory of France long after his reign had run its course; he listened patiently to the cooks who recapitulated the list of exotic seasonings they had put into the soups he had served by the barrelful to his guests and his gathering army, and the tons of lamb, beef, pheasant and veal he had caused to be served; and, like God, he surveyed his creation and saw that it was good. "Good, good," he murmured, leaving Duprat to pay the bills.

Now, at the head of his army who were as supremely confident of victory as he, he was departing from his capital for Italy and the triumphs he was certain to win, triumphs more glorious than Marignan.

Duprat watched the long cavalcade of laughing cavaliers as they left. "On such a day, so might have left the poor innocents of the Children's Crusade," he murmured, suddenly fearful of the future.

Yet he had done all a faithful and able minister of the Crown could do. Night after night, far into each night, till his eyes burned for lack of sleep he had pored over sheaves of provisioners' manifests purporting to list supplies that had been delivered to the army. On most, without reading too carefully, he would scrawl the letters "LD" — *licet* (it is permitted) — *D* (Duprat), authorizing payment. But here and there he would scrutinize a manifest suspiciously, sometimes because it read too smoothly, sometimes because it was carelessly drawn, sometimes for no reason at all except that it was time: at least every tenth contractor was dishonest, he knew. Examination of every tenth document might not accurately pinpoint the malefactors, but the proportion was right. That manifest he would set aside. He would then have each item searchingly authenticated by the chancellery accountants, and woe betide the unfortunate contractor if so much as a sou was misrepresented or so much as a hundredweight proved to be short in weight. The hapless provisioner, caught in the web of statistics, would languish in jail till his account was audited, subject to confiscatory fines if a fault were discovered. Since supplies had a way of shrinking, through theft or legitimate evaporation — a wagonload of fodder is honest weight in damp weather but criminally short weight if the sun happens to shine and dry it out — Duprat's provisioners always gave him full measure and a bit more, out of fear of his auditors. Monumental bribes found their way into his purse under the guise of donations to his favorite charity. "They would bribe anyone else who paid their bills," Duprat consoled his conscience, shrugging. "Why not me?" In the end, he knew, all came out even: he forced them to oversupply to an extent of about ten percent, and he took ten percent for himself. Thus King Francis's armies were one hundred percent provisioned, and the quality was prime.

Duprat would have liked more gunpowder and cannon, but the engineers who owned and fought the fearsome new weapons were civilians, not army men. They were a secretive independent group, speaking a queer scientific jargon among themselves that was impossible to understand: trajectories, ratio of charge to weight of ball, delayed-action fuses. They were black-faced with powder mixing; they drank a good deal of beer so as to be able to supply the large quantities of urine with which the best gunpowder was "corned," or pulverized; they were contemptuous of the lily-tabarded heralds who had no other military duties than to blow the silver trumpets, and the heralds in turn looked down on the black-faced engineers. Individually they're the best artillerymen in Christendom, Duprat knew, but they compete among themselves to gain greater prestige and profits. Each contractor made a different caliber weapon; no contractor's cannonballs would fit the cannon of any other contractor. In time I will regularize all this and force the adoption of uniform standards and draft them into the army, Duprat resolved. If there is time.

One had to deal patiently with civilian contractors since one had no military power to coerce them. It had happened in the heat of battle that artillerymen deemed their fabulously expensive cannon in danger of capture, and then they would simply withdraw from the field with their property, leaving the knights and archers to fight it out as they always had before the invention of the new weapons. It had happened that the knights after such a desertion, hotheaded and bloody from the fray, would turn about and slaughter their own artillerymen. This, though understandable, was foolish, since no cavalier knew how to fire a cannon and would not have touched the ugly thing if he knew. Since every nation suffered the same difficulty in integrating artillery with the older-fashioned methods of classical warfare Duprat was hopeful. The French engineers, with all their faults, were better than the Emperor's. Their weapons were more mobile, and above all, they spoke the same language, whereas the Emperor's armies were composed of Germans, Dutchmen, Spaniards, Austrians, Italians.

"In spirit we surpass our enemy," he mused, admiring the passing cavalcade. "That is what wins in the end."

Near the city gate in a poor part of town where peasants from the countryside exposed the produce of their truck farms for sale on market days, Duprat had caused to be erected a reviewing stand, sheltered with a canopy and provided with chairs for the Queen Mother and Queen Claude. From this vantage point the dignitaries of the realm could bid Godspeed to the king and his army and Duprat could deliver his blessing.

There was a silvery sound of treble trumpets, trumpeting a fanfare with a beat to which horses and men could march; the trumpeters wore tabards and their horns were decorated with velvet pennants resplendent with pearl-white embroidered fleurs-de-lys on a shield of azure. Jesters in cap and bells danced and turned handsprings, clowning and chattering among the crowds who lined the street, scoffing at the enemy over the Alps. Bagpipers piped in marching bands, supplying a drone bass to the march rhythm, and a squad of drummers emphasized the beat. There were troubadours with twanging harps and fiddlers who scraped with their bows on lute-bellied fiddles. Circulating among the crowds were fortunetellers, relic-sellers and painted women plying their trade, venders of good-luck charms and monks hawking dispensations to speed to Paradise the souls of those who would not return, and to pardon the sins, as yet uncommitted but certain to be, soon, of those in the crowd who were in a bibulous holiday mood and looked forward to a night of revelry.

Riding beside their cavaliers were their ladies, mature mothers, slim daughters, wives pale but smiling, and of course the painted others, all mingling in the common democracy of women whose men may not return, men loved with the helplessness that goes with knowledge that the temperamental rascals, whom no sensible female can ever understand, are off on one of their hunts to kill or be killed, a periodic madness for glory that afflicted them and was incomprehensible to creatures whom God fashioned to produce, not to extinguish, life. They were beautiful, the women, in their lace and brocades; their cheeks were red, and the men, who smelled of leather, gunpowder and sweat, sensed in the air a perfume like a summer garden, and rededicated their souls to kill: for the prospect of a booty-rich homecoming; for the sanctity of the mothers who bore them; for the purity of their brides; or simply to have funds to buy a jeweled pendant to hang round the neck of a mistress or cut a fine figure among the trollops of a favorite tavern. Thus, from the highest level to the lowest, love of women spurred them on to greater deeds of danger.

Indeed, the departure of the army presented to Duprat

the aspect of a hunt breakfast rather than the grim business of war. "Yet who am I," he pondered, "to state that France should go to war in the gloomy efficient manner of the Emperor Charles Quint? I suspect we are better off just being ourselves." On a statistical and geographic basis France hadn't a chance: the Empire was five times as big, could muster five times the fighters, and surrounded the territory of France on all sides save the sea. "But the Greeks hadn't a chance against Darius either," Duprat remembered. "And the Greeks won."

Queen Claude was pale and weak, but she sat in her throne-like chair and smiled as her husband approached, lifting a thin white hand to him in greeting. Francis gave her a most graceful bow, lifting his hat and pirouetting his horse, which was beautifully trained, so that it too bent on its spirited forelegs and seemed to curtsy before the reviewing stand.

The crowds broke into a cheer, *"Vive le roi, vive la reine!"*

"Wonderful, no?" Francis said, grinning, to Anne d'Heilly, who was riding beside him.

"Sire," she smiled, "you are always wonderful."

Duprat did not hear the interchange but he had to concede that the king's reverence to the queen was spectacularly executed and had had a good effect on the adoring spectators. It had also served to soften the astonishment that many experienced when they saw that lovely little Anne de Pisseleu d'Heilly was riding straddlewise like Joan of Arc, in a tight-fitting bodice of cloth-of-silver to simulate armor. It clung like a skin.

Giulietta rode in an inferior position to his left. She was called Giulietta again; the "Juliette" that had marked her status as *maîtresse en titre* had been dropped by common consent, as if she no longer had a right to a French name. She felt the change as a reproach and her eyes shot smoky fire if anyone dared address her to her face by her Italian name. "I am madame la Marquise de Meung." Shortly she would have another name.

Smiling regally for the benefit of the crowds, but stricken in her heart, the Queen Mother watched her son depart for war. *Cher garçon, cher roi, cher fils,* she thought. And fatuous no end! But she loved and admired him, as did all other women in France, down to the lowest tavern wench; and the men, who wished they were like him, loved him too.

Directly behind the king came his guard of honor, privileged courtiers of proven merit who had fought with him at Marignan. Among them was Henri de Tonnerre, with Marie riding side-saddle beside him. Her pregnancy was noticeably advanced now, but she refused to stay at home. "Everyone else will be there," she said.

"You shouldn't take chances," he cautioned.

"That's why I'm here," she said, smiling. "There are entirely too many attractive women around."

Henri laughed. His hand was still in the mechanical device that Dr. Paré had fitted on, and the swelling was subsiding every day.

"There is one young man who will not be casting his life away," muttered Duprat, sighting him in the cavalcade, gratified that he had protected him. He had protected Marie too. It was one of the perquisites of power. He had ordered them back to Tonnerre, to care for their physical disabilities which neither seemed to take seriously enough.

"Everybody has babies," Marie had said to him. "And I," Henri had said, "am fit as a fiddle."

"You will retire to your estates," the chancellor said positively, "till you both are over your troubles. The king so commands." The king, on the advice of his chancellor, had indeed so commanded, signing an order that Duprat had prepared in advance. "Can't get away for a while, eh, Duprat? Pity. I'd have liked him to share in the first victory." Faced with the king's *bon plaisir* Henri had had no recourse but to obey.

"Your great-uncle has a heavy hand," he grumbled to Marie, who smiled mysteriously.

"Yours is very sore," she said.

"Did you have anything to do with this order?"

"On my honor, no. You will join the king when your hand is well again."

"My father takes this very hard."

The old Comte de Tonnerre, Henri's father, was desolated that his son had had the poor taste to let himself be incapacitated by a pistol shot. A sword gash or a spear in the chest, yes; but a pistol shot, never! A new-fangled inglorious weapon without tradition or honor that ought not to be turned against anyone of noble blood! If this sort of thing kept up the time would come when wars would be fought by engineers. He did not wish to live to see that time.

"Soon as you're better, son," he admonished, "follow that king of ours. He knows how to win battles properly." The old count had then voiced some scathing remarks about devil-black sulphur-sooted artillerymen and the vile art of corning gunpowder. "A baby pisses when it's born and a dead man pisses when he falls in battle; that we know; it has always been so; but pissing to make an explosive is a reproach to the soldierly way of life."

Henri knew that a fallen cavalier, when the life departs from his body, fouls his breeches and requires washing by his squires before he is fit to be buried and decently mourned by his relatives; but he also knew that there was no better way of making gunpowder, and without gunpowder no future war could be won; and so he stood between two worlds trying in vain to be part of both. But above all he was angered by Duprat's underhanded contriving to keep him out of action.

"One must admire your great-uncle," he said to Marie. "He gets what he wants."

"What I want too, Henri."

"And in this he is much like the Italians, who calculate and scheme and add subtlety to bravery."

"I just don't see why you admire the Italians so much," Marie said. She was still jealous of Giulietta.

"Marie, I've forgotten that vixen long since."

Giulietta, Juliette, the Marquise de Meung, whatever name they knew her by, according to their personal prejudices, she still occupied the second place of honor, riding at King Francis's left. "I cannot just send her packing," thought the king. "I must let the people know that I am not fickle." He was also content to let the people know that two mistresses simultaneously loved him, and flaunt his *bon plaisir* by a public display of both in front of his cheering subjects; and as for Queen Claude? Had he not made a point of bowing splendidly before her? It never occurred to him that she might object to Anne or Giulietta, or that the humiliation of their presence on an important state occasion might further weaken her already weak will to live.

Marie said fondly, "I wish you were king."

"Good Lord, Marie!"

"You're infinitely sweeter than King Francis."

He reached over and squeezed her hand. "I'm afraid that doesn't qualify me for the throne. Antoine Duprat would make a king, not I."

"Uncle Antoine practically is."

Bringing up the rear, after the foot soldiers and archers, were the rumbling cannon, with wagonloads of barreled gunpowder and beer. The crowned heads and the dignitaries would have left the reviewing stand long before they arrived.

An untoward incident occurred at the city gate, which dampened the spirits of the crowd and caused a certain amount of foreboding among the more ignorant and superstitious, though it did not affect King Francis.

The forward elements of the cavalcade had just passed the reviewing stand. The Queen Mother had smiled, Queen Claude had waved her adieu to her husband. There was a dark area under the archway in the city wall from which the portcullis and oaken doors had long since been removed, the city having been deemed secure for a century; but it was still known as "the gate." Clustered under and around it were little shops and stalls where beggars congregated and itinerant merchants hawked their wares.

From one of these inconspicuous little stalls, as the king passed, a man with the face of a fanatic, in obvious disguise, darted out. There was madness in his eyes and murder in his heart, or so they said of him after the event.

He was dressed like a beggar, but on examination of the corpse, after the surgeons reassembled it, his clothing was discovered to have been of costly material artificially soiled and ripped to simulate a beggar's rags; the black under the fingernails proved to be ink, and the evidence of toil had been freshly applied to the hands from the dirt of the street. The horny hands of a laborer cannot be counterfeited, and the characteristic hands of the intellectual will show through a coating of one-day mud. But he had tried to the best of his ability to look like one of the people. As Duprat probed his motivation he came to the conclusion that the would-be assassin had wished to convey the impression that the common man was against King Francis. In another guess also Duprat correctly surmised that the assassination attempt was ill conceived: the man had no colleagues. In a properly planned killing there is always he who strikes the blow, confederates in the crowd who cover his retreat and some swift means of conveyance to whisk the plotters away from the scene while all is confusion and shock. With such proper planning the man could have got away. "That is how I should have planned it," Duprat thought; but few had the genius of Duprat and this man had tried to do it all on his own.

He suddenly emerged from the shadows, dagger drawn and shouting, "Death to the tyrant!" and hurled himself, arm upraised, upon the king. The king, being on a horse, was elevated by at least four feet above the assailant who was on foot, and at worst could have sustained only a wound in the thigh. He sustained not even a pinprick. The man, having called attention to himself by a shout when he should have struck in silence, was of course quickly spotted and set upon.

Henri, seeing the man dart forward with a blade in his hand, cried out, "Gare! L'assassin!" He was the first of the men to realize that an attempt was being made on the life of the king.

Giulietta sensed it quicker. She screamed, reverting to her native Italian, "Beloved one! Quickly! Defend yourself!"

From the elevation of his horse and the exultation of the moment the king looked down on the slender little creature with a little knife in its hand, and the thing that was happening seemed absurdly remote and inconsequential, as if it were happening to someone else in some other place. This was the place of his glorious departure for war.

Giulietta slipped from her saddle and threw herself between the assailant and the king, a surge of strength electrifying the lithe body and long limbs that once had fled through impoverished alleys to the hovel of her youth, through which she would run after stealing a chicken. It was an instinctive reaction to an elemental threat, similar to hunger but stronger by far, since it sprang from love of the man she adored and who now was in peril.

Still screaming in Italian she blocked the assassin's way. His greater weight knocked her down. She fell backward almost under the hoofs of the king's horse. The man's dagger rose and fell, burying itself in the froth of lace at her throat. Meteor trails of colored light streaked through the air, and star points of brilliance flashed from the cobblestones as the dagger point ripped a necklace to shreds and jewels bounced into the gutter.

High-pitched and hysterical the man's voice cursed her. Later it was determined that he too was screaming in Italian, though the legend persisted for years, repeated in whispers at night around the hearth fires of superstitious peasants, that his curses were mouthed in a pre-Adamite tongue that Lucifer spoke when he rallied the fallen angels to fight against God, and that the assassin was not a man but a demon.

Blood appeared on Giulietta's breast, staining her bodice as she screamed and clawed and fought. The attack on the beautiful girl was horribly like a public rape of a virgin, and the crowd, already surcharged with emotion, roared like one monstrous collective beast.

Giulietta's leap from her horse and rush at the man filled perhaps eight seconds of history. During one of those eight seconds, perhaps the third or fourth — since his mind was full of other matters and the event was totally unexpected — Henri too leaped from his saddle and struck the first armed blow at the king's assailant: Giulietta had only blocked with her body and struck with her fists.

Deep into the man's unprotected back, accurately aimed at the heart beneath the ribs, Henri plunged his dagger. It was said that the man died instantly, but that cannot be true. Time was moving by semi-seconds, each tiny division fraught with intense and concentrated activity. Before the assailant actually died there was ample time for his body to suffer before the mob reduced it to pieces incapable of pain.

"Instantly" (so read the annals of King Francis's reign) "the king's guard disarmed the man, who had not harmed His Majesty, His Majesty graciously saying, Let the unfortunate fellow be kindly treated and fairly tried, and inquire into what grievance has caused him to act in this fashion, and, if it have merit, let it be redressed."

But these are the pens of the chroniclers speaking long after the event.

Therefore "instantly" is not how he died. A full twelve

seconds had elapsed since the man first rushed out of the shadows.

Nor did the king make the speech about grievances; Francis was incapable of suspecting that grievances existed under his *bon plaisir*. At the moment of the attack he was gazing fondly at Anne de Pisseleu d'Heilly, gracefully complimenting her on the originality of her silver costume. "A delightful farewell, my dear. Something for a soldier to remember during long lonely nights on the tenting field, and to bring him the sooner back to his love."

Then he heard screams and turned his head.

"What is happening?" he said.

His guard and the crowd closed in and snatched at the body of the assailant. They dragged him off Giulietta and threw him into a gutter, where they kicked him in the face. Then, during the span of perhaps one minute more, the complex history of the evolution of man's weapons repeated itself, from the stone hand-hammers of primitive savages, on through the discovery of the bruising and cutting weapons, as cudgels and knives were found and used, to the last and most modern weapon of all, the pistol. Kicked, bone-crushed and beaten, the body of the assailant, which still had some seconds to live, was snatched by the mob who hacked it to pieces and hurled the detached members onto widely separated dungheaps. Then a soldier with a pistol put a bullet into the largest piece remaining in the gutter.

When it was explained to the king that an attempt had been made on his life he remarked, "The man must have been crazed to try to kill *me*," and shook his head in bewilderment for some moments.

"Are you all right, my pet?" he asked Anne.

✳ ✳ ✳ 12 ✳ ✳

T HE PERIOD FOLLOWING the king's departure was
full of noise and confusion. It fell to Duprat, as it
always did, to restore some semblance of order.

"King Francis is consistent," he sighed. "Brilliantly
chaotic." How characteristic that after His Majesty's passage there should lie in a street the dismembered body of a
would-be assassin and the wounded body of a discarded
mistress, her jewels now broken and bathed in blood and
the mud of a gutter.

He ordered a contingent of his own soldiers to escort
the Queen Mother and Queen Claude back to the Louvre,
lest an attempt be made on their lives too. He could not be
absolutely sure that this was the work of a single fanatic;
it might be a widespread conspiracy. He never took
chances.

He ordered the Mother Superior of Saint Mary of the
Walls, a convent conveniently near and conveniently obscure, to take Giulietta and care for her till she was well
again or until she should die. This, like all else he did,
was a soundly calculated move.

He ordered a cordon of soldiers to surround the spot where the jewels had fallen, since they were beginning to attract the crowd; and two sharp-eyed agents to spy on the soldiers, who might otherwise be tempted to swallow a gem or two on the sly. "Let it be rumored that I know the exact count of the jewels in her necklace," he said, "and that I expect every one to be accounted for, to me personally." By the time they were returned he would have found out the exact count.

He ordered the body of the assailant to be put piece by piece upon a litter and conveyed to a private place for study and identification. Although dressed in his archiepiscopal robes he strode through the gutters and dungheaps to make sure no piece was overlooked. There might be a letter in the pocket of the doublet; there might be a ring with a crest on the finger of a hand. All must be scooped up and examined.

He ordered Henri back to Tonnerre.

"This very day, chevalier," he said. "I will give you a guard of honor. You acquitted yourself nobly and did honor to my house."

"I have my own guard, Your Eminence." Henri said.

"They are all pensioners, Henri." Henri, though he could not go himself, had sent his best soldiers with the king. "Marie will be with you. I will not entrust her to an escort of feeble old men in times like these."

He eyed Henri for a moment, smiling. "And you might be tempted to slip over the Alps before you are fit to fight."

Henri answered, "Your Eminence, I do not know whether you are giving me a guard of honor or placing me in protective custody."

"You should not have ripped off that thing you wore on

your hand," Duprat said. "It seems to have done you good. My opinion of young Dr. Paré is rising. It's a pity he went with the king. I could have used him today."

Henri suddenly realized that his hand was normal in size; it had functioned well when he plunged the dagger in, and he had struck with all his might.

"It is cured!" Marie breathed.

"Officially he is still invalided out of the king's service by the king's special order," Duprat said sternly.

"Then it *is* protective custody," Henri said.

"Henri, King Francis can get along very well in Italy without one of his chevaliers; and I have greater work for you here at home."

"There is no greater work than victory, sir."

"That is true. That is why you will remain and work for it here. Give me your word, chevalier, that you will not sneak over the Alps without my leave. If you refuse I'm afraid I shall have to double your guard."

"Give it, Henri," Marie begged.

"I give it," he said, so grudgingly that Duprat chuckled.

Marie had witnessed with horror the brave act of Giulietta. All her old jealousy faded away. "I hate to think of the poor girl in a cold nunnery, Uncle Antoine. She is used to a palace, and she may be dying."

"She may be," said Duprat, "but I do not think so. Her necklace turned the point and blunted the force of the blow."

"We could take her to Tonnerre and nurse her back to health. She would be more at ease among friends. Henri knew her once, didn't you, Henri?"

"Oh yes, casually; in connection with the Mona Lisa, I think."

"Yes, that was it."

"She will be better off among the holy women of Saint Mary of the Walls," Duprat said coldly. He knew Giulietta's star had set. She had no friends. She had lain wounded in a gutter and the king had not even dismounted to look at her, as he might have done to immense applause. The Queen Mother had never liked her. She would never re-turn to the palace. Anyone who took her in would be suspect. Duprat did not fancy Marie and Henri suffering the Queen Mother's displeasure now that the Queen Mother was about to be Regent of France during the king's absence.

"Your sweet and compassionate thought does you credit, Marie, but it is quite impracticable till I inquire into Giulietta's condition. Has it occurred to you, my dear, that that girl might be party to the assassination attempt?"

"She couldn't be!" Marie said. "She loved him."

"Exactly," said Duprat. "That's why she could be."

Henri stated later, "I think your Uncle Antoine is the wisest man I ever knew."

"I think he's cold as a fish," Marie said. "What a hateful thought, to want somebody killed because you love him!"

Duprat also ordered the date set for the drawing of the national lottery, and prepared a proclamation ordering a second to be launched immediately after awarding the prize for the first. He was still determined that the drawing was to be absolutely honest, but the element of un-certainty in a lottery was beginning to trouble him. The king had bought thousands of tickets. Suppose His Majesty should win! Who would believe that the whole scheme had not been corrupt from the outset? The richest source of revenue ever devised would dry up overnight. Would it not be wiser in the interest of honesty to eliminate some of the uncertainty so that the wrong person did not win? Giulietta also held hundreds of tickets, as did Anne de Pisseleu d'Heilly. How would it look if one of them should win? It would look like the most cynical sort of dishonesty. There was more to honesty than chance. Honesty must also look like honesty. And there was the uncomfortable possibility that one of the thousands of nobles and chevaliers now with the king might win. It would do no positive harm, of course, if some brave warrior who had impoverished himself to equip a fighting force and follow his king into battle should recoup his fortunes on a draw of pure chance; but on the other hand, such a winner would not be in Paris on the day of the draw to receive the prize. The publicity value of the drawing would be totally ruined. The whole matter required study.

In the days when the Louvre served as a fortress it contained many large underground storerooms, and rows of barred cells for prisoners of war. The cells were now used as wine caves, the damp walls and low temperatures supplying a climate ideal for the preservation of vintage flavors. The storerooms were largely abandoned now, since King Francis disliked the salt meats and hard fare of his ancestors and preferred daintier food.

One of the largest rooms, however, was still in use. It had once been a cooper's repair shop; the forge on which barrel hoops had been heated and brazed was still there. Since Duprat's accession to power the forge was occasionally needed again in the process of judicial interrogation when it was necessary to extract a confession from a stubborn criminal. Beside the forge, ranged out with a neatness that bespoke a master's pride in his craft, were the branding irons, pincers, crushers, needles and knives of the professional torturer. Cruder machines that any hangman might employ were also in evidence: the rack, the whipping post and great flat stones for the *peine forte et dure*. All was tidy, well lighted and clean. The door was solid oak and tight-fitting. No sound from this room could penetrate to the palace above, where the exalted personages who dwelt there did not even suspect its existence.

A veteran soldier, stone deaf and blinded in one eye by a gunpowder explosion in battle, stood staring expectantly at a little bell above the lock. When he saw it jerked by the pull cord he knew it was tinkling, his signal to open the door. He turned the heavy key in the lock; the well-oiled bolts shot back as noiseless to those outside as to himself, and a distinguished group entered the room.

Duprat seated the chief surgeon at a writing table in full view of the rack. Here usually sat a clerk of the court, who would take down the confession verbatim as it was uttered, or screamed, and later guide the criminal's hand as he made his mark or signed his name to the statement that his confession was voluntary. Today, from this vantage point, the surgeon would point with his long staff to the pieces of the corpse of the king's assailant and direct his assistants in its washing and reassembly.

Admiring the cleanliness and efficiency of the place, the surgeon remarked, "I should have thought a chamber of interrogation more terrifying, Your Eminence, full of smoke and dancing ghouls, something like Hell. This looks like a well-run operating room, rather better than most."

"It serves its purpose without theatricalities," Duprat said.

The assistants, skilled at performing amputations with a minimum of waste motion so as to reduce the period of the patient's suffering, worked rapidly at the reassembly of the body, which was taking on some semblance of human shape on the rack.

The guard at the door stood spellbound, as if he were watching a miracle. "I have seen them torn apart on that bed," he muttered, "but put together again, this is something I never saw."

"Caution your men to proceed slowly," Duprat said in a low voice to the surgeon. "I want everything carefully restored."

"They are trained to speed," the surgeon replied proudly. "They work better fast than slow."

"There is no need for speed in this case, only precision."

"Very well, Your Eminence; I shall caution them. But I'm afraid they'll make a botch of it."

"Do it the way they know best then," sighed Duprat. "Be sure he is recognizable." But the face was so badly mutilated that Duprat had begun to despair of identification.

Shortly the body of a slender young man with a narrow chest lay on the rack, almost complete.

"Master, shall we cauterize the wounds?" one of the assistants asked brightly.

"It is customary, isn't it?" the surgeon replied sternly. "Your Eminence, I am afraid it will take some time to complete the operation. The forge is cold."

"Dead men don't bleed," Duprat said.

"Very well, Your Eminence, but it is customary."

"I'd rather you sewed him together, as I have heard can be done."

The assistants looked at each other in disdain, and their master patiently expalined to Duprat, as to one who is perhaps expert in his own field but totally ignorant of another's, "Only the quack Paré employs sutures, as he calls them. No self-respecting doctor of medicine will sew up the human body like an old woman mending a garment. The only treatment for wounds is the cleansing cautery, applied red hot. I cannot raise my young men to be charlatans like Paré. The oath I take to my profession forbids me to teach them bad habits."

"I respect your scruples, *maître,*" Duprat said. "Nevertheless, this body must be sewed together so that it does not fall apart when I have it moved. The witnesses who are to examine and try to identify it cannot be brought to this place. There would be comment."

"I do not see why, Your Eminence. It looks admirable to me."

"No doubt," said Duprat.

One cannot force a professional man.

"Since you deem it offensive to do the sewing yourself," Duprat said, "I shall have someone else do it."

"No surgeon would touch it, sir."

"I was thinking of an undertaker."

"Ah, yes. That is a wholly different matter. I know the very man. My nephew is an *entrepreneur de pompes funèbres,* a great artist, a man with infinite tact, with a wonderful way of comforting the bereaved and making them a little happier when their loved ones are gone. He is still young, but he will go far. I refer many of my patients to him."

"Where can your nephew be found?"

"In a charnel house, delivering a lecture to some appren-

tices who admire him and plan to make careers as under-
takers."

"Well, it's a lucrative craft."

"I will send for him."

"No, *maître,* I will send for him."

Duprat dismissed the assistant surgeons, but said to their
master, "You had best remain behind. Your nephew may
arrive in a state of some bewilderment and need reassurance. May I assume that your men will not chatter about
the location or character of the chamber? I am sure they
would not wish to return, but if they chatter, they may."

"We learn early to hold our tongues in the healing art,"
the surgeon replied shakily. The assistants turned pale at
the threat and hastily departed.

Shortly, with a mask over his eyes, a mask that hid his
identity while he was hurried through the streets under
guard, a mask through which he could not see, so he did
not know where he was going, the surgeon's nephew was
ushered through the door.

"Shall I light the forge, Your Eminence?" the guard
asked.

Duprat shook his head. Behind his mask the nephew
could not see the negative answer; but he smelled the smell
of death, he felt the chill atmosphere of a dungeon and he
heard grave voices echoing in low and hollow tones.

"What have I done?" he cried.

Duprat motioned to the guard, who took off the man's
mask. His eye fell on the body on the rack, then on his
uncle, the surgeon, who sat at the writing table, then on
Duprat.

"The chancellor! Uncle! Why am I here?"

"There is nothing to fear," his uncle said. "His Eminence has a commission for you."

Duprat made a motion, as if tipping a glass to his lips, and the guard immediately brought him a glass of cool wine. Duprat smiled, doubled his fist and pointed at the trembling undertaker. "Oh, him, eh? And stronger! Yes, Eminence, the restorative, at once, Eminence."

"The old fellow's a faithful soul," Duprat observed in a kindly voice. "He doesn't like employment in this place, but he'd starve without it. When he does not wish to see he closes his eye. I chose him because his deafness is an asset. He can neither repeat what is said here nor does he suffer the unpleasantness of the noises that I must sometimes listen to. Please be at ease, young man. I want nothing from you but your skill, of which your uncle speaks highly."

The guard gave a cup of brandy to the nephew, who gulped it, choked, and felt better. It was spiced and fiery, usually employed to restore feeling of body and clarity of mind to those who showed sings of losing consciousness under interrogation. Clearly, thought the guard, this was a most unusual day. The newcomer had not even been touched, and already he needed the restorative. Further than that he had no curiosity. His deafness, coupled with a placid good nature and innate stupidity, had isolated him from the world, patient and stolid as an ox.

The surgeon explained the mission to his undertaker nephew. The chancellor explained why he had been blind-folded. "Your Eminence, I understand."

At closer sight of the body he was taken with a violent fit of trembling. "It is the king's assailant. I saw it happen!"

"Do you know who he is?"

"No, Your Eminence."

Duprat leaned forward, leveling a cold stare at him.

"Do you know who he is!"

"No, no!"

"What *do* you know, monsieur, that makes you shake with guilt?"

In a small voice the undertaker confessed, "I have his other hand."

"Shame!" said his uncle.

"It is a heavy offense to conceal evidence," Duprat said. Now indeed the chancellor's face was the face of an inquisitor. "I was particularly anxious to get all the pieces. Where is it, undertaker?"

"I found it on a pile of garbage. It was a beautiful specimen, long, delicate, beautifully articulated."

"I must have it at once," Duprat said.

"I dissected it," the undertaker said miserably.

"He wanted to be a surgeon," his uncle said disgustedly. "You can see why we wouldn't have him."

"Where is the hand now?"

"I was terrified at breaking the law. I burned it, Your Eminence."

Duprat frowned and hesitated, wondering for a moment, but only for a moment, whether to institute suit against the man who so casually admitted the breaking of a law, and decided against it. A greater matter was at stake and the undertaker had little or nothing to confiscate. Moreover, he knew that the old law of Louis XI, a reform in its time, that permitted the bodies of four executed criminals, and only four per year for the whole realm of France, to be lawfully dissected by the surgeons of the University of Paris, was broken every day by unorthodox enthusiasts like Dr.

Paré, who robbed graves if they could get cadavers no other way. He had little patience with the inquisitiveness of these daring new men, far less for a mere *entrepreneur de pompes funèbres*. But Dr. Paré's mechanistic turn of mind had had good results in Henri's hand. Even the old ecclesiastical prohibition against the "desecration" of the human body was softening under the tolerance of the present pope. Duprat could disapprove, but he could not turn back the tide of change that seemed to be engulfing the world. However wrong the man who stood trembling before him might be, he was transparently telling the truth; and the curiosity that had led him to pick up and dissect the assassin's hand might be put to good use now.

"Did the hand wear a ring?"

"No." He paused. "Oh no! I wouldn't steal! There were jewels of the Marquise de Meung all over the street. Had I wished to steal I'd have stolen those, Your Eminence."

A keen observation, thought Duprat.

"What sort of hand was it?"

"A student's hand, unused to work. In the solution all the grime melted away and the skin was fair as a girl's."

"You have dissected female hands too?"

The uncle looked frightened, but the nephew merely lowered his eyes in confusion.

"No, Your Eminence, but I have had occasion to feel the texture of a girl's skin."

Duprat repressed a smile of approbation: here was no ghoul, like some of the tribe.

"Was there grime under the nails?"

"Yes, Your Eminence. It melted out. It had not colored the flesh, like worked-in grime, nor stained the nails."

"Grime like the grime over there on the right hand?"

The undertaker looked at the hand of the body on the rack.

"No, that is ink. The other was mud, probably from the street."

"Ink? How do you know?"

"Most students have ink-stained fingers; some put it there to flaunt their superior position as clerks; others, who write fast, acquire it through pure carelessness."

"Like this?" Duprat held out his own right hand.

There were the stains.

"Oh, Your Eminence!"

"He's not impertinent, just stupid," said his uncle.

Duprat laughed heartily.

"That is a matter I shall decide for myself."

The guard glanced at the trio and at the dead body, and smiled in sympathy. There was seldom laughter in this room, and he liked it.

"Now sew me up that creature so it won't dismember itself again the minute it's moved," Duprat ordered.

"He hasn't got his tools," his uncle said.

"Sh-h!" said Duprat. "He'll find tools. Let's see if he does."

The young man walked to the instruments beside the cold forge and chose a long curved needle and a length of strong linen thread. He threaded the needle with a steady hand. The eye was very small; it required skill to do so. The guard looked on; usually he looked away at this point. The needle and thread was employed in the most painful and elaborate of all forms of judicial interrogation. Sturdy young malefactors, who could stand hours of the *peine forte et dure*, quailed at the threat of it and, if they lived after it had done its work, lived to be spat upon and scorned by the lowest of women of the street as they walked with a curious and characteristic stiff-legged gait to the gallows.

While the work of repair was in progress the chancellor sipped a glass of wine and the surgeon had a bite to eat.

"He is deft, for a stupid undertaker," observed his famous uncle.

"I shall have a word with you about him when he finishes," Duprat said.

"Yes, Your Eminence?"

"Nothing bad," Duprat said reassuringly.

When all was done that could be done the guard, who had edged closer to watch, murmured, "It's so nice to see the process in reverse!"

Duprat warned him back to his post at the door with a stern gesture.

"Well, it is!" the guard mumbled.

"He's a goodhearted old simpleton," Duprat said.

"I'm afraid there's not enough left to make much of a face," the undertaker said.

"Build it up with clay," Duprat said, "as you do for a funeral when a man lies in state."

"Your Eminence, I can make him look handsome as Hermes or ugly as Pluto, but I cannot make him look like himself. I was in the crowd behind him, and I saw only his back."

"Make him look like his hands, the hands that stabbed a girl and tried to kill a king," said Duprat.

"Ah, that I can do. I take your meaning. I understand."

He asked for certain materials of his trade. They were sent for: putty of pulverized marble, paintbrushes and paint. Under his sculptor's hands a face took shape. The

239

forehead was high and intellectual, the chin strong and somewhat prognathous, the cheekbones prominent. There was a suggestion of the ascetic in the pale hollow cheeks. The mouth was wide and full-lipped.

Duprat nodded, pleased. It was the face of a devotee, an enthusiast, a zealot with strong passions perpetually at war with a strong will: today the passions had won. Had those eyes been open and wild, had that mouth been open and screaming instead of silent and shut in the peace of death, it was the face of a dangerous fanatic.

"He now looks like his hands," the undertaker said, laying down his tools and wiping his hands, "but I do not know if he looks like himself."

"We shall soon find out," Duprat said. He dismissed the undertaker, who was escorted, blindfolded as before, from the interrogation chamber.

Turning to the surgeon, Duprat said, "Your nephew has great talents, *maître*."

"Your Eminence, then, will not hold it against the poor fellow that he stole and dissected a hand, contrary to the law?" The uncle's voice was pleading. "I reproach him only to chasten him, only to wean him away from his dangerous ways. He is my own flesh and blood and I love him despite his weird and unorthodox fancies."

"He is wasting his talent in a paltry profession," Duprat said sternly. "He should be a surgeon, to save life, not glorify death. You should teach him your healing art and assure his future."

The surgeon's face hardened.

Duprat continued, "You have great influence in your profession. You should admit him promptly as your own protégé to one of your classes at the University. If you do

240

so I have no doubt that the crime he confessed to can be overlooked and explained away as a lawful part of his training in surgery."

The surgeon looked dubious. "It isn't customary," he said.

"Otherwise I shall unquestionably be obliged to press charges against him," Duprat said, smiling unpleasantly.

"Your Eminence! He is enrolled as of this instant as my chief assistant! I am grateful to Your Eminence!"

"France will need surgeons in this war and the wars to come," Duprat said wearily. The long session in the interrogation chamber had fatigued him; but more work must be done, starting that very night.

He ordered the body of the king's assailant decently clothed in the remnants of the garments it had worn at the time of the attack. All were now washed and clean, having first been searched for anything that might help in the identification. There was nothing in the pockets, nothing in the purse but a student's pen, not a sou of money. "If only he had bought a lottery ticket!" thought Duprat. Then in the gathering dusk he had the body swiftly conveyed by litter to the crypt of the chapel of the Convent of Saint Mary of the Walls.

Giulietta had seen him face to face, the only person who had. Now she must see him again.

The Mother Superior of Saint Mary of the Walls greeted Duprat at the convent gate with some trepidation. Not in her lifetime nor in the lifetime of her predecessor had an Eminence honored by his presence her dilapidatd house, which subsisted on the coppers of the poor of the neighborhood and the sporadic assistance of one or two pious lords;

but through the years, as the district had deteriorated and country houses become fashionable, the gentry had moved away. The Mother Superior had little hope that Saint Mary's would outlast her own tenure of office. Now, however, the run-down convent was temporarily bathed in the glare of publicity: hospitalized therein was the king's ex-mistress; on her threshold stood the redoubtable chancellor of the king's *épargne*.

"Your Eminence!" she whispered, awed.

She had put on her least-patched habit and prepared a little speech. She had planned to say it was fortunate that a house of refuge still existed in this slum area, for a slum area needed a house of refuge far more than a rich and fashionable area, since so much more work needs to be done among God's poor than among the Devil's rich. While still in the world, the Mother Superior had been a strapping peasant girl and she still spoke with a rich country accent; she still believed that the rich somehow belonged to the Devil and the poor to God. But it suddenly struck her that the chancellor was reputed to be one of the richest men in the world; an archbishop simply could not belong to the Devil; and so her tongue was tied with the confusion of contradiction, and her little speech of welcome faded into two words, "Your Eminence!"

Duprat saw the patches in her threadbare habit; his keen nose smelled the sour odor of cheap tallow candles; he hoped they were not on the altar, an inexcusable lapse. "But she did not ask me for a sou, not a sou!" he marveled. Seldom did he visit an ecclesiastical house without being subjected to a tedious request for funds.

"Reverend Mother, I wish Madame de Meung to attempt identification of the body of the king's assailant, which my men have placed in the crypt of this house," he said, kindly, but coming directly to the point.

"She is sleeping, Your Eminence. I will waken her if I can."

"Is she lucid? Is the wound serious? I'm afraid you must waken her in any case."

The wound, said the Mother Superior, was superficial. "The girl was bleeding some, but I rubbed in a good handful of thick cobwebs I got from the garret and the bleeding stopped. Then I put a plaster on and put her to bed. No need to pay a surgeon for a little thing like that. We get worse every day here. Them and their branding irons! You wouldn't treat a hurt horse like that, would you?" Duprat conceded that he would not. "Why, they charge even *us* for treating us! Oh, that is terribly wrong, I think. Besides, she's a pretty girl and she wouldn't want to be disfigured."

Duprat shrugged. Her disfigurement did not concern the welfare of the realm.

"She was in a terribly emotional state," the Mother Superior continued, and Duprat saw in her face the prodromal shadow of guilt that means to the skilled confessor that something of consequence is about to be uttered. "I gave her a cup of Muscat wine with — with — with —"

"With what, Reverend Mother?"

"With a touch, just a touch, of a country herb to make her sleep," she said, twisting the beads of the rosary to which was suspended the cross on the breast of her habit.

"What herb, Reverend Mother?" Duprat's face was impassive, neither approving nor disapproving.

It was a kind of mushroom she knew about, she said; it calmed the nerves and made them sleep. "She was so upset."

Duprat knew about it too. He knew about many herbs and drugs that were put in the restoratives of those whom it fell to him to interrogate. Some lessened the pain and loosened the tongue; those were the best. Some merely lessened the pain; those were useful when the culprit signed the statement that the confession was voluntary. Some produced a state of mind queerly akin to insanity: the person under interrogation vehemently agreed with the slightest hint from the interrogator and even elaborated upon it; those were the worst, since after their effect wore off the person had no memory of anything he had said and wondered pitifully what had happened to his broken body.

"But is she lucid?" he asked.

"Oh yes, and she'll chatter like a magpie when I get her thoroughly roused. I did not know Your Eminence would talk to her tonight or I'd not have given her the draught."

"You did not necessarily do wrong, Reverend Mother."

She sighed, relieved, and went to waken Giulietta.

Duprat observed that Giulietta's pupils were dilated by the drug when she appeared in the crypt to view the body. She wore the coarse linen nightdress supplied by the house to transient female guests of the laity who through sudden illness or sickness or assault were taken in from the streets and nursed. The nuns had put on her feet a pair of leather sandals to protect her from the chill of the stone flagged floors, for she seemed abnormally sensitive to the cold of the place. Her lustrous hair was confined in a not-too-clean snood of some heavy castoff remnant of a garment. In such a costume Giulietta looked remarkably like a condemned criminal clothed for the stake.

"Who is this man?" Duprat asked, leaning forward, eying her intently and pointing to the corpse at her feet.

Giulietta drew back her lips in a sneer like the snarl of a mad dog and spat into its reconstructed face.

"He killed my love!"

"Madame de Meung, this is the body of the man who made an attempt on the life of King Francis. Who is he?"

"He killed my lover, he killed my love!"

"Madame de Meung, he killed no one but himself."

"You don't understand," Giulietta sobbed.

"She isn't lucid after all," said the Mother Superior.

"I think I do understand." Duprat sensed that the girl was saying that the man had "killed" her illicit love affair with the king. "Did you ever see him before, Madame de Meung?"

"Not before he rushed out at Francis."

"This is all my fault," the Mother Superior whispered.

"She is lucid," Duprat said, and asked her, "What did he say in Italian? He was shouting in Italian."

"He said Death to the Tyrant! But my love was not a tyrant; he was the dearest, sweetest friend a woman could dream of having; how they dreamt of him, and how ready with love was my love!"

"She speaks madly, as if the king were dead," the Mother Superior whispered. "I gave her too much mushroom."

"To her he is dead. Be silent, Reverend Mother." And again to Giulietta he questioned, "What sort of Italian did he cry out when he struck? What dialect? From what city?" Duprat knew that Italy, like France, possessed scores of distinctive dialects; the citizens of Venice spoke an entirely different Italian from the citizens of Florence, just as the people of Paris spoke an entirely different French from the people of Marseille.

"Just Italian," Giulietta said.

Duprat nodded. "Your home was in Marignan, was it not?"

"*Sì,* in Marignano."

Clearly, concluded Duprat, the assailant was Milanese. Since Giulietta detected no accent, hearing "just Italian," they each spoke the Italian of the duchy of Milan. This was significant. It meant, unfortunately, that a large portion of the Milanese, whither King Francis was bound, were hostile to France and favorable to the traitor Duc de Bourbon. He had made some progress in the identification of the would-be assassin, but it boded ill for France.

"You never saw him before he attacked you?"

"No."

"His face has been partially reconstructed. The populace mutilated it in their righteous anger against him when he burst out to slay the king."

"Good! Good! Good! I hope he hurt, oh, how I hope he hurt!"

"No doubt he did. Is the face as it was before?"

"It looks the same. But it is kindly and peaceful now. The Devil is out of it. The face is the same though. I hate it!" She was shivering.

"Go back to bed, Madame de Meung. You have been of great assistance to us and to the king. You will be mentioned to him as deserving of his gratitude and generosity."

"*Mai più, mai più, mai più,*" Giulietta sobbed.

"*Mai più,*" said Duprat to the Mother Superior, "means *not any more* in Italian."

The Mother Superior said, "Poor girl."

The nuns took her back to bed and gently tucked her in, the corpse remaining in the crypt for other witnesses to view. Duprat remarked to the Mother Superior, "You are somewhat ill equipped to house a distinguished convalescent like the Marquise de Meung. But she must remain here till she is thoroughly cured. Thoroughly. Do you understand? Madame de Meung is a controversial figure now. Do you understand?"

"I think I do, Your Eminence," the Mother Superior said hesitantly.

She understood better next day when a group of stonemasons and ironworkers appeared to repair her walls and place bars on Giulietta's hospital chamber.

"The chancellor might have saved himself the cost of those bars," mused the Mother Superior. "The girl won't want to leave. What is there for her now in the outside world?" The mule-load of fragrant wax candles, however, rejoiced her heart. "Enough for the altar for years! But the chancellor doesn't know a thing about women, not a thing."

Students from the Italian "nation" of the University were summoned next to view the remains; but none recognized him nor did any of the professors who lectured there. "No, he was not an enrolled student."

Grocers and beggars and tavernkeepers from the district were herded in to attempt an identification; but he seemed to have been too poor to give alms to beggars, who always remembered their benefactors, and he seemed never to have frequented taverns. Nor could a lodginghouse proprietor be found who claimed him as a lodger. Here the chancellor's reputation for thoroughness worked in the interest of justice: he had offered to pay the corpse's back rent if any were due. Many a shabby innkeeper of the district would have liked to identify the body and pocket the prize; but not one did. The man was simply unknown.

Duprat concluded that the would-be assassin had only recently departed from Milan, after war was inevitable, and come into France, acting on his own; but, always significantly, a part of a widespread dissident population of the Italian duchy.

Examination of the corspe, which had not been embalmed, took some days. It had now become offensive.

As a final witness Mario Campi was called. By this time the chancellor was holding a clove-scented handkerchief to his nose.

"No," said Campi, "I never saw him before. The doublet is good work, very expensive. But no coat of arms, no insignia. Probably some son of a rich merchant. That's bad. That means there's bourgeois money against us. Has Your Eminence searched the pockets, purse, sleeves?"

"Everything," Duprat said. "We found nothing."

"If Your Eminence please, may I search?"

Duprat shrugged.

"There may be a winning lottery ticket there. Who knows? Everybody buys lottery tickets. Would it not be an interesting coincidence if the winning ticket were to be found on the corpse of the king's assailant? The prize would instantly revert to the Crown, would it not? Confiscation?"

"It would if it proved to be the winning ticket," Duprat said.

"Let me look."

"If you can touch the creature."

Campi made an expressive gesture. "It is nothing. Even in the highest sense, it is nothing at all. How does it differ from what it was a hundred years ago, from what it will be a hundred years hence? From dust of the past to dust of the future there intrudes a transitory manifestation of elaborate carrion, that is all. Excuse me, Your Eminence; I shall not take long."

Campi's fingers flew, deft as a purse snatcher's for all their pudginess. "Ha!" he said and from a rent below the pistol hole he drew forth a lottery ticket. "I thought so. Sometimes they sew them into their clothes."

"Give it to me," said Duprat.

"But Eminence! It might win! In fact, with a bit of assistance from divine providence, and the proper man to make the draw, it will win; and millions of confiscated prize money need not be paid but will pour into the *épargne*, subject to the usual taxes, to the glory of France. No?"

"Give it to me."

"Oh, very well. But in Italy we'd make the most of a windfall like this."

Duprat tore it up.

"Well, that one won't win," said Campi.

Duprat was outraged at Campi's cynicism, but he was forced to concede in his innermost thoughts that the wretch's scheme had a certain twisted merit. It appalled him to contemplate the cruel law of chance that could favor this potential regicide as much as, say, the deserving old veteran in the chamber of interrogation. So many people must *not* win, if the next lottery, absolutely essential to the treasury, were not to be shunned as dishonest by all the good Frenchmen who so far had evinced such faith in the scheme. "Bend a little, Antoine Duprat," he adjured his scruples. "Let not the ugly whisper of corruption sully the project that works for the salvation of my king, that glittering misfit, my beloved country, and myself, lest I be cast aside and no longer able to serve them."

He ordered the body of the assailant placed in a hole in unhallowed ground and covered with quicklime. All dissolved in bubbles and a stench save the built-up marble face, and shortly that too fused in the magma of hot lime and its lineaments were destroyed. Somewhere in Italy, Duprat supposed, a father might be mourning a son. But many Italians were about to die and many Frenchmen too, and Swiss and Austrians and Swabians and Savoyards and slant-eyed Hungarians from the eastern reaches of the Emperor's domains, all, all the sons of somebody; and what was one disappearance, more or less, in the battles that would be storming over Italy?

In the Convent of Saint Mary of the Walls, now suddenly become fashionable, Giulietta healed and viewed her confining bars with somber disdain. "The chancellor might have spared himself the expense," she mused. She gave her rings to the Mother Superior to adorn a chalice. One blood-red ruby, which the Reverend Mother said she had dug from the flesh of her neck where the point of the dagger had buried it, she kept. "I've a use for this," she said. "Child, it's your ruby," the Reverend Mother said.

On his estates in Tonnerre, Henri received an urgent message from the chancellor.

✲ ✲ ✲ 13 ✲ ✲

T HE FRENCH ARMY burst through the Italian Alps like a whirlwind and descended upon the Lombard plain. The beginning of the war was marked everywhere by spectacular successes. Town after town fell before King Francis. His mobile artillery, brilliantly commanded and skillfully serviced by his engineers, battered down city gates and cut great breaches in city walls. Through the rubble and dust the demoralized defenders would sally forth to fight hand to hand with the French cavalrymen, and were pinned to the ground by gaily decorated spears and slaughtered by maces, arrows and swords. The courtly traditional feudal weapons were marvelously coordinated with the terrible new weapon of gunpowder. The combination bore down all resistance, and soon it appeared that the war would be short. King Francis, the First Gentleman of Europe, was rapidly acquiring a reputation as Europe's first general.

Milan, capital city of the duchy, fell after a token resistance. Since Marignan, Milan had acknowledged French overlordship. King Francis, exalted by victory and prompted by his own instinctive generosity, now assumed an attitude so statesmanlike as hardly to admit of improvement; and Duprat was forced to concede, "Sometimes that man seems inspired!" But then, he remembered, a man so active, a man who did so many things, must occasionally do exactly the right thing. The laws of chance predestined it.

King Francis entered Milan at high noon in bright sunlight at the head of his cavalcade. Armor shone, pennants fluttered, the visors of the chevaliers were open, their handsome young faces were smiling. The ugly cannon were left outside the walls. He let it be known that he regarded the Milanese as loyal friends, temporarily led astray by traitors like the Duc de Bourbon. He proclaimed a general amnesty. Many cheered him as a liberator.

He took up headquarters in the Ducal Palace, sent back to the Louvre some paintings and statuary that caught his eye and wrote a series of happy letters home.

To Duprat he said, "I shall return by spring," and asked for money to pay an enormous bonus to his troops. The chancellor gladly complied. To the Queen Mother he wrote, *"Madame ma Mère:* All goes well. The Italian weather is beautiful. Soon you may lay down the tedious state duties you have so generously assumed for me, for soon I shall be in Paris again, not without some additional military laurels as you may have heard." To Anne de Pisseleu d'Heilly he wrote a love poem and hid it in a jewel casket filled with rose petals and pearls, bidding her wear the pearls for his love and water the rose petals, which were fragrant but dry, back to life with the lonely tears that he knew she must be shedding for him during his absence. To Giulietta he wrote nothing; she had quite slipped his mind.

Then he was informed, to his utter amazement, that the city of Pavia, twelve miles to the south, scarcely the distance covered in a brisk morning's hunt, was dissatisfied with him and that a considerable force of Italians, Imperial troops and dissident Frenchmen, adherents of the Duc de Bourbon, had gathered there to oppose him. He set out at once to chastise the impudent rascals and finish off the nuisance.

He marched headlong into disaster.

He ordered his artillery to beat down the walls, as had proven so successful heretofore with other towns, and the maneuver was started. Pavia was strongly defended and amply provisioned, but no one expected it to stand up for a longe siege under the bruising of the wonderful French cannon. Aware that sieges were going out of style, the Emperor Charles sent a flying column of Imperial troops up from Naples to relieve the city before it fell. When the column appeared the French simply swiveled round their cannon and pumped grapeshot, stones, iron nails, anything that was little and scattered and killed, whistling into their ranks. Broken, they fled in terror.

Shouting "They are ours!" King Francis led a mounted charge in pursuit, with the intention of taking them all prisoner. In that instant his reputation as a general was destroyed, for he imprudently placed all his shining cavaliers and his own priceless person directly in the line of fire of his own cannon. The dumbfounded artillerymen swore and stopped shooting. Their matches smoldered out and their guns grew cold; the king had masked their target. Had he not pursued he might have won the day and spared himself a year of the most humiliating experience that could ever befall a man of his stamp.

The defenders of Pavia, seeing the French guns silent and turned the other way, sallied forth and overwhelmed them, dragging them into the city together with their crews.

Francis, spurring for the hunt, made contact with the fleeing quarry and began to hack them down. But there now ensued a tactical surprise for which he was not prepared: more new weapons, more gunpowder.

There were fifteen hundred Spanish arquebusiers in the retreating column. The French had neglected this portable version of the cannon, but the methodical Emperor had been impressed by it, a German invention, in one of his Dutch provinces and equipped his Spanish troops, the best disciplined of all his soldiers, with thousands of them. These arquebusiers were drilled to fire at will, not waiting for orders. They had also perfected a tactic of letting themselves be surrounded, then shooting in all directions at once in a sustained and concentrated volley, "pointing their weapons now here, now there, in a deadly manner marvelous to behold," as the bemused chroniclers set down in their records. Within the memory of men still living the voice of battle had consisted of the shouts of men and the clang of steel on steel. Then had come the new thunder of cannon. Now had been added another sound, the continuous barking of portable firearms, guns that could pierce a knight's armor and kill at four hundred paces. Truly, the voice of battle was changing, ever less courtly, ever more murderous.

Laboring and sweating in the battle, laying about him with his sword when his spear snapped in the body of a gorgeous Italian knight who opposed him, while bullets picked off his best chevaliers and hurled them from their mounts, King Francis sustained an uncomfortable thought: The glory of war had departed, and war itself might soon become obsolete in a world where cruel small and impersonal pellets, no respecter of persons, could cut down the knight and the churl indiscriminately — at four hundred paces.

It was often the custom of mounted men to spear to death an opponent's horse, for then one's opponent was forced to fight on foot where, awkward and sluggish by reason of the weight of his armor, he could easily be killed or, more profitably, captured and held to ransom. The Spanish arquebusiers did not often kill horses; they did not need to; they preferred the mounted men. As the French cavaliers toppled dead from their mounts the horses went wild, snorting and charging through the ranks, fearful of the new noise of the arquebuses, trampling down their late masters, adding immeasurably to the confusion.

In this sad and sorry battle King Francis found himself surrounded by a group of grinning arquebusiers, who leveled their guns at him and demanded surrender.

Francis shouted, swore, brandished his sword and charged into their midst. They shot his horse dead and he tumbled into the dust, his sword falling out of his hand.

A powder-grimed arquebusier, a captain of some sort, picked up the royal sword and, while strong hands held the king, replaced it in its scabbard. "For that at least I thank you," Francis said. The fellow replied in French with a characteristic Spanish lisp, "Your Majesty is welcome," and the First Gentleman of Europe was roughly hustled from the field out of danger, with sweat and tears of shame streaming down into his scented beard.

Behind him the French cavalry, leaderless and decimated, turned tail and took flight.

In Paris the chancellor sat down to contemplate the appalling situation now presented to his eye by the map of Europe. To the north across the English Channel King Henry VIII was a wily neutral, courting both sides and content for the moment to see them weaken each other. Dynastically he was extremely close to the Emperor Charles, for he had married Catherine of Aragon, the Emperor's maternal aunt. But Henry was tired of her; he had long contemplated divorcing her; and he was in desperate financial straits. "He should institute a lottery," Duprat chuckled. "But the English wouldn't take to a lottery. No imagination." On the whole, with the aid of some cautiously placed bribes in Henry's privy purse, England could be counted on to remain neutral as long as Henry's financial, marital and (it was whispered) medical problems continued.

Southward beyond the Pyrenees glowered the haughty kingdom of Spain, the Emperor's most loyal nation, rich, powerful and implacably hostile. But the Pyrenees interposed a barrier against invasion.

On the Mediterranean coast of France the port of Marseille was invested by sea, but Andrea Doria was coming with a fleet to its rescue. Doria was a fascinating Italian admiral, an orphan from his youth, rootless, stateless, a soldier of fortune who had entered Duprat's service for a fortune in bribes from the king's *épargne*. "He would leave me if the Emperor paid him more," Duprat knew, "but the Emperor won't, and so he'll be faithful." He had a genius for winning battles.

Thus King Henry was poor and the Emperor was stingy,

and thus was made secure the English Channel and the Mediterranean coast, while mountains secured the Spanish frontier.

But to the east, the map of Italy, where the war was being fought, was leprous with trouble spots. Some towns were held by the French, some by the Emperor. The Lombard plain was the battleground, the duchy of Milan the prize. After Pavia the native Milanese found their duchy entirely occupied by foreigners, half French, half Imperialist, each holding out in strongly defended cities and towns. In the countryside between, the happy Italian peasant trudged his produce to French or Imperialist markets indiscriminately: never had prices been so high. Few battles were fought during this leaderless period, but in one disastrous skirmish the Chevalier Bayard was slain by a bullet from an arquebus.

The king's captivity and Bayard's death plunged all France into gloom and despondency. What was left to cling to, what was left to believe in, when one national hero was behind bars and the other was in his grave?

Duprat knew only one weapon to fight the power of gunpowder: the power of gold.

In the dark and uncertain days that followed upon the capture of the king, even the brave Queen Mother wavered. From Italy Francis had scrawled her one line; the courier's sweat or seepage from some shower through which he had ridden, or perhaps the king's tears, had blurred it: *Tout est perdu fors l'honneur.* All is lost, save honor.

She asked Duprat, "Wouldn't they let him write more? To tell me where he is, or how he fares, or even whether he is wounded? Chancellor, this is a heavy burden for a mother's heart to bear."

Duprat could give her little comfort other than to assure her that captive kings are royally treated and that he knew from eyewitnesses of the battle that Francis had not been wounded when captured.

Then news came, not from the Emperor but from an English agent in Duprat's pay, that the king had been removed to Madrid in the hard and barren heart of Spain. He was not being royally treated. He was actually confined behind bars in a dilapidated Moorish castle on a high hill where the air was thin, the nights were cold and the sun shone mercilessly hot in the daytime. Close by were the remnants of local forests, rapidly disappearing under the axes of hungry peasants who cut them down to burn charcoal, and a luxurious hunting lodge that a mentally defective Spanish king had built in the days when the rainfall was more plentiful and the forests more extensive and full of game. In recent centuries a drought seemed to have settled over the area and blighted it. Beyond the stunted forests was nothing but sand and rocks and clay from horizon to horizon. To this wild and desolate spot the Emperor came often, because it suited his melancholy temperament and because it benefited his asthma. In this place of maximum security and discomfort he chose to confine his pleasure-loving royal prisoner.

"They are trying to break his spirit!" the Queen Mother cried, near to tears. "Chancellor, you must hurry."

"Madame, I will smash his iron bars with bars of gold!"

It was at this juncture that Henri received the urgent message from Duprat, "Monsieur le Chevalier de Tonnerre: I need your strong right arm. Come."

"Thank God the chancellor finally relents!" Henri cried. "At last I shall have a command." He had chafed at the inactivity forced upon him; but the vigilance of Duprat's guard of honor had never relaxed, nor had their instructions changed. They were always with him, and would now accompany him up to Paris.

Marie smiled. "Uncle Antoine sometimes has a wry sense of humor, Henri. It is surely something important, but do not be too downcast if it isn't a command."

Henri cautioned her against riding and sudden movements. "I should have liked to be here when my son is born," he said, "but that cannot be."

Marie smiled. "Perhaps you will."

He shook his head; her time was close; he would be far away in Italy. He kissed her and spurred up to Paris. He took with him a troop of his own men. They had been filtering back from Italy for some time. One of them said, "I have not heard, chevalier, that troops are now being sent into Italy. Things look pretty well stalemated there."

"That's just the time when the chancellor will strike!" Henri said. "Will he not?" he asked one of Duprat's officers. But the officer knew nothing of Duprat's plans. No one ever did.

Paris was in a festive mood. Church bells were ringing, the populace was in holiday dress, and great piles of brush were being gathered in the market places for bonfires that night. At first Henri assumed that a great victory had been won or that the king had been released. But the talk in the streets was all of something else: this was the day of the draw in the national lottery. Looking at the excited crowds Henri mused, "Every one of those poor devils expects to be a millionaire by suppertime."

His admiration for Duprat soared. To be able to distract

a whole nation at a moment of national calamity, to give each man hope and something to live for touched on the miraculous. Even more of a miracle was a shout he heard from the street. Some tipsy reveler, foretasting the sweets of winning, cried *"Vive Duprat!"* Round him a cluster of good-natured companions amused themselves by guiding the fellow into a tavern, to keep him drunk and preserve the illusion of riches as long as he provided entertainment. Henri heard their remarks as he passed: "Well, really how do we know it is an illusion?" "Maybe he's got the second sight." "Well, he's certainly seeing double now." "Maybe he'll actually win!" "No, maybe I'll be the one." "Maybe it'll be me!" *"Vive le chancelier de l'épargne!"* The hated prelate who formerly never set foot outside his archiepiscopal palace without being hissed was now being cheered in the streets.

"And even when all these poor people lose except one, as assuredly they will," Henri realized, "they will still lose only a sou." No one would suffer. It was a game. It was entertainment. Everyone would hope for better luck next time, demanding a new and bigger lottery as soon as possible.

In front of the Louvre an elevated platform had been erected with a gay canopy to shield it from the weather, though the weather had been fine for a week and every rheumatic in Paris predicted it would continue fair. He could feel it in his bones.

The platform was cordoned off by a line of archers in holiday tabards. A huge wicker basket shaped roughly like a churn and fine woven, big enough to hold a team of horses, stood in the center of the platform. It was mounted on an axle and it could be turned by a crank, also much like certain types of country churns. Everyone knew what it contained, and the contents would be thoroughly mixed before the draw.

Inside were all the tens of thousands of possible winning numbers, each written on a slip of paper and sealed in a nutshell. The churn would turn, the shells would tumble, a man would thrust in his hand and draw one out, a clerk would read the number, a crier would shout it to the crowd, and someone — man, woman or child, nobleman, peasant, beggar or thief from the Paris gutters — would read his ticket (or be told, if he could not read) that he was a millionaire. Provision had been made to expose the winning number under a sheet of glass for all to see after the draw, so that everyone would know that the draw had been honest.

Henri mounted the steps of the Louvre suffused with high hopes and elated by a great expectation. Guards saluted as he followed a black-habited friar down long halls; doors opened before them. "I am one of the chancellor's secretaries," the friar said amiably. "His Eminence is expecting you and will see you at once."

"What does he want me for?"

"Who can say?" said the friar.

Henri grinned. "You could, if you would."

He was ushered into the chancellor's private apartment, startlingly bare and severe in contrast with the rest of the luxurious palace.

Duprat was thinner and grim, but his face was alive with nervous energy. He sat at a desk, his pen flying over a sheaf of papers, writing his signature. Without looking up he said, "Sit down, Henri."

Henri sat down on the only other chair in the room.

Duprat signed the last of the documents, pushed aside the pile and reached for the little bell at his elbow. Before it stopped tinkling another secretary glided into the room, silent as the shadow of some quick scurrying animal, removed the papers and disappeared.

"Criers will be shouting the names on those papers all over town in an hour," Duprat said, nodding his head toward the door that had shut on the secretary. He looked at Henri for the first time and smiled thinly. "A lot of unworthy persons are going to be made very happy tonight. Those, Henri, were pardons. Nothing adds to a celebration like emptying the jails. Of course I'll have to fill them up again tomorrow, probably with the same rascals. But tonight they'll add to the cheering, poor fools."

"Marie is well and sends you her love, sir," Henri said uncertainly.

"I know how she is. Did you think I didn't know? I would not have summoned you otherwise. But it is good to hear you confirm it." Duprat dipped his handkerchief into a glass of water in which floated a single rose and refreshed his forehead and inhaled the scent. "Ah," he said. "That's much better."

He looked faint with fatigue; Henri wondered when last he had slept.

The chancellor continued, "Tonight, just before supper, while it's still light you are to draw the winning number in the lottery. That is why I sent for you."

Henri felt his heart sink. Was this the mission? Was this the command he had hoped for?

"Why me, Your Eminence?" His distress showed in his face and Duprat chuckled.

"Bayard is dead. The king is captive. Follow in their foot-

steps, Henri, and you will end like them, glorious and in-
effectual. I read in your angry eyes that you would not fear
such a death or such a captivity, deeming a brave extinction the ultimate sacrifice for France; and indeed it is a
reputable notion that one can do no more for honor, country and king, than lay down one's life. I tell you one can
do more. What if, for example, that easy lazy sacrifice were
futile? Worse, if it were out of tune with the times? Worst
of all, if it fell short of what one could do to be of genuine
service? What good to France is one more brave dead
chevalier when I have better use for him alive? Are you
quite sure that you do not desire a command simply for
your own self-glorification?"

Henri blushed. "I will never concede that."

"Your color concedes it; it is one factor in all ambition
and convicts you of falling prey to the common temptation
of military glory. So fell Bayard. So was captured the king.
My dear nephew, do you suppose for one instant that I
would hesitate to send you to Italy and your death if I
thought you could thus win the war? I would also send you
to Madrid, even though it meant widowhood for Marie, if I
thought you could bring back the king."

"Sir, I could try."

"I cannot afford trials. I must have certainty. To achieve
certainty only mountains of gold will suffice, mountains
more when I spend the first."

"All I have is yours, sir."

Duprat snorted. "I want the treasure of Jacques Bonhomme, not the hereditary rents of a few devoted chevaliers.
That treasure is in that basket outside the door, Henri, in
the form of lottery tickets. And I have chosen you to make
the winning draw."

Again Henri asked, "Why me?"

"Because you are the typical Frenchman, Henri; not so blindly feudal as Bayard, not so madly modern as the king; not so dull as a peasant, not so wily as a statesman; not so noble as a *duc,* not so humble as a bourgeois. You are neither so young as to be totally irresponsible nor so old as to be impossibly conservative. Those who know you esteem you, yet you are not so well known as to be a target for violent popular emotions, as is the lot of those who are famous or notorious. In short, my dear nephew, you are that extraordinary phenomenon: the average good man."

Henri colored furiously. The chancellor chuckled.

"With a healthy temper," he added.

Later when Henri told Marie of the interview he said, "It sounded like my epitaph: *ci gît le chevalier sans nom et sans renom.*"

She replied, "Uncle Antoine was tired, Henri. You've name and renown enough for me. How did the draw go?"

"Oh that," Henri said. "A truly deserving old veteran won."

As dusk began to fall the chancellor appeared on the balcony of the Louvre and addressed the huge crowd that had gathered around the high platform to witness the draw. He pronounced a short prayer for the safety and quick release of the king and reminded the multitude that their pennies would contribute towards his ransom, would bring him home and assure victory to France in the war. Then he blessed them all, with a special blessing for the fortunate unknown person who, in the next few moments, would find himself a millionaire through the working of pure chance.

Then he gave a signal to the man at the crank and the great wicker basket began to turn.

Then he retired to his chapel. Kneeling, with his head unbowed, his eyes wide open and looking straight up to Heaven, he prayed, "Father, forgive me. I knew not what else to do," and waited for an answer.

It came, as he knew it would, from the square outside. There was a blare of trumpets and a number cried out in a stentorian voice.

"Henri will have stuck in his thumb and pulled out the plum," Duprat mused.

There was a moment of silence and then a mighty shout.

"Someone will have told the deaf old guard of the chamber of interrogation that the laws of pure chance have singled him out," Duprat murmured, nodding his head, listening.

Then came the name of the winner, roared out by the wildly cheering crowd. Duprat nodded. It was the right name. Nothing had gone wrong. He cocked his ear to detect a hiss or a boo in the ocean of cheers. He heard not one. "I knew he'd prove popular," Duprat thought. An unlikelier winner could hardly be imagined. "They are satisfied it was honest."

Now they'll be escorting the bewildered old fellow up the steps, the chancellor continued in his thoughts. I must go out and congratulate him.

As he left the chapel he cast a farewell glance at the calm stone faces of the saints that looked down at him out of their niches in the walls. He shrugged his shoulders in an eloquent Gallic gesture of helplessness. "What else could I have done?"

On the steps of the Louvre he raised the stunned winner

from the kneeling position to which he had fallen, shook him by the hand and exhorted him to lead an honest life and contribute generously to charity out of his new-found wealth.

The crowd, having discovered that the winner was deaf as a post, roared with laughter, cheered the winner, cheered Duprat, cheered the king, cheered Chance and carried the millionaire on their shoulders in triumph through the streets.

The chancellor smiled benignantly on the crowds, raised his voice and cried, "Listen, all you who are lucky enough to be able to hear! In your celebration tonight do not spend your last penny. Save one for tomorrow! Tomorrow new tickets for the new lottery go on sale! Good luck to you all!"

Then he clapped his hands, the signal for music to sound, and the general celebration began, starting with the broaching of free casks of wine and the lighting of an enormous bonfire in front of the Louvre. This was Duprat's own personal bonfire and he lingered a moment to make sure it was well alight before he retired into the palace.

Workmen with buckets of oil soaked the platform on which the draw had just taken place. Others heaped faggots of dry brush underneath and on top till the basket was surrounded like a criminal at the stake. Torches were applied and the entire structure blazed up in a pillar of fire and smoke. Guards kept back the crowds, lest someone get hurt — and lest someone pick up the nutshells before they were consumed.

Every shell contained the same, the winning number.

The half-wit printer who had struck off the slips was returned to the lunatic asylum from which he had been taken for this, his last job, and shut up in permanent solitary confinement.

The blind cripples and blind beggars who had inserted the numbers were released again to hobble the streets, praising the chancellor for giving them alms and a day's employment. They had seen nothing, and so could do no harm.

All over Paris other bonfires were lighted. Far into the night a glow hung over the city. Fireworks streaked into the sky, roman candles exploded in showers of colored sparks like falling stars. From the countryside it looked as if the city were under siege, and madly, absurdly happy to be so. The chancellor retired early and slept peacefully, his conscience clear, and smiled when he heard the music of dancing and laughter in his dreams.

Well could he rest and relax. Never had his policy of aggrandizing the *épargne* seemed so farsighted and successful. Never had he personally been so powerful. That very night, while he slept and congratulated himself, a courier was riding to Madrid under a flag of truce with an offer to the Emperor: France was willing to negotiate for the king's ransom and any reasonable demand would be met.

The chancellor had no doubt of the outcome.

14

A S MARIE'S TIME drew close, then imminent, then
hourly expected, Duprat promised himself a holiday.
Not every day does a man become a great-grand-uncle.
Childless and lonelier each year as his power increased in
the state, trusting no one, suspicious of everyone, he cherished Marie because she asked nothing of him and he
shared her Montholon blood; and he was prepared to
cherish her child also, and prayed daily it would be a boy.
"I shall be very old when he grows up to be a man, but I
vow to stay alive to make him something great in the
world!" It was nepotism of the most flagrant sort, he knew;
but he grinned, "Nepotism be hanged! Who's to stop me?"
He fretted because Marie took so long about the business
and he sent daily couriers to Tonnerre. They returned
with the message, Not yet.

Then a death intervened to delay his holiday further. "It
is as if she knew this would happen and held things back
just to help me out. Bless that sweet dutiful girl!" He
smiled indulgently.

It was a major state death, that required several days of attention and much diplomatic correspondence if the most was to be got out of it.

Poor Queen Claude, having long since lost the will to live, simply breathed her last alone in her bed one night shortly after the drawing of the lottery. She, who had been impotent and neglected in life, became powerful in death, a highly negotiable pawn in French diplomacy, since, with her passing, King Francis was a bachelor again. Though a prisoner, his prestige rocketed; he became the most eligible prince in Christendom. Numberless alliances were now open to France, and Duprat set out to encourage them all. He elaborated a month-long period of mourning, and sent his couriers spurring throughout the Christian and heathen worlds with the momentous news.

In England King Henry VIII put on a cloak of violet, mourning in the color reserved for a French prince of the blood, reminding Europe that he still numbered among his titles "King of France"; and looked around for some likely English princess to offer King Francis. Henry was worried about the Emperor's victory at Pavia and wished to restore the balance of power in Europe, to say nothing of the pleasant possibility of a half-English prince in line for the throne of France if an English marriage should prove fruitful. Henry had also accepted an enormous subsidy from Duprat and was grateful to be freed from an irksome Parliament, who were forever meddling with his expenditures and his personal life.

As far away as Turkey the Sultan, Suleiman the Magnificent, mourned Queen Claude and inquired of his favorite wife, Roxelana, who was a Christian, whether there might not be among his Christian subjects some pretty princess whom Francis might fancy. There were many, she told him: the slim and seductive Hungarians, the extraordinary sophisticated Greeks, adept at love and hence able to influence the French king, who was known to be fond of women, as well as exotic ladies of noble families in Transylvania, Trebizond, Moldavia, Persia — a veritable *embarras de richesses*. "Riches never embarrass me," the Grand Turk said smiling. "This Antoine Duprat, this chancellor of the *economies* of France, as they call their extravagances, has sent me a most noble gift of French gold, and suggests an alliance, and asks only in return that I harry the Eastern provinces of the Empire. Such is always a pleasure. Naturally I shall oblige." Shortly the Sultan did.

Thus, with bribes of gold and promises of alliances, among those who were outright infidels and those who were toppling on the brink of schism, the chancellor clawed and gnawed all around the frontiers of the Emperor Charles's vast complex of nations, corroding the edges, till the world wondered whether the kingdom of France or the Holy Roman Empire was encircled and threatened.

In Madrid the Emperor sulked and refused to see his royal prisoner; but he removed Francis's bars, allowed him to hunt and surrounded him with luxury. "It was high time I was treated like a king!" Francis wrote to Duprat. "Poor Claude could not have died at a more convenient time." And to Anne de Pisseleu d'Heilly he wrote, "My Precious: You would hardly have known your friend yesterday, so bristly and savage was my appearance. How I should have frightened you! Can you imagine, my dear one, I was not even permitted my barber!" Now, however, he felt himself again, and was, as he said, bursting with love. Duprat intercepted the letter, sighed, sealed it again and sent it on to the girl. Then, having done all that could be done for France for the moment, he took his holiday. The people cheered him all the way, but his mood was grave. The dispatches from Tonnerre still read: Not yet.

From the Louvre in Paris to the country seat of the counts of Tonnerre one traveled a short distance as reckoned in miles, but an age away as Time was reckoned. Here all was as it had been for ages, before the ferment of the Italian New Learning burst over the world and upset the good, old, but vastly uncomfortable feudal way of life. Here the chancellor, who in Paris was accounted a reactionary, was deemed a most modern statesman, some said dangerously modern.

The dowager duchess of Montholon had traveled to Tonnerre to be present at the birth of her grandchild, stoutly declaring that the process was a normal and natural one and that she had no apprehension, glaring malevolently, however, at Henri, who was the author of all Marie's pain.

"Mothers-in-law can't help hating us at a time like this," chuckled the old Comte de Tonnerre. "You should have heard your grandmother, Henri. Tongue like a serpent when you were born. One would have thought I had forcibly violated your mother. But my mother-in-law got over it, and yours will too."

The directness of the old man's allusion offended Henri; but then, his father had not had the advantages of the new liberal education, and in any case the old are always a little gross. Yet he was aware that this was the father, this was the ancient château in which he had grown up, and at this crisis in his life it was comforting to have around him the familiar stiff traditional atmosphere of his youth. He wondered if he would ever seem rough and crude to his son, now knocking at the portal of this world. He supposed he would. And after his son, his son's sons — what would they think of him in the after-centuries? In the tenseness of the moment, awed that his body was being perpetuated in the infant body of a child in the miracle of birth, his mind leapt ahead to the France of 1600, 1700, 1800, 1900. Would there be a France in such an unthinkably distant year? If there were, there would be counts of Tonnerre.

"I think, sir, that the birth of an heir works a great change in one's sense of values," he said to his father.

"Eh, boy? What?"

Henri repeated his observation, somewhat sententiously.

"Can't say I remember," the comte said rubbing his chin. "The change didn't last in me, if I ever felt it."

Marie's mother was abrupt with everyone, scarcely picked at her supper, looked pale and found excuses to visit the chancellor several times during the night. Duprat had stationed himself in an antechamber outside the closed door beyond which the birth was in progress.

"Nothing to worry about," Duprat said smiling, nodding, encouraging.

"That's what I came to tell *you!*" said the dowager duchess. "You ought not to be pacing the floor like a silly young first-time father. That dreadful Henri ought to be doing that."

"Henri is pacing elsewhere, I am informed. And I call to your attention, Agathe, that I am not pacing. I am seated most comfortably. Who said I was pacing?"

"I heard you when I listened at the door before I came in."

"Madame," he chuckled, "permit me to offer you a place in my service. Where would you like to spy? England? Turkey? Canada? Spain?"

He lifted her out of her mood and made her smile. But when she heard a stifled cry through the door she said, "I think I shall go to my room now."

A servant whom she had not noticed before ushered her out and she hurriedly departed. An unpleasant odor of faded lilies emanated from him. She wondered how Duprat with his sensitive nose could tolerate it. But then, the chancellor was always surrounded by odd creatures and no doubt this one had its function. Then too, the odor might be something the midwife was using in the birth chamber. In this the anxious mother hit very near the mark.

Henri too came into the anteroom from time to time, but Duprat chased him away. "Go to your father, boy. You're no good here."

Again a stifled cry from beyond the door. "She needs me," Henri cried.

"You're the last person she needs," Duprat growled. "She'll need you tomorrow."

It was comforting that the chancellor thought there would be a tomorrow for Marie. Like everyone else who came in contact with Antoine Duprat, Henri bent to his will, and indeed was content to retreat out of hearing of Marie's cries. "But she should cry louder," Henri muttered as he left the room. "She's holding back. That's no good. Pride, pride, pride!"

"A mortal sin, no doubt," Duprat said, "and perfectly admirable. Go to your father, Henri."

During the night, when the cries grew louder and came at shorter intervals, Duprat suddenly stood up and said, "I cannot stand it any more."

The servant at the door nodded, pulled out of his jerkin a goosequill full of a white powder, bit off both ends and boldly entered the birth chamber.

The *sage-femme* squealed in outrage, her assistants drew back from the intrusion of a man, an unheard-of presence at a birth. The man approached the pierced chair where Marie was in difficult labor in the birth position.

He inserted the goosequill first into one nostril, then the other, and blew. The powder penetrated the nasal cavities and entered her throat, causing her to choke and sneeze violently. Then the man left the chamber.

"They'll think the sneezing did it," the man said, aggrieved, to Duprat.

"Who cares what they think, so long as it's done."

"But I am an apothecary, Your Eminence! I have my pride. The drug does far more than cause sneezing. Indian tobacco can do that. It contracts the belly, it expels the burden —"

"Would you be here if I didn't know what it does? Now take your stench out of my presence!"

"Yes, Eminence," whined the little apothecary, and scuttled away from the great man's ire. "I have left the wine."

"Out!"

But in the morning the apothecary was handsomely rewarded.

Suddenly there was another cry, high-pitched and a trifle absurd, for as yet it expressed no emotion, neither pain nor pleasure nor anger nor fear, the first cry of the newborn who as yet have not learned that breathing does not require such frantic expansion of the lungs.

"So men are born, so men die, gasping," thought Duprat, slipping to his knees and thanking God, his smile verging on the beatific.

After a suitable interval, while the women inside were doing what was necessary with cobwebs, scissors, water and thread, Duprat knocked impatiently at the door.

"Well?" he said sharply. "Does it take all this time?"

"One moment, one moment, Your Eminence!"

The voices were flustered but happy; he could hear in their tone that all was well.

Then the door opened and the *sage-femme* presented him with an armful of lace out of which came an astonishing volume of lusty cries.

"A boy!" the *sage-femme* pronounced, proud as if she personally were responsible.

"How is the mother?"

"As well as can be expected after that *man* came in and complicated things."

"Send for the father. I am going in."

"I wouldn't, Your Eminence."

He thrust her aside and entered the birth chamber.

Marie's face was white as the pillows on which her head rested; her hair clung damply to her brow. Duprat felt his spine tingle. Death had passed very close, might still be lurking in the room. He had sensed the same dread Presence in the chamber of interrogation.

He was prepared. He raised her head and held to her lips the goblet of wine that the apothecary had left. "Drink, Marie," he said, and Marie took a swallow. "Another," and she obeyed automatically. "Another!" But she shook her head and said, "No more."

Duprat smiled. When they could speak again as soon as the second swallow there was a sufficient reserve of strength in the body for the restorative to work upon and stimulate, and they almost never died. They remained alive to be questioned next day. "But this is so much better!" Duprat thought. It was the greatest satisfaction he had ever received from the specialized knowledge he had acquired as a criminal interrogator.

"What is the baby, uncle?"

"A hulking boy with leather lungs."

"Where is Henri?"

"Racing to this room this very moment, if I know him."

"I look a sight!"

She tried to smooth her hair, but her hand dropped weakly against the pillow.

"Shame on you for such vanity," he said in mock reproach. She saw him smile and smiled in return; an excellent sign, he thought.

Henri burst into the room and knelt at her bedside and kissed her. Duprat retired to the background and noted with satisfaction that she had enough strength in her arms to embrace him.

"Marie, my darling!"

"It's a boy," she said.

"I saw him."

"He nearly split her in two, the rascal, that big little man," cooed the midwife, proudly exhibiting the shrieking bundle.

"Silence, woman," Duprat hissed.

"Well!" she said. "I don't know where the little mother would be without *me*."

"Neither do I," Duprat agreed, "but please be quiet and do not disturb her." He had unbounded respect for the midwife's skill. She had a spotless reputation. Queen Claude herself had employed her services in the delivery of the two little royal princes.

"Humph!" said the midwife.

Shortly the room filled with relatives and well-wishers: the grandparents, the count's chaplain, the midwife's assistants, the captain of the household guard and certain other privileged retainers like the major-domo and the chief cook. A surgeon in a long robe was also admitted now that the child was safely delivered; he felt Marie's pulse, nodded gravely, and ordered the windows closed and some chicken feathers burned to purify the air. Then, the patient being somewhat weak and pale, he ordered a handful of medicinal leeches applied to the inside crook of her arm and removed only when they had doubled their size with gorged blood. Then the surgeon left, overwhelming the gathering with many a dignified bow, with murmured congratulations and a cautiously voiced hope for the future of mother and child. Duprat wrinkled his nose at the smoke and foul air, but he was satisfied that Marie was getting the best care that devotion and science could provide. A queen had received no more. In a little while, whiter than before, Marie fell asleep. Everyone but the midwife tiptoed out of the room. She remained behind to sit beside the bed, having first pulled the curtains snugly around it to guard against draughts.

Only one voice was raised in protest. "I have heard that in Italy they do not bleed a parturient mother," Henri said,

277

frowning, "and that the peasants there, who are noteworthy for their strength and good health, bear their infants in fresh air."

He was silenced by scathing glances from all sides. "My grandson is not a peasant," the dowager duchess said severely.

Duprat said, "I think we can safely trust the midwife whom the queen herself trusted."

Queen Claude, of course, was dead; but Henri could not lay her death to improper care when the princes were born, princes who had safely passed through childhood and soon would be adolescent. Nevertheless, he fretted and worried, wavering between the traditional old and the uncertain new waves of thought that were sweeping over the world of France, wondering whether the *homme universel* would be a Chevalier Bayard or a King Francis. But inordinately proud, as any new father in any age has a right to be.

The dowager duchess now took Henri's arm and smiled at him. "You men always make such a fuss about a simple little thing like a birth! Why, I was telling Uncle Antoine only a little while ago that everything was going to be all right. Was I not, uncle?"

"Indeed, that is just what you said," Duprat agreed.

"Marie *is* all right, isn't she?"

"I am sure she is."

"You see, my dear son? Even the chancellor says she's all right," the dowager duchess assured Henri.

The old Comte de Tonnerre whispered in Henri's ear, "It would appear that you are forgiven for existing. I thought you'd be."

"May I ask what you two are snickering about, *monsieur le comte?*" the dowager duchess asked.

"Madame," said the Comte de Tonnerre, tongue in cheek and favoring her with a stiff old-fashioned bow that made her blush with pleasure, "I was congratulating my son on his son, suggesting a good supper, with music, to celebrate this happy event." He nudged Henri in the ribs and chuckled, "You see, they do get over their tantrums, these mothers-in-law!"

Duprat smiled indulgently at this family interchange and felt warm and comfortable at the lessening of tension between them. Here he was at home. Here the stresses and strains of his high office seemed far away, and he could relax. Here he need not be modern, and to the chancellor of the king's *épargne* that was a godsend.

"Henri," he sighed, "I would not for the world be as young as you."

"Sir," Henri grinned, "I would for all the world that I was as young as my son."

"You would be *most* objectionable," said the dowager duchess. "Nothing but a constant care, all wet and soggy, and nothing on your horrid little male mind but the satisfaction of your horrid little male demands. I think you men will never change. Uncle Antoine, you will not be going up to Paris *too* soon, I hope?"

The Comte de Tonnerre added his voice to the invitation. "I hope everybody will stay here at Tonnerre, at least till the christening."

"I shall certainly stay for that," said Duprat.

It would be ten days or two weeks. The chancellor looked forward to a solid recuperative rest in the country. Like Marie, when she needed the restorative, he felt a thirst to drink deep of the calming and fortifying strength that rose from this unchanging French way of life, these unchanging manorial French acres. He would also be at hand to watch over Marie. There was no doubt that she needed care, more care than he had dared hint to Henri. Well, he would be there to supply that watchfulness, a simple welcome wholesome recreation for a confessed nepotist, while the great affairs of the world lapsed into the stalemate of wordy negotiations involving the king's ransom. Time, that most precious of all life's boons, had been granted him.

Then, in the twinkling of an eye, Time was snatched away from him. A contemptuously correct Spanish courier was waiting in his room after supper. Of all the Emperor's subjects the proud and unbending Spaniards irked the chancellor most, with their calm assumption of superiority. Duprat was prepared for bad news, and it came.

With a bow that appeared to convey a favor, the courier handed him a dispatch from the Emperor. Duprat scanned it and had difficulty hiding his confusion and fury. His most trusted weapon was blunted. The treasury of France was scorned. Money was of no interest to Charles Quint. He refused to accept ransom for the king.

But he was sending him home. One would have thought that a father was sending home an erring child with a spanking. He was sending him home, he said, because King Francis had concluded a peace which was satisfactory. Scarcely crediting the evidence of his own eyes the chancellor read the following:

King Francis, from his prison cell, on his own authority, scorning the counsel of his peers, with a flick of his pen, had signed a treaty that cast away Italy and alienated to the enemy half the territory of France.

15

D UPRAT CAST A LOOK of sadness upon the quiet
estates of Tonnerre, which he must now leave and
return to Paris and salvage what was salvageable from the
king's disastrous action. Not for a thousand years, not
since the incursions of the barbarian Vandals and Huns,
had the land of France stood in such danger of foreign
domination. But the man now dismembering France was no
barbarian, he was the First Gentleman of Europe; no foreigner, but the king of France himself. And, incredible
irony, fitter for a Greek tragedy than sober history, the king
who was witlessly working the ruination of his own kingdom bore a name synonymous with that kingdom: Francis.

It was too much.

For the first time in his adult life Antoine Duprat wept.

Further provisions of the treaty became known as the
complete text of the agreement arrived from Madrid by
courier and was widely published. Duprat made no attempt to suppress the appalling document. Let the people

know! Frenchmen would rise in their wrath to unite and resist as one man! Here is what Francis agreed to do in addition to pulling back French boundaries on the north and east to indefensible positions, to giving away whole French provinces full of loyal French subjects and renouncing all claim to any part of hard-won Italy: Francis agreed to reinstate the traitor Duc de Bourbon in all his former titles, territories and privileges. The least loyal of Frenchmen was to return in triumph from fighting against France, and be honored for his treason.

But the ultimate humiliation was the provision for the king's remarriage. The throne of the Queen of France, deeply revered and so recently vacated by the death of Queen Claude, was to be filled forthwith by an archenemy. King Francis agreed to marry the Emperor's sister.

"Small wonder the Emperor refused mere money when he could exact concessions like these!" Duprat thought. Nevertheless, he blamed himself for a serious error of judgment. He should have foreseen how Francis would behave in captivity with all his pleasures denied him.

Patently the treaty would have to be disavowed, and to that end the chancellor set in motion all the intricate and powerful machinery of government over which he had command; but all must be done in secrecy till the royal butterfly once more set foot on the soil of France.

"Henri," he said, "you shall have your command! Not too long hence I am sending you to Italy." He disclosed no more at that time, and Henri asked no more. It was enough that protective Uncle Antoine had relented and was sending him into action.

Henri kissed his son and kissed Marie good-by. "This

time he means it, he needs me, he's letting me fight!" he whispered.

She answered, "I need you too. But if he lets you go, he needs you more."

The chancellor doffed his churchly garb. Vested in steel — she cannot hear my heart — his features grim under an iron mask of self-control — she cannot read my thoughts — girded and spurred, he watched the two people he loved most kiss farewell. He bent forward and kissed her forehead. "I will send you a nursing sister to look after you till you are stronger and up and around again, though in truth," he hastened to say, "you look strong already. Adieu, my dear."

From the walls of Tonnerre the old comte and the dowager duchess waved farewell to Duprat and the warlike party that accompanied him. "She's weak as a kitten and he knows it," the old comte said.

"He changes his character as rapidly as he changes his garments," the dowager duchess said. "But in all his troubles and stresses he did not forget Marie."

"He came for a rest. Little rest he got!"

"Marie is quite strong, of course," the dowager duchess said, reassuring her own nagging fears which she considered a weakness unworthy of the Montholon blood. "Still, it was thoughtful of him to think of sending a nursing sister. Some superannuated old nun, I suppose, that I shall have to take care of."

Much happened very soon in the great world of the chancellor's multifarious enterprises where his mind was;

283

in the little world of Tonnerre, where his heart was, the great and saving thing that happened was the arrival of the nursing sister whom Duprat had chosen because of her total dedication and absolute selflessness. For reasons of her own, and because there could be no possible objection on the part of her superior, she had taken the name "Maria" when she took the veil. Underneath the concealing black skirts of her order were the same lithe limbs that had run through the squalid Italian slums when she stole food to keep alive, and, for a brief moment of power and passion, had embraced the king of France; and the hands that once wrung the chicken necks and tweaked the king's scented beard, and done other things he long since had forgotten, since Anne de Pisseleu d'Heilly could do them too, now counted beads and clasped in prayer and devoted themselves to healing. It was not, after all, thought Duprat, so unusual a situation, when men like the king did no more than simply be themselves: in battle they leave behind a swath of broken bodies, in love a swath of broken hearts, and go on to the next.

Giulietta Leone, when she made her vows of poverty, chastity and obedience, swore solemnly to possess no property of her own throughout the rest of her life, and she readily relinquished the riches King Francis had showered upon her. But one object she held back and hid in her nun's sleeve, "and if it costs me some centuries in Purgatory," she thought shrugging, "I do not care." It was the ruby which the point of the dagger, destined for the king, had driven into the flesh of her neck and which had been removed. "I've a use for it," she thought; and her smile was as lovely as when Henri had watched her haggle with the merchant for the linen to wrap the Mona Lisa.

Marie said incredulously, "You, Giulietta?" when her nurse appeared.

"I will go away if you do not want me," said Sister Maria.

"But I do so want to stay."

"Stay, then, Giulietta. I am glad you are here," Marie said weakly.

The dowager duchess, after some preliminary misgivings, welcomed the nurse, who was unquestionably competent. And well it was, for complications set in. "What bewilders me is her unfailing devotion! She seems never to sleep. She is up all hours of the night, caring for Marie and the boy."

"Oh, I don't know if that's so unusual," said the Comte de Tonnerre. "If she couldn't get Henri she still can get something, by helping his wife and his son. Lots of people are like that."

"Well, I wouldn't be like that," said the dowager duchess.

"That's why I don't think the chancellor would have chosen you to nurse Marie back to health," the comte said severely.

"Monsieur le comte, we must not quarrel."

The Bidassoa River is an inconsequential little stream on the French side of the Pyrenees. Its sole claim to fame was the fact that it marked the boundary between France and Spain. South of it King Francis was a prisoner. North of it he was an absolute monarch. To arrange the crossing, which an arrow could traverse in three seconds, the chancellor devoted much planning, much money and many pounds of dispatches, which were carried to all quarters of Europe and into the heathen Eastern regions beyond, where the Emperor's enemies were. At length the crossing was arranged.

But the Emperor had grown wary. He now demanded hostages, namely, the king's two sons.

Duprat sacrificed them, thinking of Abraham offering Isaac, stayed by an angel, and hoping for a similar deliverance. And if the Good Lord was tardy in sending an angel, Duprat counted on the Parliament of Paris, backed by all the provincial parliaments of France, to disavow the treaty and work such a threat against Charles Quint that he would be glad to return them. And yet, if all went wrong, what were two little hostage lives compared with the life of the king of France?

Francis himself proved remarkably agreeable to the exchange. Bluff and hearty he reminded the boys that this was perfectly in accord with knightly tradition; he bade them be good and learn their manners and obey their "cousin," the Emperor.

They were very young and they waved their father adieu on the banks of the river, wide-eyed at the adventure, and marched bravely into Spain and bowed respectfully, but with the dignity of their blood royal, to their captor, a dark man in a dark cloak with a forbidding face.

They were safer than they knew. Already the chancellor's wily schemes were bearing fruit. By the time the king crossed the river a disaster was preparing for the Emperor, a stain on his name that the apologists of centuries would never efface: and for Antoine Duprat — since he never did anything to his own disadvantage — a cardinal's hat and the thanks of the pope himself. For the chancellor trapped the Emperor into the most stupid blunder a Christian can make: armed might against the Holy See. ("And Charles calls himself the *Holy* Roman Emperor," he chuckled when all was over.)

King Francis, in a brand-new helmet with gorgeous feathers, crossed the Bidassoa on an imperial barge. On the French side he sprung upon a warhorse, brandished his sword and shouted, *"Je suis encore roi!"*

"Yes," said Duprat, the ecclesiastic again, in cope and miter, making the most of the Emperor's plight, "well can he cry 'I am still the king!'" But the chancellor wished in his heart he were dealing with a Charlemagne, or a Philippe Auguste, or a Louis XI.

Said Francis, "How fares my little Anne?"

"Your duty," so read the directive of Duprat to Henri, "is to cut off supplies from the army of the Duc de Bourbon. On no account attempt to destroy him or his men. That is a chivalrous notion which will occur to you, but put it sternly down. He has twenty thousand mouths to feed. See that nothing gets through to them. See that they get no pay. See that they go hungry. Burn, ravage, destroy all that might contribute to their sustenance. Then the great traitor, already eccentric, will go mad and make a mistake. We cannot predict what it will be, but we know it will come. Watch for it."

It was vague, but it was comprehensible.

Henri's values had changed. "I mistook the character of the *homme universel,* when I wanted to be one, when I escorted the Mona Lisa home," he mused. "I thought all that was required was to excel in battle, love, art and learning. But the true *homme universel* is a chancellor Duprat. And he's a rascal!" The age had need of such a rascal. That was why, he supposed, every age always produced one.

In Tonnerre, as Marie languished and developed a fever, Sister Maria chased away the chancellor's physician, who arrived with more leeches in a glass jar. "Get out, you ghoul!" she cried. The physician retired with the bloodsuckers. "Do not lay her death to me," he warned. "I must represent to the chancellor at once that my services are refused."

"Represent all you please. They are. Begone."

"One imagines you care very little about yourself," he said, bewildered.

"Not myself."

Giulietta brewed her invalid soups and spoon-fed her until, miraculously, her fever abated and the color returned to her cheeks.

"When your charge is well," wrote Duprat, amid all his other cares, "depart, and return to your nunnery."

"She is well," Giulietta could report after some weeks, and departed.

She left behind her ruby. "I would like to think," she said as she left Marie, "that the boy might one day wear this in his sword. Or if it is no longer fashionable to wear jewels in a sword-pommel he might wear it in his ear. Men's styles are so changeable. Or if men no longer wear earrings in the year 1550, when he will be a man, that he make a ring of it and give it to his love. It came," she said softly, "from the king."

In Marseille the Italian admiral, Andrea Doria, superbly provisioned and armed by Duprat, bore down upon the port with a fleet and raised the siege. The Emperor's forces retreated. The south was safe.

In the north French armies held firm against the Germans.

In the inscrutable East, subsidized by Duprat, the Grand Turk attacked the Emperor's rear.

In Italy, Henri finally had his day.

At the head of his command he nibbled and scratched and worried and bit like a terrier. When the Duc de Bourbon attacked he retreated, scorching the earth, destroying all supplies: the bulls, the cows, the goats, the gardens, the hoarded fodder in peasants' barns and the salted meats in peasants' kitchens. When the Duc de Bourbon retreated he attacked; but it was noted that there were few casualties among the Imperialists: Henri's men seemed more intent on robbery than on killing, so that after a skirmish his soldiers returned burdened with armor, money, food, horses and guns rather than with prisoners, whom they left alive to regroup around their leader, and hound him.

The problem of accumulating loot embarrassed Henri. Duprat sent explicit instructions: Distribute it among the refugees and blame the Duc de Bourbon for rendering them homeless. Let it be known that he, not we, brought war to their country.

It would stand in the chroniclers' annals that the French ravaged the Milanese plain as it had never been ravaged before, and that the Emperor got the blame.

Swiftly the strategy took its toll. Mule trains laden with silver from the New World, destined to pay some part of the long overdue wages of the Duc's mercenaries, were intercepted. Some of this treasure went to alleviate the plight of the homeless Italians, just enough to render them friendly to the French, but most of it went to France and into the king's *épargne*.

Fodder was lacking for the Duc's horses. Food became so scarce that the Duc's men began openly to threaten. The Duc, who disliked meat and preferred roots and herbs and nuts, sarcastically suggested that they eat their shoe leather. They ate their horses.

Twenty thousand rebellious carnivorous mercenaries posed an insoluble problem to the Duc de Bourbon's delicately balanced mind, and, pushed beyond all endurance, it snapped and solved all the chancellor's problems.

The Duc ranted, "They lust after the fleshpots of Egypt! Oh faithless, oh cannibals, oh the nauseating brutes, so be it! I will give them what they want!"

He issued a venomous general order to his troops, couched in bitter terms against the king of France, blaming France for the starvation they suffered, blaming also the Eternal City of Rome, greatest city of the miserable country where they found themselves, saying: "I will lead you to the fat heart of this land, corrupted by the French, and there you will find riches beyond your power of imagining! Forward! To Rome! *En avant! Victoire!*"

Now followed a spectacle which disgusted Christendom and set the heathen world to roaring with cynical laughter. The Duc de Bourbon, starving on the Milanese plain, struck south with his ragged, unpaid, desperate army and besieged the Holy City of Rome. Sanctimoniously the Emperor had Masses said for the safety of the pope, but he did not call off his dogs. The French army followed the Imperialists, harrying their rear. The result was to goad the Duc into further excesses.

While the whole Christian world stood aghast at the Emperor's minions' profanation of the capital of their faith, the chancellor seized upon the moment when public sympathy was veering in favor of France to disavow King Francis's treaty. With the Queen Mother he convoked the Parliament of Paris. Simultaneously all the French provincial assemblies met. There was only one question they had to decide: Could a king of France, even a king who ruled *du bon plaisir,* alienate the sacred soil of France? The unanimous vote of every parliament in the kingdom was that the king could not.

It is likely that this would have been their opinion regardless of legal precedent; and since they spoke the voice of the whole of France, now vehemently aroused and united, the treaty would have been disavowed whether legal or no. But there was ample precedent for the disavowal, namely, the king's solemn vow at his "sacring," or consecration. For more than a thousand years French kings had been anointed with holy oil before the crown of France was placed upon their brows, with all its high privileges and heavy responsibilities. It was an awesome ceremony. The oil of anointing was from the same little phial, *la sainte ampoule,* that tradition said, and no one could disprove, had been flown down from Heaven in the beak of a pure white dove for the baptism of King Clovis. Thenceforth a French king was a man set apart from the ordinary run of men, partaking of the ecclesiastical character: he could assist at the altar at Mass, as if he were in holy orders, and his person was inviolable. Francis had been anointed like all other kings since the days when the Franks beat back the Huns and sent them retreating into Asia whence they had erupted; and on that solemn occasion, while vowing never to be a heathen but always to cleave to the Christian faith, Francis had sworn also to rule, serve and faithfully defend the land of France and never to alienate so much as a handful of her soil, on his honor, on his faith and before almighty God.

It was the measure of his profound statesmanship that

the chancellor had appealed to this broad principle in breaking the treaty, rather than to the lesser detail that Francis was under duress when he signed it.

When Francis was apprised that his pact with the Emperor was a nullity he was delighted and exclaimed, "What an imbecile Charles must be not to have remembered that! The rascal deceived me!" He was equally delighted not to have to marry the Emperor's unattractive sister.

"I suppose the war will go on now, will it not, chancellor?"

"Yes, Your Majesty."

But the king had been fatigued by his irksome incarceration and took no part in war for some time. There was Anne de Pisseleu d'Heilly to welcome and refresh him, and much hunting and dancing to do, all the delightful things that had been denied him. Meanwhile the little princes remained in Spain.*

No sooner did Henri find himself in Italy, directing a successful campaign and coming again into contact with the vibrant culture he had admired and desired to emulate, than he met a man who punctured his affection for the New Learning and caused him to say to himself, *"Mon Dieu!* Is this creature the end result of *homme universel* in Italy? If it is, as it seems to be, I shall turn feudal again, and let who will condemn me as old-fashioned!"

The genius who staggered into his camp outside the walls of Rome was a youngish man of enormous personal magnetism, a ready (though somewhat drunken) smile, and a

---

* The Emperor freed them four years later. The elder died shortly after his release. The younger grew up to reign as Henry II. He was cold, haughty, melancholy, bigoted and dull, characteristics which Hispanophobes traced to his captivity in Spain and his Spanish education at an impressionable period of life.

casual amorality that surpassed anything Henri had ever known. His surname, he said, was Cellini. His Christian name was Benvenuto. He was at pains to explain to the illiterate Frenchman that *benvenuto* was the same as *bienvenu,* namely, *welcome;* and he hoped he would be, since he was on King Francis's side.

Henri said anybody on King Francis's side was welcome. He thought the laborious etymological approach superfluous and patronizing. Did the Italians consider the French on a par with the Huns? But he had heard the name Benvenuto Cellini spoken of with respect, and he treated his tipsy guest like the gentleman which he was not.

First he fed him, for Cellini was hungry. The gypsy-like character wolfed down the food, absorbed three bottles of wine in quick succession and pronounced the quality atrocious.

"We are engaged in a war," Henri said, "and perhaps you find our fare a bit austere."

Having fed, Cellini said, "No doubt you will wish to be paid," and flipped a diamond, big as a bean, across the table.

Henri was so incensed at the fellow's arrogance that he let it bounce, till it fell off the table and lodged in a crack of the tent flooring.

"Thank you very much," Henri said.

A servant picked it up and held it out to Henri. It was tear drop in shape and exquisitely faceted. "Here it is, sir," the servant said.

"Inform my cook that a qualified guest compliments the artistry of his supper and wishes to pay for it, and give it to him," Henri said.

"Oui, mon chevalier," said the servant; for when Henri

de Tonnerre's color rose he had learned not to argue.

Cellini watched the servant hurry off — to deliver the priceless gem to a cook! — and raised his penciled eyebrows and bared all his strong white teeth in a smile of surprise and approval.

"Upon my word, monsieur de Tonnerre, you are civilized. I like you."

Henri was interested, but he could not honestly say the same.

"I came as a pauper, naked and hungry," Cellini said, dramatically raising both delicate (but curiously powerful) hands to his breast in an expressive Italian gesture. "You took me in, and you did not even know who I am. Or did you? Am I so little known you do not?"

"I knew, but it didn't matter," Henri said. "The Devil himself would be welcome here if he fought on King Francis's side."

Ah, that was precisely the thing, Cellini said sighing, full of wine, self-righteousness and good humor. At this very moment, all unjustly, he was being accused of being a devil. But did not all artists partake in some measure of the diabolical? He had been unjustly accused before. His beautiful natal city of Florence had exiled him for a triviality, the stabbing in the back of the slayer of one of his brothers. Was ever a homicide more justifiable? He was certain he had stabbed the right man, though the city fathers disagreed. In another municipality, whither he had fled, the authorities escorted him roughly to the city limits and bade him begone and never return, for the ridiculous detail of dismissing a model who, being six months with child by him, could of course no longer pose for a slender

Leda with the swan, and turned up in a canal; he had substituted her cherub-cheeked young brother. "Actually, the brother was much more attractive," Cellini said, "but the confounded night watch broke in and took a dim view of my research in the configuration of the human body in passion, the dolts!" But later the Holy Father, recognizing his genius — "There is no question concerning the universality of my genius," Cellini said — had given him sanctuary in Rome and commissioned him to sculpt statues, paint frontals, engrave dies and finally — "Since no one has ever produced such exquisite work as mine" — had entrusted him with the intricate task of resetting the jewels of the papal tiara.

"Dio mio, such jewels!" exulted Cellini. "Turquoises from Persia, polished without facets in the old cabochon way, round and smooth like a breast; amber from the Baltic with insects imprisoned in it like souls in Purgatory, expiating their sins but destined for salvation, since of course in time the amber wears away; Indian rubies, Byzantine emeralds, pearls from the Red Sea so old and lusterless I had to wrap them round the fragrant limbs of a pubescent girl — ha! I saw to that to restore their fire! — and a crystal of tin from Britain that Saint Patrick had worn in a miter, primitive, wonderful; and diamonds, diamonds by the dozen, tracing the progress from Apostolic times to the matchless present, as more and more faceting appeared. In these jewels one could grasp at a glance the forward march of art, if one is endowed, as I am, as the Holy Father concedes, with the Jovian view."

"No one doubts your skill, Benvenuto Cellini."

"Skill? I spit! It is art."

"Then it is art. Once I thought I understood it. Now it merely bewilders me."

"Of course it would," said Cellini.

But then, continued Cellini, when his artistic life was going so well, had come this war. Italy was in chaos. One never knew where to turn for privacy. The intruding sounds of guns and crumbling walls were everywhere. In the midst of a delicate operation of melting a mix for a bronze statue, in the midst of experiments to determine whether egg-white or oil is best for a portrait of the Madonna, in the midst of tracing the grain of a block of marble, in the midst of critical research with a boy and a girl or a dog, observing the play of the facial muscles and how the body contorts and whether it sweats, for if it does one applies a glaze, comes an inopportune distraction and strangers rush into the studio, full of loud words and politics, taking the artist's attention off his work and vitiating his concentration on all that really counts.

"You must have had a hard time," Henri said.

"Harken what happened to me!" Cellini said. "How exquisitely I had draughted the Holy Father's tiara! In color, on parchment, with my most delicate tools. It set forth the sublime history of the Faith from the first rude beginning, the tin, down to the glorious present of faceted jewels, which can never be surpassed unless I myself decide to polish gems one day. *That* would surpass the lapidaries who work such wonders, *non è vero?*"

"I do not know," Henri said.

"How could you, a soldier! But I assure you it would. Then I was wrenched from my work. The Duc de Bourbon attacked Rome. I was furious. What could I do but bury the papal jewels outside the walls and wait for a calmer time to finish the tiara? I am still outside. And — can you credit your ears? — I am accused of stealing them! Was ever such injustice? Was ever a great artist so put upon?"*

Henri smiled and did not ask where the cook's diamond had come from. Presumably not all the jewels were buried, and the artist, like the chancellor, had taken his tithe.

"What are your present plans, monsieur Cellini?"

"Peace," grumbled Cellini, "to finish the pope's commission. I can do nothing in all this noise."

"I will send you to France if you like. King Francis is a devoted patron of the arts."

"So I have heard. He exhibits interesting possibilities. Some day I shall fashion him a masterpiece that only I can give. He is said to be saucy, in the old and delightful sense of the term. Perhaps I should explain."

"I try to hobble along," Henri said.†

"But first I shall kill your absurd and distracting Duc de Bourbon," Cellini said, as if he were sweeping his studio. "But for him I should have finished the pope's tiara."

"Nothing would please me more," Henri said. "Kill him."

Among Henri's most treasured mementoes of the Italian expedition was a note in the chancellor's own handwriting: "Your shrewd employment of the mad artist Cellini was praiseworthy. One is sometimes moved to discount these eccentrics. Nothing could be more shortsighted; to recognize their value bespeaks much talent. I have recommended

---

* Cellini was later cleared of the theft of the papal jewels. He remained a bachelor most of his life, marrying only at the age of sixty-five, dying at seventy-one, full of honors. Art critics dispute the excellence of his work; but no one denies its vigor.

† Cellini, for the saucy king, made a solid gold salt cellar, composed largely of naked male and female figures with little place for the salt. It still exists and many people admire it.

a peerage for you to the king; it will surprise me if he declines." Here the note would have ended for the ordinary field commander, but for Henri he added, "My grand-niece and great-grand-nephew do well. Marie's nurse, the Sister Maria, has broached to me the subject of a hospital for the sick poor near the Gate. It is a worthy cause and I shall advance it."

It was signed, "Your Uncle Duprat."

Benvenuto Cellini, still without the walls, under the cloud of stealing the papal jewels and thirsting to get back to his foundry, his palette and his graving tools, loathing the Duc de Bourbon for interrupting his work, joined Henri's army. He was little understood but made as welcome as his name.

Among his many accomplishments Cellini had experimented with the new gunpowder. It was not that he wanted a more effective means of killing. He had done very well in effecting his personal assassinations with daggers. It was simply that the ballistic mystery challenged him. Why does an arrow fly true if it has a feather in its tail? Why does a bullet wobble in flight and miss the mark? Why does a top spin upright? Would a spinning bullet fly truer, stable like a top?

With his amazing metallurgical craft he had fashioned a hand gun — there were many in use, but they were smooth-bore — and cut spiral grooves in the barrel with his engraving tools to give the missile a top-like twist in flight. It shot astoundingly far and straight. He decorated the little weapon with a languishing Venus whose svelte limbs slithered into the silver handle. "Seek out the Duc," he apostrophized the gun. "Destroy him, thou eternal, thou delicious, thou lethal." In his heart Cellini envied women.

The day of the attack dawned bright and clear. Beyond the walls of Rome lay food and the accumulated treasure of fifteen centuries of Christian devotion. The Duc de Bourbon led the assault. Close at his heels snarled and snapped the French army, though Henri silenced his artillery for fear of overshooting and inflicting casualties on the Romans, or even the Holy Father, who had taken refuge in the Mole of Hadrian, a massive thousand-year-old structure of indescribable strength, fortified successively by forty generations and now called the Castle of Sant'Angelo. Thus Henri squeezed the Duc and his tatterdemalion followers between the offense and the defense, between the French who harried his rear and the Romans who shot at his front. The Roman defense was weak; it was soon apparent that the Holy City would not hold out for long.

Here Henri and Cellini had a tussle of wits, and Cellini won. "Put me in charge of one of your advance parties, monsieur de Tonnerre! I have sworn to kill the Duc. I will pick him off with my gun the instant I see him scale the first ladder."

"The Duc is their general," Henri said. "He will stay at his command post in the rear, where a general belongs, and direct the assault."

"How little you understand genius!" Cellini said, "Even my own! I tell you, the Duc de Bourbon is mad and will therefore be the first man over the wall. Do I get my advance party or must I do it on my own? The result would be the same, of course."

"I should hate to see you killed going off on your own,"

Henri said smiling. He had begun to like the artist in spite of himself. "Very well, Benvenuto Cellini, be welcome to one of my advance parties."

To the captain of the group Henri said privately, "Take care that that crazy Italian doesn't expose himself and get himself killed. He is valuable."

With remarkable shrewdness, bespeaking long acquaintance with the terrain, Cellini led the French party far beyond the line that Henri had set as the limit for his troops, taking cover in the tumbledown deserted dwellings and winding streets of a slum area till he emerged a scant hundred paces from the foot of the Roman walls. He had actually succeeded in infiltrating the rear of the attackers without being detected.

Against the towering fortifications the scaling ladders were going up. Romans with grappling hooks pushed many away; they would overbalance and fall, carrying a file of screaming men to death or a lifetime as cripples, since bodies and bones were invariably broken in the crash. But one ladder, better manned than the rest, was not overturned. Up its rungs clambered the Duc de Bourbon, with his coronet on his helmet and an ermine mantle over his breastplate, shrieking defiance, brandishing his sword.

Arrows and arquebuses took aim from the walls, but Cellini was quicker.

Although he had slept not a wink the night before, spending the dark hours between assaults on a comely wench and a brace of bottles of brandy, Cellini's strong sophisticated hands were amazingly steady.

"The range is too far!" shouted the captain in his ear, above the tumult of the battle.

Cellini threatened him in the face with his slow-match,

the captain jumped back. Cellini laughed, took aim and fired.

"You very nearly spoiled my aim," Cellini said amiably.

The captain wiped the sulphur fumes out of his eyes. When he could see again the Duc de Bourbon was gone from the ladder. "Good God! You got him!"

"Certainly," said Cellini, kissing the silver handle of his gun. "Thou beauty! The doctors will find your message in his right kidney, burrowed in from the back."

A shout of fury went up from the Imperialists and mingled with a shout of short-lived exultation from the Romans. The Duc de Bourbon toppled backwards from the ladder and fell with his coronet and his ermine into the filth and debris that always accumulates outside walled cities. His breastplate had deflected the arrows but many bullets had pierced his breast and the doctors who examined the corpse after it was dug from a heap of dead bodies and identified did indeed find one bullet that had entered from the back. For this Benvenuto Cellini took credit forever thereafter. With the same hand-gun he slew, in an ambuscade in the days of chaos that overtook the city, the Prince of Orange, another of the Emperor's generals. No one could disprove his claim, which was in keeping with his character.

The leaderless Imperialists now swarmed over the walls and bore down all resistance. The Romans abandoned the fight and fled for their lives, to the shelter of their homes, which were shortly invaded; to the crypts of the city's myriad churches, where they were soon reduced to eating the candles; some even to the Catacombs, where they lost themselves in forgotten uncharted labyrinthine miles of ancient tombs and went mad and perpetrated acts of cannibalism before they died and added their gnawed and loathsome bones to the tons of bones already there from Apostolic times. In the city above, the Imperialists abandoned themselves to scenes of slaughter, loot and rapine. The Wine of Communion was guzzled by ruffians with blood still wet on their hands in drunken orgies after a day of pillage. Next day the sack of the city and the abuse of its inhabitants resumed. For weeks the night sky was red with the fire of burning buildings: humble homes, patrician palaces, even churches if they were found, or thought to be found, sheltering soldiers of the defending army. Irreplaceable works of antique Greek and Roman art were wantonly destroyed: oddly, the noses and genitalia of the ancient masterpieces were particularly attractive targets for the maces of the marauding bands of ignorant victors, who gaped and gibed at their pagan perfection of nudity and took special pains to deface them.

At night from the roof of Sant'Angelo the pope would peep over the battlements and watch the Holy City burn. He was timid and indecisive by nature. He had a deep-rooted fear of mob violence. His father had been assassinated in a political conspiracy. A stubborn whisper about his legitimacy had long haunted him and was only silenced among his friends by a special decree of his predecessor and never silenced among his enemies. He had many. England was about to separate. Germany was already sundered by Luther. He was a wretched administrator and he could neither calm nor control the passions convulsing the Church in his century of ecclesiastical earthquakes. But he was a cultured man of a princely family. And now he trembled and watched the city he loved go up in flames set by the torch of the Holy Roman Emperor.

Duprat, apprised of the carnage, sent a severe dispatch to all his field commanders, ordering them to draw back. "In such disorder," he warned, "the Romans cannot tell friend from foe. Retire, therefore, to the Milanese plain, and secure the north."

To Henri he sent a fuller note: "The two opposing forces must fight it out in the city between themselves. I order you particularly, who are in closest contact, to withdraw. It must never be said that the French had any part in the desecration of the Holy City. I am also attempting to use my good offices to work the release of the Holy Father."

French gold, the bubonic plague and the Emperor's shame came to assist the chancellor in this successful endeavor.

✻ ✻ ✻ 16 ✻ ✻

BAD NEWS TRAVELS FAST, and soon all Europe knew of the sack of Rome and the continuing depredations there of the Emperor's Imperialist troops. Time now worked for France. The northern portions of Charles's Empire were delirious with joy, dreaming that their Reformation had conquered and would supplant the Old Religion. Catholic Spain was appalled and began to murmur against the Emperor, who, since he ruled both Germany and Spain, was in a dire dilemma.

Then in the fallen city, with the dead unburied and rats feeding upon the corpses, with a stench in the streets and the pope still a prisoner in Sant'Angelo, the dread scourge of the Black Death broke out in a particularly virulent form, adding to the misery and desolation. Christendom was festering at its heart, and the Emperor looked for a way out of his troubles.

It was supplied.

The Emperor who had scorned to ransom King Francis now agreed to ransom the Holy Father and permit him to exile himself in a place of greater health and safety. For four hundred thousand scudi, some of which was supplied by Duprat, the Emperor sent a body of soldiers to Rome, which was now open on all sides, and spirited the frightened pope out of the city. The papal banner still flew from the battlements of Sant'Angelo as a deception, but the Holy Father was no longer there. Weeping and in disguise, he took the winding road to Orvieto seventy-eight miles to the north. There, in a fortress atop a bleak sheer rock six hundred and forty feet above the surrounding plan, subject to cold nights and every inconvenience after the splendors of the Vatican, but safe from the plague and the fear of assassination, the weak old man brooded and waited for better times.

The chancellor smiled when he heard how the Emperor claimed credit for his daring "rescue" of the pope. The scandal of the ransom did not leak out for some time. Spain was satisfied and Germany was appeased, for along with the four hundred thousand scudi the Emperor had exacted from his exalted prisoner a promise to call a council that would give every consideration to the Lutheran claims. Thus the Holy Roman Empire remained intact and the war with France could continue.

But the fury of the war had abated; it seemed wearing on to a close, with France the victor.

King Francis now sustained an inspiration.

"Milan is safe for France now, is it not, chancellor?"

"It seems so, Your Majesty."

"Permanently?"

"Unless Charles wins a battle, which is unlikely at this time."

"They tell me Rome is a desert!"

"I fear much has been destroyed. The Imperialists are decimated by the plague, and the population who have not died have left for other places."

Hs was surprised and pleased that King Francis was showing interests other than hunting and his amours.

"But Rome is the repository of great art!" Francis said. "This is very sad."

It would be worse, the chancellor said, if the Emperor had won the war.

Then Francis divulged his inspiration.

"I will end this war, chancellor!"

The king's plan, which he seriously proposed, was that he and the Holy Roman Emperor should meet in single combat at a suitable jousting field and fight it out alone. Whoever won the match would win the war.

"I have sent my personal *défi!*" the king said proudly.

"You have *what*, Sire?"

Hesitantly, as if he were being chided and wished to justify himself, the king exhibited a copy of a scroll which a courier was even at that moment rushing to Madrid.

The remarkable document notified to its recipient that Francis, King of France, considered himself grievously insulted by his good cousin, Charles, the Holy Roman Emperor, and challenged the aforesaid Holy Roman Emperor to single combat to the death, or until one or the other yielded, the Emperor having the choice of weapons.

"Francis, did you actually send this challenge?" the chancellor asked, calling the king by his Christian name for the first time since the days when he was his tutor.

"Of course I did. Is it wrong?"

"No, sir, it is not wrong; and I would to God that wars were as simple as that."

"It cannot be used against France?"

"No, Your Majesty; and it will add luster to your name. But the Emperor won't answer it."

The Emperor instantly published the absurdly romantic document and attempted to ridicule it, and he did not of course answer it. But many knightly persons on both sides, to whom the stench of gunpowder was an abomination and the fiery ideal of chivalry still a guiding light, thought like the chancellor that it would be a good thing in this world if wars could be settled so simply.

From Italy, after a period of time while the war dragged on and ended in stalemate, came a notification from the pope. Though Rome was desolate and deserted, the Holy Father still exercised his supreme spiritual powers. Antoine Duprat, chancellor of the king's *épargne,* was created a cardinal. He grew scandalously rich, he showered his relatives with favors at the treasury's expense, his palaces and châteaux were unconscionably lavish. But he never fell, as Wolsey did, and France never succumbed to the Emperor; and he curbed his king's more disastrous impulses so ably that the reign of Francis the First rests in the chroniclers' annals as an age of magnificence, brilliance and beauty.